PENGUIN CLASSI

UNCLE REMUS:
HIS SONGS AND HIS SAYINGS

Joel Chandler Harris was born on December 9, 1848, near Eatonton, Georgia. Little is known about his family, except that they were poor and his mother was a seamstress.

In 1862, Harris began a four-year apprenticeship as a printer at the Turnwald plantation in Putnam County, Georgia, where the journal *The Countryman* was published. Through this position he was able to publish his first writing compositions. In 1866 he began his career as a journalist, working for a number of newspapers around the South, including the Macon, Georgia *Telegraph*, the New Orleans *Picayune* and *Crescent*, and the Savannah *Morning News*. In 1876 he began his work at the Atlanta *Constitution*, where he eventually became an editor. During this time he also married Esther LaRose. Together they had five children: Mary Esther, Lillian, Linton, Mildred, and Joel Chandler, Jr.

Harris was also an avid student of black folklore and wrote several collections of stories based on his studies, known as the *Uncle Remus Tales*. The first volume, *Nights with Uncle Remus: Myths and Legends of the Old Plantation* was published in 1883. Other works include *Daddy Jake, the Runaway, and Short Stories Told After Dark* (1889), *Little Mr. Thimblefinger and His Queer Country* (1894), and *The Chronicles of Aunt Minervy Ann* (1899). In 1900 Harris resigned from the *Constitution* so he could concentrate on his fiction. He founded *Uncle Remus's Magazine* in 1906.

Harris died in Atlanta in 1908 after a long liver illness.

Robert Hemenway is Professor of English at the University of Kentucky. He is the author of *Zora Neale Hurston: A Literary Biography* and the editor of Hurston's *Mules and Men*, Taylor Gordon's *Born to Be*, and Paul Allen's *The Late Charles Brockden Brown*. Mr. Hemenway's essays on F. Scott Fitzgerald, William Faulkner, Charles W. Chesnutt, and others have appeared in such journals as *American Literature*, *American Studies*, *The Black Scholar*, and *Modern Fiction Studies*.

Uncle Remus
HIS SONGS AND
HIS SAYINGS

by

Joel Chandler Harris

Edited with an Introduction by
ROBERT HEMENWAY

PENGUIN BOOKS

PENGUIN BOOKS
Published by the Penguin Group
Penguin Books USA Inc.,
375 Hudson Street, New York, New York 10014, U.S.A.
Penguin Books Ltd, 27 Wrights Lane, London W8 5TZ, England
Penguin Books Australia Ltd, Ringwood, Victoria, Australia
Penguin Books Canada Ltd, 10 Alcorn Avenue,
Toronto, Ontario, Canada M4V 3B2
Penguin Books (N.Z.) Ltd, 182–190 Wairau Road, Auckland 10, New Zealand

Penguin Books Ltd, Registered Offices:
Harmondsworth, Middlesex, England

Uncle Remus: His Songs and His Sayings first published in
the United States of America by D. Appleton and Company 1880
First published in Great Britain by
George Routledge and Sons 1881
Published in The Penguin American Library 1982
Reprinted in Penguin Classics 1986

11 13 15 17 19 20 18 16 14 12

Introduction copyright © Viking Penguin Inc., 1982
All rights reserved

LIBRARY OF CONGRESS CATALOGING IN PUBLICATION DATA
Harris, Joel Chandler, 1848–1908.
Uncle Remus, his songs and his sayings.
(Penguin Classics)
Originally published: New York: D. Appleton, 1880.
Bibliography: p.
Summary: Presents the legends, songs, and sayings
of Uncle Remus, following the text of the first
edition of Joel Chandler Harris' attempt to
record traditional black stories of his time.
1. Afro-Americans—Folklore. 2. Tales—United States.
[1. Folklore, Afro-American. 2. Animals—Fiction]
I. Hemenway, Robert E., 1941–   . II. Title. III. Series.
PZ8.1.H233Un   1982   813'.4 [398.2]   82-7482
ISBN 0 14 03.9014 6   AACR 2

Printed in the United States of America
Set in CRT Caslon

ACKNOWLEDGMENTS
I wish to thank Professors Bruce Bickley,
William Bradley Strickland, Joseph Griska, and Florence Baer
for their help in preparing this edition.
                                        —Robert Hemenway

Contents

Introduction:
Author, Teller, and Hero

"I read your stories to the little folks nearly every night of my life," said Edith Roosevelt to Joel Chandler Harris, "and they never tire of their beloved 'Uncle Remus.' " Edith's husband thought Uncle Remus "one of the undying characters of story"; he invited Harris to a private White House dinner. "Presidents may come and presidents may go," Teddy said, "but Uncle Remus stays put."

Uncle Remus: His Songs and His Sayings, a collection of thirty-four black folktales, four pages of proverbs, ten songs, and twenty-one character sketches, sold 7,500 copies in the first month after being released for the Christmas book trade in November 1880. It has been constantly before the American reading public ever since, in more than sixty reprints of the original edition. There have been ten Uncle Remus volumes in all, published over a seventy-year span, containing 220 tales. The stories have been translated into dozens of languages, including the African tribal dialects in which some of the folktales originated.

Few characters in American literature have held the popular imagination like Harris's venerable black storyteller. The Ralston-Purina Company, in return for a box top from Ralston Wheat Cereal, once mailed out thousands of "Draw-Your-Own Uncle Remus Comic Strips." A steel company manufactured Tar Baby nails, "Guaranteed to hold-on-tite." Always with a nose for the box office, Walt Disney starred Uncle Remus in a feature-length movie in 1946, *Song of the South,* an

7

Oscar-winning combination of actors and animation that grossed millions and played neighborhood theaters for the next twenty years. Withheld from circulation in the late sixties because of criticism that it portrayed blacks in stereotypical roles, the movie has apparently transcended American race relations. The centennial of Uncle Remus's first appearance, fall 1980, found black and white parents, kids in tow, waiting in long lines to view the reissued movie once again, to hear Oscar winner James Baskett sing, "Zip-a-dee-do-dah, zip-a-dee-ay, My oh my what a wonderful day."

Any character who has persisted so long and become so fixed in the American imagination deserves thinking about, and Uncle Remus deserves more thought than most; no one questions his historical and cultural significance, but there is considerable confusion about just what he means.

One can make sense of the collision of ideas and images surrounding Uncle Remus by distinguishing among Joel Chandler Harris, Uncle Remus, and Brer Rabbit. A fictional character, Uncle Remus was created by an author with a sentimental attachment to a plantation memory. Bald, bearded, bespectacled, Remus is a former slave who does odd jobs around the plantation after emancipation. He tells his stories night after night to a little white boy, son of the plantation owner, unfolding to him in grandfatherly fashion the "mysteries of plantation lore." Remus has, Harris tells us, "nothing but pleasant memories of the discipline of slavery." This fictional creation of a white Southerner was welcomed by an audience that wanted to believe Remus was a representative of his race; Uncle Remus is a cousin of those nineteenth-century minstrels who blackened their faces to entertain with jokes and songs. He is, in a way, white.

Brer Rabbit, on the other hand, was created by black storytellers long before Joel Chandler Harris heard animal tales being passed on from one slave generation to the next. Virtually every single Brer Rabbit tale written down by Harris, told by Remus, had been a staple of Afro-American folk expression prior to 1880, and the tales continue to be told, free of Harris's influence, to the present day. Shaped by a long line of oral artists, Brer Rabbit is black from the tip of his ears to the fuzz of his tail, and he defeats his enemies with a superior intelligence growing from a total understanding of his hostile environment. He is the brier-patch representative of a people living by their wits to make a way out of no way.

These two images, Uncle Remus's semiminstrelsy and Brer Rabbit's cunning tricksterism, complicate the interchange between tale and teller in Harris's famous book. Uncle Remus is literature, artifice, a Victorian relic whose plantation manners embarrass the modern reader. Brer Rabbit is folklore, a communally created universal outlaw whose revolutionary antics satisfy deep human needs. Joel Chandler Harris works between the two of them, investing a part of himself in Uncle Remus, struggling to understand Brer Rabbit's appeal.

Joel Chandler Harris was pathologically shy, so self-effacing he often found himself unable to speak in the presence of strangers. He habitually stuttered in an unfamiliar environment, struggling to achieve speech. As a young printer, he couldn't repeat the initiation oath of his typesetter's union. Honored at a New York banquet, he suffered through the formal proceedings, then sprinted to his hotel room in a panic, leaving town and canceling all further engagements. Totally at ease only around a few friends and his family, Harris admitted that he lacked "the polishment, so to speak, that enables a fellow to get on with other fellows." About to celebrate his closest friend's silver wedding anniversary, he fled at the front gate, leaving his wife to make his excuses. Harris himself said it best: "I am morbidly sensitive. . . . It is an affliction—a disease. . . . It is worse than death itself. It is horrible." Over the years he grew more and more eccentric, wearing unfashionable clothes and refusing to remove his hat even indoors, perhaps to hide his conspicuous red hair.

Harris told his publisher it was his "keenest regret" that he had ever allowed his name to appear on his books. He refused to read from *Uncle Remus* despite lucrative offers, and he avoided telling Brer Rabbit tales, even to his own children. His correspondence expresses a staggering humility. He felt his literary reputation unmerited, since his role in the Uncle Remus tales was that of a mere "compiler." "I am perfectly well aware that my book has no basis of literary art to stand upon," he told Mark Twain; "I know it is the matter and not the manner that has attracted public attention." He called himself only a "cornfield journalist," admitting, "Nobody knows better than I do how far below the level of permanence my writings fall."

One might explain away the self-deprecation as an admirable modesty, or a coy authorial game, similar to Faulkner's claim that he was a mere farmer. In Harris's case, the disparagement was so consistent, and extended over such a long period of time, that clearly it was obsessive behavior. A vague, deep-seated guilt lay somewhere beneath Harris's shyness. In 1886, an author already so famous that a national magazine begged him for a biographical essay, Harris called his fame "accidental" and disclaimed: "I . . . know nothing at all of what is termed literary art. I have had no opportunity to nourish any serious literary ambition." He was "embarrassed" by his success: "People persist in calling me a literary man, when I am a journalist and nothing else."

Harris was obviously of two minds about his fame— on the one hand he sought it by continuing to write, on the other he felt unworthy of it—and those two minds were seldom very far from the surface. In an extraordinary letter to his daughter, well after he was a national figure, Harris personified the two sides of his personality:

As for myself—though you could hardly call me a real, sure enough author—I never have anything but the vaguest ideas of what I am going to write; but when I take my pen in my hand, the rust clears away and the "other fellow" takes charge. You know all of us have two entities, or personalities. That is the reason you see and hear persons "talking to themselves." They are talking to the "other fellow." I have often asked my "other fellow" where he gets all his information, and how he can remember, in the nick of time, things that I have forgotten long ago; but he never satisfies my curiosity. He is simply a spectator of my folly until I seize a pen, and then he comes forward and takes charge.

Sometimes I laugh heartily at what he writes . . . it is not my writing at all; it is my "other fellow" doing the work and I am getting all the credit for it. Now, I'll admit that I write the editorials for the paper. The "other fellow" has nothing to do with them, and, so far as I am able to get his views on the subject, he regards them with scorn and contempt . . . He is a creature hard to understand, but, so far as I can understand him, he's a very sour, surly fellow until I give him an opportunity to guide my pen in subjects congenial to him; whereas, I am, as you know, jolly, good-natured, and entirely harmless.

Now, my "other fellow," I am convinced, would do some damage if I didn't give him an opportunity to work off his energy in the way he delights.

Harris's psychological complexity was masked by an uneventful biography. Born in 1848, he grew up illegitimate in a small rural village, Eatonton, Georgia. Harris's biographers have long suggested that his birth out of wedlock explains his anxieties. Perhaps so, but the fact also remains that Harris was a kind and loving father and husband, nowhere exhibiting in his domestic life the kinds of inadequacies he apparently felt in the larger world. He also was a competent, conscientious, and professional journalist all of his adult life; his journalism displays authority and wit; there is no hint of the shyness of the man himself, perhaps because, as he once wrote, "You know, of course, that I do most of my talking with the pen." Walter Hines Page, visiting Harris shortly after the initial success of *Uncle Remus,* could only remark, "It was impossible to believe the man realized what he had done. . . . Joe Harris [the journalist] does not appreciate Joel Chandler Harris."

Reared by a strong-willed mother who refused to act as a community outcast, who stimulated her son's literary ambitions by reading to him nightly from *The Vicar of Wakefield,* Harris left home at the age of thirteen to learn the printer's trade on the only newspaper ever published on a plantation, Joseph Turner's *The Countryman,* printed at "Turnwold," nine miles from Eatonton in Putnam County.

Turner was an unusual man, "good" to his slaves, literate, cultivated, and eccentric, and he shaped Harris in many ways, serving as a kind of literary father. He placed his large library at Harris's disposal and both encouraged and demanded the discipline necessary for a young writer. Harris began publishing juvenile pieces in *The Countryman,* displaying considerable wit for a printer's devil.

Harris's semiautobiographical account of his years at Turnwold, *On the Plantation,* reports that he befriended a runaway slave shortly after arriving, an act of kindness that caused Turnwold's black citizens to treat him with special respect: "There was nothing they were not ready to do for him at any time of day or night." Two slaves in particular took him under their wing. Masters of the tale teller's art, "Uncle" George Terrell and "Old" Harbert shared with him their repertoire of folktales. Terrell owned a Dutch oven in which he made ginger cakes each Saturday, then sold them to the children of planters. At twilight, by the light of the oven's fire, he told stories to the Turner children and Joe Harris.

Harris left Turnwold in 1866 after *The Countryman* stopped publishing and spent the next decade building a newspaper career, including among his stops Forsyth, Georgia (1867–70), where the town gardener was named Remus. In the fall of 1876, a yellow fever epidemic forced him to leave a paper he had edited in Savannah and bring his family to Atlanta. Well known for his humorous paragraphs widely reprinted across Georgia, Harris was quickly hired as a columnist and editorial writer by Atlanta's major newspaper, the *Atlanta Constitution.*

The *Constitution* had for some time been using "an antebellum darky" named Old Si for comic comment on its editorial page. Written in dialect, the Old Si sketches had been a great hit, but their creator was leaving the paper. The new staff member was given the assignment; he told his employers, "I know the old time Middle Georgia Negro pretty well."

A character named Remus appeared briefly in the October 31, 1876, issue, followed by Uncle Remus himself on November 28; for the next three years Harris periodically published sketches about this first Uncle Remus, an elderly ex-slave who occasionally dropped by the *Constitution* offices to beg from the staff and talk his darky talk. This Uncle Remus, little more than a delegate for white Atlanta's views of Reconstruction blacks ("W'en freedom come out de niggers sorter got dere humps up, an' dey staid dat way, twel bimeby dey begun fer ter git hongry, an' den dey begun fer ter drap inter line right smartually"), eventually gave way to a second Uncle Remus, the "old time Negro" of the Brer Rabbit tales, whom Harris remembered as "a human syndicate . . . of three or four old darkies whom I had known. I just walloped them together into one person and called him Uncle Remus."

This second Uncle Remus tells animal tales, the first of which appeared in the *Constitution* on July 20, 1879. Five months later he reappeared with the tar baby story, and from then until May 1880 he became a regular feature of the *Constitution*'s Sunday edition. The stories received such a favorable response and were reprinted so widely in other newspapers that in early 1880 the New York publisher D. Appleton contacted Harris about bringing out a book-length collection. Harris had already received over a thousand inquiries about the Uncle Remus tales, and the publisher was impressed. Appleton's J. C. Derby stopped in Atlanta, contract in hand, on his way home from Alabama, where he had just collected Jefferson Davis's memoirs, *The Rise and Fall of the Confederate Government.*

Released in November 1880, although officially published in 1881 as part of Appleton's catalogue of humorous publications, *Uncle Remus: His Songs and His Sayings* found instant praise, partly because white reviewers wanted to believe the book granted a glimpse of life behind the veil. The *New York Times* called it "the first real book of American folklore." Northern readers unfamiliar with the South were urged to buy the book; one of Harris's New York correspondents wrote him that the stories "are, to people here, the first graphic pictures of genuine Negro life in the South." The *Dial* followed this lead, praising the book for giving the "sentiments and habits of the negroes themselves." The *New York Evening Post* proclaimed *Uncle Remus* the most significant contribution to the "literature of Negro life" that had ever been made, while *Scribner's Monthly* felt Harris "had recorded in a style so true to character and tradition" that "it is safe to say that no one will ever undertake to improve his work." Shrewd book men saw immediately that white interest in the supposed "sentiments and habits of the negroes" would sell books, especially if the presentation did not threaten. Charles A. Dana told Appleton, *"Uncle Remus* is a great book. It will not only have a large, but a permanent, an enduring, sale."

Perennially shy, Harris continued to write Uncle Remus stories for the remaining twenty-eight years of his life, but avoided public acclaim. He also published nineteen other books, including a number of collections of local-color stories about Georgia, and a Reconstruction novel, *Gabriel Tolliver,* which expressed his moderate views on race and politics. All of this fiction was well received, but the judgment of time has relegated most of it to minor status. Only a few of Harris's short stories, such as "Mingo" or "Free Joe," have survived to be anthologized. *Uncle Remus* made Harris's reputation, and without it he would be a relatively insignificant figure in American literary history.

Harris published a second Uncle Remus collection, *Nights with Uncle Remus,* in 1883; six more Uncle Remus volumes appeared during his lifetime, an additional two after he died. For the last two years of his life he edited and owned a family monthly, *Uncle Remus's Magazine,* which at one point had a circulation of 200,-000. He kept his job as editorial writer at the newspaper until 1900 but after 1890 went to the office in the morning, collected his assignments, and returned home to compose his copy. Harris usually did his "own writing" at night, often surrounded by his children and, later, his grandchildren. A small man who grew increasingly heavy in his later years, apparently from lack of exercise, Harris suffered from ill health for the last decade of his life. He died in 1908 at the age of fifty-nine.

Harris's life story is less important than the story of his creation, Uncle Remus, yet it becomes difficult to separate them. Mark Twain wrote of a group of children who waited eagerly to meet Harris, then turned away in disappointment after discovering he was white. The grinning illustration of Uncle Remus that appeared on the frontispiece of the first edition of *Songs and Sayings* was much better known during Harris's lifetime than his own photograph, even though it bore little resemblance to any black human being, living or dead. As late as the 1930s Coca-Cola ads prominently featured the Uncle Remus image.

Harris's self-deprecation deflected public attention away from the author and onto his stories; appropriately, since the only part of the stories really created by Harris is Uncle Remus himself. Afro-Americans had been telling the same Brer Rabbit tales to each other for 150 years, and the tar baby story had even been published by a folklore collector, Thaddeus Norris, eight years before it appeared as an Uncle Remus tale in the *Constitution*. Harris merely added a new context for tale telling in the figure of an "old time Negro" entertaining and teaching a young white boy. The fictional Uncle Remus, Harris's literary contribution to *Songs and Sayings,* grew from both a personal and a historical necessity.

Harris apparently had a deep need to imagine himself as Uncle Remus. When the "other fellow" took over his writing in the voice of Uncle Remus, that fellow was a black man of Harris's childhood, a plantation figure who told stories that Harris's conscious mind had long forgotten. Harris told Walter Hines Page that he could "think in Negro dialect," that if necessary he could speak whole passages of Emerson as a Negro would. The retiring Harris sometimes overcame his habitual fear of strangers with dialect jokes; he once took on the identity of Uncle Remus to entertain Andrew Carnegie. There is an element of the minstrel show in all this, though Harris's dialect was fairly accurate, thereby distinguishing Remus from the "Honorable Pompey Smash" and other characters of the minstrel stage. The

very authenticity of Harris's dialect reveals his investment in the Uncle Remus role. Psychologically, there
were benefits to blackface, particularly since there was
never any danger of actually being mistaken for a
Negro. In mimicking black speech, often calling himself
Uncle Remus, signing his letters Uncle Remus, hearing
himself referred to by the President of the United States
as Uncle Remus, Joel Chandler Harris assumed an identity well suited to the "other fellow" dualism of his creative life. By donning the black mask of Uncle Remus,
Harris liberated a part of himself.

After the publication of *Songs and Sayings* Harris confessed to a folklorist that "not one [tale] nor any part of
one is an invention of mine." He wanted to present his
stories so that "it may be said that each legend comes
fresh and direct from the Negroes." This was admirable
honesty, but also an act of creative identification. In each
Uncle Remus story, Harris addresses a narrative introduction, in standard English, to what he assumes is a
white audience; then the "other fellow" takes over, in
Remus's black dialect. Harris's psychological investment
in the Remus persona is startlingly revealed in the introduction to *Nights with Uncle Remus.* The painfully shy
author who cannot find his tongue in the presence of
strangers describes an evening of folklore collecting in
Norcross, Georgia, in 1882. Waiting for his train,
Harris observed black railroad workers at their ease at
the end of a long day: "They seemed to be in great good
humor, and cracked jokes at each other's expense in the
midst of boisterous shouts of laughter." He was moved
to sit down "next to one of the liveliest talkers in the
party," and after listening and laughing awhile, he told
the tar baby story "by way of a feeler." The story was
"told in a low tone, as if to avoid attracting attention,
but the comments of the negro . . . were loud and frequent. 'Dar now!' he would exclaim or 'He's a honey,
mon!' or 'Gentermens! git out de way an' gin 'im

room.' " Before the end of the story had been reached, the other men had gathered around and made themselves comfortable. Harris swiftly moved into two other stories, and for the next hour the group swapped tales. In a revealing aside, Harris admitted that a couple of the storytellers, "if their language and their gestures could have been taken down, would have put Uncle Remus to shame."

There would be nothing remarkable about this event if someone other than Joel Chandler Harris had taken part in it. Harris apparently lost his shyness in the presence of black people; no one can be sure why, but clearly he was liberated by the storytelling identity he temporarily assumed with the workers. He wanted to think that he was one of them, their language shared, their stories mutually possessed.

Whatever the psychological imperatives leading to Harris's creation, Uncle Remus must stand on his own and bear the scrutiny of a more radically self-conscious age. Under such gaze, Uncle Remus appears too often as less human being than Southern myth. He was meant to be, in Harris's phrase from another context, "the old-fashioned, unadulterated negro who is still dear to the heart of the South." Remus is as humble toward whites as Harris was toward the world. He gives to the white boy constantly, yet receives only tea cakes and an occasional piece of mince pie in return. He loves and caresses, strokes the child's hair, props him on his knee, constantly says, "Bless yo soul, honey." Merely outlined in *Songs and Sayings,* Remus's character develops further in subsequent volumes until he comes to fulfill all the classic characteristics of the loyal family retainer.

Yet having said all of this, one must also admit that Uncle Remus goes beyond stereotype. Black critics have grudgingly admitted as much, Darwin Turner suggesting that he "transcends" his origins. Sterling Brown complained bitterly of the "first" Uncle Remus of the Atlanta sketches, calling him "a dialect-talking version of a Georgia politician," but Brown also agreed that the Uncle Remus of the animal stories was "finely conceived," and was in fact "one of the best characters in American literature."

This power of Uncle Remus as a character explains much about Harris's own popularity. The Uncle Remus stories create a racial utopia in which black and white love one another and share a childhood, just as Harris thought he had done at Turnwold. Uncle Remus's cabin constitutes one of the most secure and serene environments in American literature. In the half-light of evening, in the flickering shadows of the fire, black man and white boy enjoy an intense and loving bond. Time stands still while animals walk the earth like natural men. Parental authority has retired to the big house, and the confusing world of racial caste disappears at the slave cabin's door. Two human beings share an atmosphere of mutual care and respect, a frozen moment of innocent childhood purity.

That only one of the participants is actually a child goes unnoticed; that it is an unnatural environment is beside the point; that it never really existed historically is forgotten; Uncle Remus's antecedents in both the dialectology of the American minstrel show and the antebellum myth of the contented slave fall by the wayside. For a brief moment, history is suspended in the firelight's flickering glow.

Yet only for a moment. Uncle Remus as a phenomenon of American cultural history quickly reappears, even before the child leaves for his bed in the big house. Harris is the captive of a plantation tradition that includes, in Brown's words, the courtly planter, the one hundred percent Southern belle, the dueling cavalier, and the bighearted mammy. In a strange way, Uncle Remus in the quarters was intended to serve as a sign-

post on America's "road to reunion," a uniting symbol
for South and North.

An editorial writer for the *Atlanta Constitution,* Harris
joined the paper's chief editor, Henry W. Grady, one of
the region's most dynamic leaders, to manipulate public
sentiment toward the goal of reuniting the country—
Northern capital joining Southern labor in a new indus-
trialism. As Grady put it in his famous essay entitled
"The New South": "The Old South rested everything
on slavery and agriculture. . . . The new South presents
. . . a diversified industry that meets the complex needs
of a complex age." Grady's ultimate purpose, as expressed by Harris, was "to draw the two sections together in closer bonds of union, fraternity, harmony and
goodwill."

Uncle Remus became a historical instrument promot-
ing closer bonds of sectional harmony, representing an
image of black people around which Northern and
Southern whites could unite. Harris borrowed Uncle
Tom's faithfulness but did away with his harsh masters,
took the minstrel's grin but added a loving demeanor,
affixed to them his hazy, romantic memories of life at
Turnwold, and created a figure who could contribute to
the country's reunification. Uncle Remus reassured
Southern whites about their darkest fears: free black
people would love, not demand retribution. At the same
time he assured Northern whites that abandoning black
people was not a failure of moral responsibility. Uncle
Remus, immensely popular, witnessed that black people
would turn the other cheek, would continue to love, despite all the broken promises of American history.

Invented as Federal troops withdrew from the South,
Uncle Remus was the perfect figure to allay Northern
uneasiness about the abandonment of the Negro. Uncle
Remus promised the North that Southerners could see
the Negro's virtues and could even celebrate them,
which was proof that rehabilitation had occurred and

that force was no longer necessary to ensure that black people would be treated with justice by their former masters. In an editorial written in the same year that *Uncle Remus* was published, Harris claimed that the South had made "a disastrous and demoralizing mistake" after the war by "refusing to take their old slaves into their care and confidence." The solution, so obvious that it hurt, was, "We had only to hold out our hands to these poor, unfortunate people to renew the confidence and affection that had always existed between the white and colored races in the South."

For moderate Southerners of Harris's stripe, slavery now seemed a blot on the civilization that had produced Washington and Jefferson. There was a reluctant admission that slavery was wrong, even though the means of ending it had seemed an outrage. Harris himself believed that the South would have abolished slavery, in all deliberate speed, without the Civil War. By referring to the romantic tradition of the plantation, a warm, mythic memory that had existed in the South since the proslavery fiction of John Pendleton Kennedy in the 1830s, Harris reinforced a historical theory of slavery that began with the premise, widespread in his generation, that the human relationships of the peculiar institution had been close and mutually supporting. There is relatively little truth to this assertion, especially from black people's point of view, but it was a premise that could be manipulated to enlist support for the cause of the New South. Since slavery had receded into the past, and Reconstruction had brought such violence, blacks and whites were losing sight of the virtues of those former days. Unce Remus, an "old time Negro," reminds Southerners of what was "good" about slavery, becoming a wish-fulfillment fantasy for a populace forced to deal each day with black people considerably less docile than the plantation darky.

Remus's dialect especially supports this fantasy. The

standard English used by the author to frame the tales contrasts with the vivid dialect in the stories themselves, suggesting that black language is colorful but ignorant, that black people are picturesque but intellectually limited. Remus's language helped whites forget that one of Georgia's Reconstruction congressmen was a black man who spoke nothing like a plantation darky; that Frederick Douglass, writing in commanding, imperial prose, published the final version of his autobiography in the same year that *Songs and Sayings* appeared.

Uncle Remus, a black man who knows his place, who never threatens, helped heal the sectional scars. Teddy Roosevelt praised Harris as an author whose work was always a force for the "blotting out of sectional antagonism." This "blotting out" occurs particularly in the Uncle Remus sketch that begins the last part of *Songs and Sayings*, "A Story of the War." It tells of a Federal soldier, wounded in battle, recuperating on Remus's plantation, where he falls in love with his nurse, the one hundred percent Southern belle. After the war they marry and produce the male heir Remus watches over. Harris claimed this story was almost "literally true," but if so, what of the *Constitution* version three years earlier, which ended with the soldier's being shot and killed by none other than Uncle Remus himself? Harris revised the story, as he created the character, to support the political cause of reunification.

While advocating sectional brotherhood, Harris also defended the South, one reason the long-dormant Brer Rabbit stories came back into his waking consciousness. In December 1877, *Lippincott's Magazine* printed some animal tales in an article entitled "Folklore of the Southern Negroes." Harris read the essay and realized that "the curious myths and animal stories" he had "absorbed" at Turnwold held "literary value"; moreover, he knew this material better than most white people, including the article's author, William Owens. Harris mentioned the article in the *Constitution,* complaining about the transcription "Buh" for "Brer" and about omissions by Owens. He admitted later, "The article gave me my cue, and the legends told by Uncle Remus are the result."

Because Harris recreated oral tales on the written page, readers think of him as a literary artist rather than a folklorist. Because Harris was white, many see the tales as tainted by a white perspective, the proof of which is Uncle Remus himself. Some black people resent Harris and Uncle Remus, and some school libraries have gone so far as to ban the Uncle Remus volumes as offensive. Although Uncle Remus has a place in the gallery of racist stereotypes that includes Aunt Jemima and Uncle Ben—and Harris held a full complement of the racist views of his age—there is also the danger of throwing out the tar baby with the bandana.

Not one of the stories, Harris assured readers, was "cooked," and he spent much time and effort verifying the authenticity of the tales he used. Folklore research has largely proved his claim: Harris did not in any significant way tamper with the stories themselves. If he had merely published them in the *Journal of American Folklore,* without the Remus context, he would be thought one of the founding fathers of Afro-American folklore studies. Harris's literary ambitions cannot be ignored, and his white perspective does affect the tales in racist ways, yet there is relatively little reason to doubt Harris when he says that his first book "is composed of stories originally told to me by Negroes." At one point he titled his book *Uncle Remus's Folk-Lore.*

Brer Rabbit's status as folklore rather than literary creation explains much of Harris's guilt as the "author" of *Uncle Remus.* Harris understood that his contribution to the Brer Rabbit tales was only a context for the rabbit to do his tricks. Harris's newspaper editors had wanted an "antebellum darky," and Harris, son of the South, with a good ear for dialect, could supply one. He hid his pathological shyness behind this comic mask, escaping into the blackness that had always beckoned, but carrying along all the prejudices and paternalism of a loyal Georgian. However, the "first" Uncle Remus, a Reconstruction mouthpiece for Harris and Southern whites, the Uncle Remus who appears in *Songs and Sayings* in the twenty-one "character sketches," was nothing but a caricature. He primarily appealed to readers in need of a minstrel show.

After the *Lippincott's* article, Harris reached into the corners of his memory and discovered the significance of Afro-American folklore. Now Uncle Remus had something to say; his stories of Brer Rabbit granted Remus an authority he had never wielded before. Brer Rabbit, not Uncle Remus, commands the modern reader's attention.

The Brer Rabbit tales, shaped under slavery by black artists, function at three levels: they provide complicated insights into the slave's world view; they demonstrate what Bernard Wolfe has called the "psychic drainage system" of folktales for a captive people; and they reveal an ultimate universality reached not by transcending the individual Afro-American experience, but by penetrating to its deepest psychic meaning.

Certainly the stories can be enjoyed unconsciously. The average six-year-old who identifies with Cinderella or Brer Rabbit does not analyze his or her emotions. But folklore is a complicated system of expression, and to understand its universality one begins with its culturally specific characteristics. Folklorist Florence Baer has traced twenty-four of the thirty-two animal tales in *Songs and Sayings* to Africa. Her studies of all 220 of the tales concludes that well over half of them originally were African tales in some form.

Naturally enough, the African tales were adapted to

the Afro-American experience. Slaves told tales or the parts of tales that seemed most suited to the slave environment. Trickster tales, universal in all folklore, were especially popular because they often emphasized the triumph of the weak over the strong; they seemed ready made for a slave situation in which foot speed—escape—was a persistent hope and tricks rather than physical force were the primary recourse for survival. The point cannot be overemphasized: black people identified with Brer Rabbit. When Brer Rabbit triumphed over a physically superior foe, black people fantasized themselves in the identical situation. As one black storyteller told an early folklorist: "I allers use my sense for help me 'long jes' like Brer Rabbit." Historian Lawrence Levine states: "The white master could believe that the rabbit stories his slaves told were mere figments of a childish imagination. . . . Blacks knew better. The trickster's exploits, which overturned the neat hierarchy of the world in which he was forced to live, became their exploits; the justice he achieved, their justice; the strategies he employed, their strategies. From his adventures they obtained relief; from his triumphs they learned hope." Even Harris himself understood this side of Brer Rabbit. In *Nights with Uncle Remus,* Uncle Remus tells the boy, "Well, I tell you dis, ef deze yer tales wuz des fun, fun, fun, en giggle, giggle, giggle, I let you know I'd a-done drapt um long ago."

Yet the allegorical identification between Brer Rabbit and black people is extremely complicated, much more complex than the simple victory of the weak (black) over the strong (white) that Harris noted in his introduction when he interpreted it as a victory not for virtue "but helplessness . . . not malice, but mischievousness." To begin with, the prior existence of the rabbit as an African trickster proves that the tales originally were not racially coded for allegorical interpretation. Although it is true, as Bernard Wolfe has counted, that

Brer Rabbit appears twenty-six times in *Uncle Remus,*
encounters the fox twenty times, and soundly trounces
him nineteen times, it is also true that Brer Rabbit often
triumphs through malice and malevolence; he is seldom
merely mischievous. Above all he is violent, savagely at-
tacking not only his adversaries but also sometimes his
friends. Assisted by his children, he cruelly assassinates
the fox, imprisoning him in a chest, then pouring in
scalding water little by little until he dies. If Brer Fox
represents the white man, so be it: the slave's rage was
justified. But Brer Rabbit also contributes to the demise
of his friend Brer Possum, who is entirely innocent, to
escape punishment for stealing food. The allegory is not
always precise.

The allegorical interpretation tends to overlook the
didactic function of the tales. The Brer Rabbit tales
teach each generation anew the nature of the slave's universe. Telling the tales was a means of acculturation, a
technique of adaptation to the environment of bondage.
Brer Rabbit can hardly be blamed for his violence, since
the world he inhabits is one of unrelieved hostility. He
must be constantly on guard, never trusting, always
watching. Danger is everywhere; an assault lurks behind
every bush. He never enjoys an open road, free of troubles. If Brer Rabbit forgets for one moment the true
nature of his environment, if he once begins to think
that he has cold-conked a tough world, a lesson in hubris
lies just around the corner. The tar baby story, so famous for its reverse psychology that it has become a national metaphor for duplicity and slickness, also teaches
the virtues of internal discipline. Brer Rabbit thinks for a
moment that he can confront the world directly, loud-
talk it into submission. He gets taken in by the tar baby;
before he knows it he is trapped, as much by his own
braggadocio as by the tar baby's adhesiveness. He ends
up with head and all four limbs stuck to the tar baby because, full of himself, he has tried to bully someone

less powerful—and black. The racial ironies in the tar baby symbol—whites are intertwined with blacks, try as they may to untangle themselves—emphasize again how the tales go beyond allegory. Black people could identify with both the rabbit *and* the tar baby.

In another tale, with a moral quite different from that of the comparable version in Aesop, Brer Tarrypin outraces the much speedier rabbit by positioning relatives along the route and himself at the finish line. Brer Rabbit thinks he has sped through the race, flashing his form, but in fact he has only chased himself and lost the contest. The trick works because Rabbit assumes all members of the Terrapin family look alike. But the tale also teaches the wisdom of knowing your opponent's weakness and utilizing that knowledge. At the level of "psychic drainage," the unconscious level at which stories bring satisfactions we scarcely realize, the story offers immense satisfactions to any people denied their individuality by a system which ignores that some people run, others walk. "I am what I am, shell and all," says the tale, "and I can beat you with it."

At the most subtle levels of the narratives, Brer Rabbit teaches the world view necessary for survival. There is a constant emphasis on food as a symbol of status and power—a natural enough concern for slaves living on meager rations—and Brer Rabbit is particularly adept at stealing food. In one of the more complicated tales in *Uncle Remus,* Brer Rabbit steals Brer Wolf's fish, then, when confronted with his crime, tells Brer Wolf that if he thinks he has been wronged, he can kill Brer Rabbit's cow—which Wolf, seeking justice, proceeds to do. But Brer Rabbit, knowing Brer Wolf's fear of "patter-rollers," the white bands who enforce the slave codes, tricks him, stealing the meat back after falsely warning of a patter-roller attack. Allegorically, the tale may teach that one should not excessively fear the patter-rollers, but at another level it emphasizes the uncertainty of possession in a world where irrational violence can be invoked at any moment. There is no justice, only the search for it, and although Rabbit is on top at the end of the tale, Brer Wolf will be back with designs on the smokehouse.

Whatever our interpretation of individual tales, one constant in all the Uncle Remus stories is the psychic satisfactions that come from Brer Rabbit's acquisition of status. This characteristic of the tales can best be seen in the famous tale of Brer Rabbit riding Brer Fox. A symbolic courting tale, the story revolves around Brer Rabbit's attempt to impress "Miss Meadows en de gals" by telling them that Brer Fox used to be "my daddy's riding horse." Told of Brer Rabbit's boast, Brer Fox vows to bring the rabbit to the ladies and make him eat his words. Brer Fox tries to trick Brer Rabbit into attending a party at Miss Meadows's, but Brer Rabbit, feigning sickness, can only go if Brer Fox carries him part of the way. He tricks Brer Fox into putting on saddle and bridle, then breaks his promise and rides him right up to the front door, where "Miss Meadows en all de gals wuz settin' on de peazzer." Brer Rabbit saunters around smoking a cigar, a living reminder that the world can be overturned, the weak can ride the strong.

The story demonstrates the ultimate triumph for the slave listeners. Brer Rabbit does not kill his enemy, but treats him as a beast of burden—the legal status of slaves—and humiliates him. He also implicitly steals his woman, although Harris probably did not understand this part of the story. "Miss Meadows en de gals" have caused a good deal of inquiry over the years. Harris admitted to his illustrator he had no idea why they were there, and neither does Uncle Remus: "Don't ax me, honey. She wuz in de tale, Miss Meadows en de gals wuz, en de tale I give you like hi't wer' gun ter me." But there should be no question about their function. The "gals" represent the order of the white world, which

Brer Rabbit violates by trampling on the most sacred of white sexual taboos. In effect, Brer Rabbit takes Brer Fox's place, turning the established order of the slave world on its head.

The Brer Rabbit tales document one revolutionary turn of events after another. The world of superior force is undermined, but so is the notion that the meek shall inherit the earth; cunning often results in victory, but the trickster can also be tricked. Brer Rabbit exhibits the revolutionary consciousness necessary to survive in an oppressive system. He suggests that no order can be depended on for very long, that there are no certainties, that goodness may win this week but power the next. What is certain is the need to improvise, to hang loose, stay cool, avoid sticky situations, shun rigid interpretations of events. Brer Rabbit shows that anarchy undermines all systems which mask reality. His lessons inculcate a revolutionary consciousness because they teach that one never has to accept limitations on the self, that one can never be denied the radical possibilities of being human.

The Uncle Remus tales showcase a revolutionary black figure, Brer Rabbit, who must be sanitized for acceptance by the predominantly white American reading public of the nineteenth century. For slaves listening to the Brer Rabbit tales, the rabbit provided an acceptable outlet for an overwhelming hostility, which could lead to self-destruction if openly expressed. Black Brer Rabbit could only be assimilated into the culture of a postslavery America through the mouth of a quasi-Negro whom white readers desperately needed to defuse the stories' revolutionary hostility.

Uncle Remus always loves, and Brer Rabbit sometimes hates, but Brer Rabbit does not hate life. He glories in its manifold possibilities, the chances for reversal. He embodies a revolutionary consciousness which says that one need not accept the world as it is, that any individual, working with the mother wit at hand, can change things.

This revolutionary quality makes Brer Rabbit a universal figure. Brer Rabbit expresses archetypes of human emotion because one identifies with his liberating sense of anarchy—an imperative of liberation embedded deep in Afro-American history. The early tellers of Brer Rabbit tales, "black and unknown bards," had no choice but to interpret the world as morally unstable. If slaves had not been able to believe in the possibility of revolution, of overturning the antihuman moral structure offered by slavery, they could have scarcely endured their physical pain. If their minds could not have identified with Brer Rabbit's assaults, with his violence, they might have actually become the Sambo figures whites wanted them to be.

One arrives at the universality of the Brer Rabbit tales by examining the ways in which we are all oppressed, the limits placed upon us, the need we all have for a psychic drainage system; for nineteenth-century whites the closest analogy was that of children surrounded by an adult world of unrelenting authority, thus the popularity of Uncle Remus among white children. Harris became, in Mark Twain's words, "the oracle of the nation's nurseries." But for blacks, the oppression has been adult and immediate, even when, as in the case of Harris, the oppressor has had great sympathy with the race, has been guilty of paternalism rather than physical violence.

Black folklore is not childish, yet it has survived in a society given to treating black people as children. Human survival systems, cultural paradigms for mental health, depend on the possibility of imagining a revolutionary change. It doesn't have to be this way, Brer Rabbit says, and we listen because to believe is human.

The curious history of Uncle Remus, Brer Rabbit, and Joel Chandler Harris charts an author retreating from an adult, public world of difficult decisions, establishing a life for himself that would change as little as possible, then trying to express what remained dammed within through a medium that he could mimic but never fully comprehend. Uncle Remus, the mimetic creation, had his moment, but his importance has diminished with the passage of time; Brer Rabbit, the collective discovery of a people seeking to express their humanity, has assumed universality. Uncle Remus became more than Harris during the author's lifetime, and now Brer Rabbit has become more than both of them, because Harris could never openly embrace, or understand, a radically altered racial universe—one in which he no longer had to carry a terrible burden of guilt. It is a very American paradox.

—Robert Hemenway

Suggestions for
Further Reading

BIBLIOGRAPHICAL

Bickley, R. Bruce, Jr. *Joel Chandler Harris: A Reference Guide.* Boston: G. K. Hall and Co., 1976.

Ray, Charles. "Joel Chandler Harris." In *A Bibliographical Guide to the Study of Southern Literature,* edited by Louis Rubin. Baton Rouge: Louisiana State University Press, 1969.

Strickland, William Bradley. *Joel Chandler Harris: A Bibliographical Study.* Ph.D. dissertation, University of Georgia, 1976.

BIOGRAPHICAL

Bickley, R. Bruce, Jr. *Joel Chandler Harris.* Boston: Twayne Publishers, 1978.

Cousins, Paul M. *Joel Chandler Harris: A Biography.* Baton Rouge: Louisiana State University Press, 1968.

Griska, Joseph. "Selected Letters of Joel Chandler Harris, 1863–1885." Ph.D. dissertation, Texas A and M University, 1976.

Harris, Julia Collier. *The Life and Letters of Joel Chandler Harris.* Boston and New York: Houghton Mifflin Co., 1918.

CRITICAL

Baer, Florence. *Sources and Analogues of the Uncle Remus Tales.* Helsinki: Folklore Fellows Communications, 1981.

Bickley, R. Bruce, Jr., ed. *Critical Essays on Joel Chandler Harris.* Boston: G. K. Hall and Co., 1981.

Bone, Robert. *Down Home: A History of Afro-American Short Fiction.* New York: G. P. Putnam's Sons, 1975.

Brookes, Stella Brewer. *Joel Chandler Harris—Folklorist.* Athens, Ga.: University of Georgia Press, 1950.

Brown, Sterling. *The Negro in American Fiction.* Washington, D.C.: Associates in Negro Folk Education, 1937.

English, Thomas. "In Memory of Uncle Remus," *Southern Literary Messenger* 2 (February 1940): 77–83.

English, Thomas H., ed. *Mark Twain to Uncle Remus: 1881–1885.* Atlanta: Emory University Sources and Reprints, series VII, no. 3, 1953.

Levine, Lawrence. *Black Culture and Black Consciousness.* New York: Oxford University Press, 1977.

Turner, Darwin T. "Daddy Joel Harris and His Old Time Darkies," *Southern Literary Journal* 1 (December 1968): 20–41.

Wolfe, Bernard. "Uncle Remus and the Malevolent Rabbit," *Commentary* 8 (July 1949): 31–41.

Note on the Text

This edition follows the text of the first edition, published by D. Appleton and Company in New York. The book was originally released in November 1880, although the title page bears the official publication date of 1881. There were three states, usually thought of as representing three separate printings, to this first edition, since Appleton had not anticipated the large demand for the book. All are usually considered first editions because they all carry the 1881 date, but the actual first edition can be identified by a few minor changes that took place in the second and third printings. In the first printing, the last line of page nine includes the word *presumptive* and page 233 contains an advertisement for Roberts Bartholow's *A Treatise on the Practice of Medicine*. In the second printing, the word *presumptive* has been changed to *presumptuous* and page 233 again advertises Bartholow's *Treatise*. The third printing repeats *presumptuous*, but Bartholow has been replaced with reprints of favorable reviews of *Songs and Sayings*.

The original edition was reprinted in 1883, 1884, 1886, 1889, 1890, and 1892. In 1895 Appleton brought out a new and revised edition, containing superior illustrations by A. B. Frost, a talented artist who would become a close friend of Harris's as well as his favorite illustrator. The revised edition was reprinted virtually every year between 1895 and 1941; the printings of 1908 and 1920 show minor changes.

It is interesting to note that a pirated English edition

appeared almost immediately, published by George
Routledge and Sons in 1881. The authorized English
edition also appeared the same year but omitted both the
songs and the twenty-one character sketches entitled
"His Sayings." The Woodruff Library at Emory University, where most of the Harris manuscripts and letters are deposited, owns a first edition of *Uncle Remus*
that Harris himself began to revise, marking it in pencil
to make the dialect more accurate. Anxious about the
book's reception, Harris apparently was concerned that
linguists would find fault with his transcriptions. Few of
his corrections, however, became a part of subsequent
editions.

UNCLE REMUS:
HIS SONGS AND HIS SAYINGS

Introduction.

I am advised by my publishers that this book is to be included in their catalogue of humorous publications, and this friendly warning gives me an opportunity to say that however humorous it may be in effect, its intention is perfectly serious; and, even if it were otherwise, it seems to me that a volume written wholly in dialect must have its solemn, not to say melancholy, features. With respect to the Folk-Lore series, my purpose has been to preserve the legends themselves in their original simplicity, and to wed them permanently to the quaint dialect—if, indeed, it can be called a dialect—through the medium of which they have become a part of the domestic history of every Southern family; and I have endeavored to give to the whole a genuine flavor of the old plantation.

Each legend has its variants, but in every instance I have retained that particular version which seemed to me to be the most characteristic, and have given it without embellishment and without exaggeration. The dialect, it will be observed, is wholly different from that of the Hon. Pompey Smash and his literary descendants, and different also from the intolerable misrepresentations of the minstrel stage, but it is at least phonetically genuine. Nevertheless, if the language of Uncle Remus fails to give vivid hints of the really poetic imagination of the negro; if it fails to embody the quaint and homely humor which was his most prominent characteristic; if it does not suggest a certain picturesque sensitiveness—a curious exaltation of mind and temperament not to be

defined by words—then I have reproduced the form of
the dialect merely, and not the essence, and my attempt
may be accounted a failure. At any rate, I trust I have
been successful in presenting what must be, at least to a
large portion of American readers, a new and by no
means unattractive phase of negro character—a phase
which may be considered a curiously sympathetic sup-
plement to Mrs. Stowe's wonderful defense of slavery as
it existed in the South. Mrs. Stowe, let me hasten to say,
attacked the possibilities of slavery with all the eloquence
of genius; but the same genius painted the portrait of the
Southern slave-owner, and defended him.

A number of the plantation legends originally appeared in the columns of a daily newspaper—"The Atlanta Constitution"—and in that shape they attracted
the attention of various gentlemen who were kind
enough to suggest that they would prove to be valuable
contributions to myth-literature. It is but fair to say that
ethnological considerations formed no part of the undertaking which has resulted in the publication of this volume. Professor J. W. Powell, of the Smithsonian
Institution, who is engaged in an investigation of the
mythology of the North American Indians, informs me
that some of Uncle Remus's stories appear in a number
of different languages, and in various modified forms,
among the Indians; and he is of the opinion that they are
borrowed by the negroes from the red-men. But this, to
say the least, is extremely doubtful, since another inves-
tigator (Mr. Herbert H. Smith, author of "Brazil and
the Amazons") has met with some of these stories
among tribes of South American Indians, and one in
particular he has traced to India, and as far east as Siam.
Mr. Smith has been kind enough to send me the proof-
sheets of his chapter on "The Myths and Folk-Lore of
the Amazonian Indians," in which he reproduces some
of the stories which he gathered while exploring the
Amazons.

In the first of his series, a tortoise falls from a tree upon the head of a jaguar and kills him; in one of Uncle Remus's stories, the terrapin falls from a shelf in Miss Meadows's house and stuns the fox, so that the latter fails to catch the rabbit. In the next, a jaguar catches a tortoise by the hind-leg as he is disappearing in his hole; but the tortoise convinces him he is holding a root, and so escapes; Uncle Remus tells how the fox endeavored to drown the terrapin, but turned him loose because the terrapin declared his tail to be only a stump-root. Mr. Smith also gives the story of how the tortoise outran the deer, which is identical as to incident with Uncle Remus's story of how Brer Tarrypin outran Brer Rabbit. Then there is the story of how the tortoise pretended that he was stronger than the tapir. He tells the latter he can drag him into the sea, but the tapir retorts that he will pull the tortoise into the forest and kill him besides. The tortoise thereupon gets a vine-stem, ties one end around the body of the tapir, and goes to the sea, where he ties the other end to the tail of a whale. He then goes into the wood, midway between them both, and gives the vine a shake as a signal for the pulling to begin. The struggle between the whale and tapir goes on until each thinks the tortoise is the strongest of animals. Compare this with the story of the terrapin's contest with the bear, in which Miss Meadows's bed-cord is used instead of a vine-stem. One of the most characteristic of Uncle Remus's stories is that in which the rabbit proves to Miss Meadows and the girls that the fox is his riding-horse. This is almost identical with a story quoted by Mr. Smith, where the jaguar is about to marry the deer's daughter. The cotia—a species of rodent—is also in love with her, and he tells the deer that he can make a riding-horse of the jaguar. "Well," says the deer, "if you can make the jaguar carry you, you shall have my daughter." Thereupon the story proceeds pretty much as Uncle Remus tells it of the fox and rabbit. The cotia finally jumps from the jaguar and takes refuge in a hole, where an owl is set to watch him, but he flings sand in the owl's eyes and escapes. In another story given by Mr. Smith, the cotia is very thirsty, and, seeing a man coming with a jar on his head, lies down in the road in front of him, and repeats this until the man puts down his jar to go back after all the dead cotias he has seen. This is almost identical with Uncle Remus's story of how the rabbit robbed the fox of his game. In a story from Upper Egypt, a fox lies down in the road in front of a man who is carrying fowls to market, and finally succeeds in securing them.

This similarity extends to almost every story quoted by Mr. Smith, and some are so nearly identical as to point unmistakably to a common origin; but when and where? When did the negro or the North American Indian ever come in contact with the tribes of South America? Upon this point the author of "Brazil and the Amazons," who is engaged in making a critical and comparative study of these myth-stories, writes:

"I am not prepared to form a theory about these stories. There can be no doubt that some of them, found among the negroes and the Indians, had a common origin. The most natural solution would be to suppose that they originated in Africa, and were carried to South America by the negro slaves. They are certainly found among the Red Negroes; but, unfortunately for the African theory, it is equally certain that they are told by savage Indians of the Amazons Valley, away up on the Tapajos, Red Negro, and Tapurá. These Indians hardly ever see a negro, and their languages are very distinct from the broken Portuguese spoken by the slaves. The form of the stories, as recounted in the Tupi and Mundurucú languages, seems to show that they were originally formed in those languages or have long been adopted in them.

"It is interesting to find a story from Upper Egypt (that of the fox who pretended to be dead) identical with an Amazonian story, and strongly resembling one found by you among the negroes. Varnhagen, the Brazilian historian (now Visconde de Rio Branco), tried to prove a relationship between the ancient Egyptians, or other Turanian stock, and the Tupi Indians. His theory rested on rather a slender basis, yet it must be confessed that he had one or two strong points. Do the resemblances between Old and New World stories point to a similar conclusion? It would be hard to say with the material that we now have.

"One thing is certain. The animal stories told by the negroes in our Southern States and in Brazil were brought by them from Africa. Whether they originated there, or with the Arabs, or Egyptians, or with yet more ancient nations, must still be an open question. Whether the Indians got them from the negroes or from some earlier source is equally uncertain. We have seen enough to know that a very interesting line of investigation has been opened."

Professor Hartt, in his "Amazonian Tortoise Myths," quotes a story from the "Riverside Magazine" of November, 1868, which will be recognized as a variant of one given by Uncle Remus. I venture to append it here, with some necessary verbal and phonetic alterations, in order to give the reader an idea of the difference between the dialect of the cotton plantations, as used by Uncle Remus, and the lingo in vogue on the rice plantations and Sea Islands of the South Atlantic States:

"One time B'er Deer an' B'er Cooter (Terrapin) was courtin', and de lady did bin lub B'er Deer mo' so dan B'er Cooter. She did bin lub B'er Cooter, but she lub B'er Deer de morest. So de noung lady say to B'er Deer and B'er Cooter bofe dat dey mus' hab a ten-mile race, an' de one dat beats, she will go marry him.

"So B'er Cooter say to B'er Deer: 'You has got mo'

longer legs dan I has, but I will run you. You run ten mile on land, and I will run ten mile on de water!'

"So B'er Cooter went an' git nine er his fam'ly, an' put one at ebery mile-pos', and he hisse'f, what was to run wid B'er Deer, he was right in front of de young lady's do', in de broomgrass.

"Dat mornin' at nine o'clock, B'er Deer he did met B'er Cooter at de fus mile-pos', wey dey was to start fum. So he call: 'Well, B'er Cooter, is you ready? Go long!' As he git on to de nex' mile-pos', he say: 'B'er Cooter!' B'er Cooter say: 'Hullo!' B'er Deer say: 'You dere?' B'er Cooter say: 'Yes, B'er Deer, I dere too.'

"Nex' mile-pos' he jump, B'er Deer say: 'Hullo, B'er Cooter!' B'er Cooter say: 'Hullo, B'er Deer! you dere too?' B'er Deer say: 'Ki! it look like you gwine fer tie me; it look like we gwine fer de gal tie!'

"W'en he git to de nine-mile pos' he tought he git dere fus, 'cause he mek two jump; so he holler: 'B'er Cooter!' B'er Cooter answer: 'You dere too?' B'er Deer say: 'It look like you gwine tie me.' B'er Cooter say: 'Go long, B'er Deer. I git dere in due season time,' which he does, and wins the race."

The story of the Rabbit and the Fox, as told by the Southern negroes, is artistically dramatic in this: it progresses in an orderly way from a beginning to a well-defined conclusion, and is full of striking episodes that suggest the culmination. It seems to me to be to a certain extent allegorical, albeit such an interpretation may be unreasonable. At least it is a fable thoroughly characteristic of the negro; and it needs no scientific investigation to show why he selects as his hero the weakest and most harmless of all animals, and brings him out victorious in contests with the bear, the wolf, and the fox. It is not virtue that triumphs, but helplessness; it is not malice, but mischievousness. It would be presumptive in me to offer an opinion as to the origin of these curious myth-stories; but, if ethnologists should discover that they did not originate with the African, the proof to that effect should be accompanied with a good deal of persuasive eloquence.

Curiously enough, I have found few negroes who will acknowledge to a stranger that they know anything of these legends; and yet to relate one of the stories is the surest road to their confidence and esteem. In this way, and in this way only, I have been enabled to collect and verify the folk-lore included in this volume. There is an anecdote about the Irishman and the rabbit which a number of negroes have told to me with great unction, and which is both funny and characteristic, though I will not undertake to say that it has its origin with the blacks. One day an Irishman who had heard people talking about "mares' nests" was going along the big road—it is always the big road in contradistinction to neighborhood paths and bypaths, called in the vernacular "nigh-cuts"—when he came to a pumpkin-patch. The Irishman had never seen any of this fruit before, and he at once concluded that he had discovered a veritable mare's nest. Making the most of his opportunity, he gathered one of the pumpkins in his arms and went on his way. A pumpkin is an exceedingly awkward thing to carry, and the Irishman had not gone far before he made a misstep, and stumbled. The pumpkin fell to the ground, rolled down the hill into a "brush-heap," and, striking against a stump, was broken. The story continues in the dialect: "W'en de punkin roll in de bresh-heap, out jump a rabbit; en soon's de I'shmuns see dat, he take atter de rabbit en holler: 'Kworp, colty! kworp, colty!' but de rabbit, he des flew." The point of this is obvious.

As to the songs, the reader is warned that it will be found difficult to make them conform to the ordinary rules of versification, nor is it intended that they should so conform. They are written, and are intended to be

read, solely with reference to the regular and invariable
recurrence of the caesura, as, for instance, the first
stanza of the Revival Hymn:

"Oh, whar | shill we go | w'en de great | day comes |
    Wid de blow | in' er de trumpits | en de bang | in' er de
      drums |
    How man | y po' sin | ners'll be kotch'd | out late |
    En fine | no latch | ter de gold | en gate | "

In other words, the songs depend for their melody
and rhythm upon the musical quality of *time,* and not
upon long or short, accented or unaccented syllables. I
am persuaded that this fact led Mr. Sidney Lanier, who
is thoroughly familiar with the metrical peculiarities of
negro songs, into the exhaustive investigation which has
resulted in the publication of his scholarly treatise on
"The Science of English Verse."

The difference between the dialect of the legends and
that of the character-sketches, slight as it is, marks the
modifications which the speech of the negro has under-
gone even where education has played no part in re-
forming it. Indeed, save in the remote country districts,
the dialect of the legends has nearly disappeared. I am
perfectly well aware that the character-sketches are
without permanent interest, but they are embodied here
for the purpose of presenting a phase of negro character
wholly distinct from that which I have endeavored to
preserve in the legends. Only in this shape, and with all
the local allusions, would it be possible to adequately
represent the shrewd observations, the curious retorts,
the homely thrusts, the quaint comments, and the humorous philosophy of the race of which Uncle Remus is
a type.

If the reader not familiar with plantation life will imagine that the myth-stories of Uncle Remus are told night
after night to a little boy by an old negro who appears to

be venerable enough to have lived during the period which he describes—who has nothing but pleasant memories of the discipline of slavery—and who has all the prejudices of caste and pride of family that were the natural results of the system; if the reader can imagine all this, he will find little difficulty in appreciating and sympathizing with the air of affectionate superiority which Uncle Remus assumes as he proceeds to unfold the mysteries of plantation lore to a little child who is a product of that practical reconstruction which has been going on to some extent since the war in spite of the politicians. Uncle Remus describes that reconstruction in his "Story of the War," and I may as well add here for the benefit of the curious that that story is almost literally true.

J. C. H.

Contents.

His Songs.

His Sayings.

LEGENDS
OF THE OLD
PLANTATION.

I.
UNCLE REMUS INITIATES
THE LITTLE BOY.

One evening recently, the lady whom Uncle Remus calls "Miss Sally" missed her little seven-year-old. Making search for him through the house and through the yard, she heard the sound of voices in the old man's cabin, and, looking through the window, saw the child sitting by Uncle Remus. His head rested against the old man's arm, and he was gazing with an expression of the most intense interest into the rough, weather-beaten face, that beamed so kindly upon him. This is what "Miss Sally" heard:

"Bimeby, one day, arter Brer Fox bin doin' all dat he could fer ter ketch Brer Rabbit, en Brer Rabbit bin doin' all he could fer ter keep 'im fum it, Brer Fox say to hisse'f dat he'd put up a game on Brer Rabbit, en he ain't mo'n got de wuds out'n his mouf twel Brer Rabbit come a lopin' up de big road, lookin' des ez plump, en ez fat, en ez sassy ez a Moggin hoss in a barley-patch.

" 'Hol' on dar, Brer Rabbit,' sez Brer Fox, sezee.

" 'I ain't got time, Brer Fox,' sez Brer Rabbit, sezee, sorter mendin' his licks.

" 'I wanter have some confab wid you, Brer Rabbit,' sez Brer Fox, sezee.

" 'All right, Brer Fox, but you better holler fum whar you stan'. I'm monstus full er fleas dis mawnin',' sez Brer Rabbit, sezee.

" 'I seed Brer B'ar yistiddy,' sez Brer Fox, sezee, 'en he sorter rake me over de coals kaze you en me ain't make frens en live naberly, en I tole 'im dat I'd see you.'

"Den Brer Rabbit scratch one year wid his off hine-foot sorter jub'usly, en den he ups en sez, sezee:

" 'All a settin', Brer Fox. Spose'n you drap roun' ter-morrer en take dinner wid me. We ain't got no great doin's at our house, but I speck de ole 'oman en de chil-luns kin sorter scramble roun' en git up sump'n fer ter stay yo' stummuck.'

" 'I'm 'gree'ble, Brer Rabbit,' sez Brer Fox, sezee.

" 'Den I'll 'pen' on you,' sez Brer Rabbit, sezee.

"Nex' day, Mr. Rabbit an' Miss Rabbit got up soon, 'fo' day, en raided on a gyarden like Miss Sally's out dar, en got some cabbiges, en some roas'n years, en some sparrer-grass, en dey fix up a smashin' dinner. Bimeby one er de little Rabbits, playin' out in de back-yard, come runnin' in hollerin', 'Oh, ma! oh, ma! I seed Mr. Fox a comin'!' En den Brer Rabbit he tuck de chilluns by der years en make um set down, en den him en Miss Rabbit sorter dally roun' waitin' for Brer Fox. En dey keep on waitin', but no Brer Fox ain't come. Atter 'while Brer Rabbit goes to de do', easy like, en peep out, en dar, stickin' out fum behime de cornder, wuz de tip-een' er Brer Fox tail. Den Brer Rabbit shot de do' en sot down, en put his paws behime his years en begin fer ter sing:

> " 'De place wharbouts you spill de grease,
>   Right dar youer boun' ter slide,
>   An' whar you fine a bunch er ha'r,
>   You'll sholy fine de hide.'

"Nex' day, Brer Fox sont word by Mr. Mink, en skuze hisse'f kaze he wuz too sick fer ter come, en he ax Brer Rabbit fer ter come en take dinner wid him, en Brer Rabbit say he wuz 'gree'ble.

"Bimeby, w'en de shadders wuz at der shortes', Brer Rabbit he sorter brush up en santer down ter Brer Fox's house, en w'en he got dar, he yer somebody groanin', en he look in de do' en dar he see Brer Fox settin' up in a rockin' cheer all wrop up wid flannil, en he look mighty weak. Brer Rabbit look all 'roun', he did, but he ain't see no dinner. De dish-pan wuz settin' on de table, en close by wuz a kyarvin' knife.

" 'Look like you gwineter have chicken for dinner, Brer Fox,' sez Brer Rabbit, sezee.

" 'Yes, Brer Rabbit, deyer nice, en fresh, en tender,' sez Brer Fox, sezee.

"Den Brer Rabbit sorter pull his mustarsh, en say: 'You ain't got no calamus root, is you, Brer Fox? I done got so now dat I can't eat no chicken 'ceppin she's seasoned up wid calamus root.' En wid dat Brer Rabbit lipt out er de do' and dodge 'mong de bushes, en sot dar watchin' fer Brer Fox; en he ain't watch long, nudder, kaze Brer Fox flung off de flannil en crope out er de house en got whar he could cloze in on Brer Rabbit, en bimeby Brer Rabbit holler out: 'Oh, Brer Fox! I'll des put yo' calamus root out yer on dish yer stump. Better come git it while hit's fresh,' and wid dat Brer Rabbit gallop off home. En Brer Fox ain't never kotch 'im yit, en w'at's mo', honey, he ain't gwineter."

II.
THE WONDERFUL
TAR-BABY STORY.

"**D**idn't the fox *never* catch the rabbit, Uncle Remus?" asked the little boy the next evening.

"He come mighty nigh it, honey, sho's you bawn— Brer Fox did. One day atter Brer Rabbit fool 'im wid dat calamus root, Brer Fox went ter wuk en got 'im some tar, en mix it wid some turkentime, en fix up a contrapshun wat he call a Tar-Baby, en he tuck dish yer Tar-Baby en he sot 'er in de big road, en den he lay off in de bushes fer ter see wat de news wuz gwineter be. En he didn't hatter wait long, nudder, kaze bimeby here come Brer Rabbit pacin' down de road—lippity-clippity, clippity-lippity—dez ez sassy ez a jay-bird. Brer Fox, he lay low. Brer Rabbit come prancin' 'long twel he spy de Tar-Baby, en den he fotch up on his behime legs like he wuz 'stonished. De Tar-Baby, she sot dar, she did, en Brer Fox, he lay low.

" 'Mawnin'!' sez Brer Rabbit, sezee—'nice wedder dis mawnin',' sezee.

"Tar-Baby ain't sayin' nuthin', en Brer Fox, he lay low.

" 'How duz yo' sym'tums seem ter segashuate?' sez Brer Rabbit, sezee.

"Brer Fox, he wink his eye slow, en lay low, en de Tar-Baby, she ain't sayin' nuthin'.

" 'How you come on, den? Is you deaf?' sez Brer Rabbit, sezee. 'Kaze if you is, I kin holler louder,' sezee.

"Tar-Baby stay still, en Brer Fox, he lay low.

" 'Youer stuck up, dat's w'at you is,' says Brer Rabbit, sezee, 'en I'm gwineter kyore you, dat's w'at I'm a gwineter do,' sezee.

"Brer Fox, he sorter chuckle in his stummuck, he did, but Tar-Baby ain't sayin' nuthin'.

" 'I'm gwineter larn you howter talk ter 'specttubble fokes ef hit's de las' ack,' sez Brer Rabbit, sezee. 'Ef you don't take off dat hat en tell me howdy, I'm gwineter bus' you wide open,' sezee.

"Tar-Baby stay still, en Brer Fox, he lay low.

"Brer Rabbit keep on axin' 'im, en de Tar-Baby, she keep on sayin' nuthin', twel present'y Brer Rabbit draw back wid his fis', he did, en blip he tuck 'er side er de head. Right dar's whar he broke his merlasses jug. His fis' stuck, en he can't pull loose. De tar hilt 'im. But Tar-Baby, she stay still, en Brer Fox, he lay low.

" 'Ef you don't lemme loose, I'll knock you agin,' sez Brer Rabbit, sezee, en wid dat he fotch 'er a wipe wid de udder han', en dat stuck. Tar-Baby, she ain't sayin' nuthin', en Brer Fox, he lay low.

" 'Tu'n me loose, fo' I kick de natal stuffin' outen you,' sez Brer Rabbit, sezee, but de Tar-Baby, she ain't sayin' nuthin'. She des hilt on, en den Brer Rabbit lose de use er his feet in de same way. Brer Fox, he lay low. Den Brer Rabbit squall out dat ef de Tar-Baby don't tu'n 'im loose he butt 'er cranksided. En den he butted, en his head got stuck. Den Brer Fox, he sa'ntered fort', lookin' des ez innercent ez wunner yo' mammy's mockin'-birds.

" 'Howdy, Brer Rabbit,' sez Brer Fox, sezee. 'You look sorter stuck up dis mawnin',' sezee, en den he rolled on de groun', en laft en laft twel he couldn't laff no mo'. 'I speck you'll take dinner wid me dis time, Brer Rabbit. I done laid in some calamus root, en I ain't gwineter take no skuse,' sez Brer Fox, sezee."

Here Uncle Remus paused, and drew a two-pound yam out of the ashes.

"Did the fox eat the rabbit?" asked the little boy to whom the story had been told.

"Dat's all de fur de tale goes," replied the old man. "He mout, en den agin he mountent. Some say Jedge B'ar come 'long en loosed 'im—some say he didn't. I hear Miss Sally callin'. You better run 'long."

III.
WHY MR. POSSUM
LOVES PEACE.

"One night," said Uncle Remus—taking Miss Sally's little boy on his knee, and stroking the child's hair thoughtfully and caressingly—"one night Brer Possum call by fer Brer Coon, 'cordin' ter greement, en atter gobblin' up a dish er fried greens en

smokin' a seegyar, dey rambled fort' fer ter see how de
ballunce er de settlement wuz gittin' 'long. Brer Coon,
he wuz wunner deze yer natchul pacers, en he racked
'long same ez Mars John's bay pony, en Brer Possum he
went in a han'-gallup; en dey got over heap er groun',
mon. Brer Possum, he got his belly full er 'simmons, en
Brer Coon, he scoop up a 'bunnunce er frogs en tad-
poles. Dey amble 'long, dey did, des ez soshubble ez a
baskit er kittens, twel bimeby dey hear Mr. Dog talkin'
ter hisse'f way off in de woods.

" 'Spozen he runs up on us, Brer Possum, w'at you
gwineter do?' sez Brer Coon, sezee. Brer Possum sorter
laff 'round de cornders un his mouf.

" 'Oh, ef he come, Brer Coon, I'm gwineter stan' by
you,' sez Brer Possum. 'W'at you gwineter do?' sezee.

" 'Who? me?' sez Brer Coon. 'Ef he run up onter me,
I lay I give 'im one twis',' sezee."

"Did the dog come?" asked the little boy.

"Go 'way, honey!" responded the old man, in an im-
pressive tone. "Go way! Mr. Dog, he come en he come
a zoonin'. En he ain't wait fer ter say howdy, nudder.
He des sail inter de two un um. De ve'y fus pas he make
Brer Possum fetch a grin fum year ter year, en keel over
like he wuz dead. Den Mr. Dog, he sail inter Brer Coon,
en right dar's whar he drap his munnypus, kaze Brer
Coon wuz cut out fer dat kinder bizness, en he fa'rly
wipe up de face er de earf wid 'im. You better b'leeve
dat w'en Mr. Dog got a chance to make hisse'f skase he
tuck it, en w'at der wuz lef' un him went skaddlin' thoo
de woods like hit wuz shot outen a muskit. En Brer
Coon, he sorter lick his cloze inter shape en rack off, en
Brer Possum, he lay dar like he wuz dead, twel bimeby
he raise up sotter keerful like, en w'en he fine de coas'
cle'r he scramble up en scamper off like sumpin was
atter 'im."

Here Uncle Remus paused long enough to pick up a
live coal of fire in his fingers, transfer it to the palm of

his hand, and thence to his clay pipe, which he had been filling—a proceeding that was viewed by the little boy with undisguised admiration. The old man then proceeded:

"Nex' time Brer Possum meet Brer Coon, Brer Coon 'fuse ter 'spon' ter his howdy, en dis make Brer Possum feel mighty bad, seein' ez how dey useter make so many 'scurshuns tergedder.

" 'W'at make you hol' yo' head so high, Brer Coon?' sez Brer Possum, sezee.

" 'I ain't runnin' wid cowerds deze days,' sez Brer Coon. 'W'en I wants you I'll sen' fer you,' sezee.

"Den Brer Possum git mighty mad.

" 'Who's enny cowerd,' sezee.

" 'You is,' sez Brer Coon, 'dat's who. I ain't soshatin' wid dem w'at lies down on de groun' en plays dead w'en dar's a free fight gwine on,' sezee.

"Den Brer Possum grin en laff fit to kill hisse'f.

" 'Lor', Brer Coon, you don't speck I done dat kaze I wuz 'feared, duz you?' sezee. 'W'y I want no mo' 'feared dan you is dis minnit. W'at wuz dey fer ter be skeered un?' sezee. 'I know'd you'd git away wid Mr. Dog ef I didn't, en I des lay dar watchin' you shake him, waitin' fer ter put in w'en de time come,' sezee.

"Brer Coon tu'n up his nose.

" 'Dat's a mighty likely tale,' sezee, 'w'en Mr. Dog ain't mo'n tech you 'fo' you keel over, en lay dar stiff,' sezee.

" 'Dat's des w'at I wuz gwineter tell you 'bout,' sez Brer Possum, sezee. 'I want no mo' skeer'd dan you is right now, en' I wuz fixin' fer ter give Mr. Dog a sample er my jaw,' sezee, 'but I'm de most ticklish chap w'at you ever laid eyes on, en no sooner did Mr. Dog put his nose down yer 'mong my ribs dan I got ter laffin, en I laft twel I ain't had no use er my lim's,' sezee, 'en it's a mussy unto Mr. Dog dat I wuz ticklish, kaze a little mo' en I'd e't 'im up,' sezee. 'I don't mine fightin', Brer Coon, no mo' dan you duz,' sezee, 'but I declar' ter grashus ef I kin stan' ticklin'. Git me in a row whar dey ain't no ticklin' 'lowed, en I'm your man,' sezee.

"En down ter dis day"—continued Uncle Remus, watching the smoke from his pipe curl upward over the little boy's head—"down ter dis day, Brer Possum's bound ter s'render w'en you tech him in de short ribs, en he'll laff ef he knows he's gwineter be smashed fer it."

IV.
HOW MR. RABBIT WAS
TOO SHARP FOR MR. FOX.

"Uncle Remus," said the little boy one evening, when he had found the old man with little or nothing to do, "did the fox kill and eat the rabbit when he caught him with the Tar-Baby?"

"Law, honey, ain't I tell you 'bout dat?" replied the old darkey, chuckling slyly. "I 'clar ter grashus I ought er tole you dat, but ole man Nod wuz ridin' on my eyeleds 'twel a leetle mo'n I'd a dis'member'd my own name, en den on to dat here come yo' mammy hollerin' atter you.

"W'at I tell you w'en I fus' begin? I tole you Brer Rabbit wuz a monstus soon beas'; leas'ways dat's w'at I laid out fer ter tell you. Well, den, honey, don't you go en make no udder kalkalashuns, kaze in dem days Brer Rabbit en his fambly wuz at de head er de gang w'en enny racket wuz on han', en dar dey stayed. 'Fo' you begins fer ter wipe yo' eyes 'bout Brer Rabbit, you wait en see whar'bouts Brer Rabbit gwineter fetch up at. But dat's needer yer ner dar.

"W'en Brer Fox fine Brer Rabbit mixt up wid de Tar-Baby, he feel mighty good, en he roll on de groun' en laff. Bimeby he up'n say, sezee:

" 'Well, I speck I got you dis time, Brer Rabbit,'

sezee; 'maybe I ain't, but I speck I is. You been runnin' roun' here sassin' atter me a mighty long time, but I speck you done come ter de een' er de row. You bin cuttin' up yo' capers en bouncin' 'roun' in dis naberhood ontwel you come ter b'leeve yo'se'f de boss er de whole gang. En den youer allers some'rs whar you got no biz-ness,' sez Brer Fox, sezee. 'Who ax you fer ter come en strike up a 'quaintence wid dish yer Tar-Baby? En who stuck you up dar whar you iz? Nobody in de roun' wor-ril. You des tuck en jam yo'se'f on dat Tar-Baby widout waitin' fer enny invite,' sez Brer Fox, sezee, 'en dar you is, en dar you'll stay twel I fixes up a bresh-pile and fires her up, kaze I'm gwineter bobbycue you dis day, sho,' sez Brer Fox, sezee.

"Den Brer Rabbit talk mighty 'umble.

" 'I don't keer w'at you do wid me, Brer Fox,' sezee, 'so you don't fling me in dat brier-patch. Roas' me, Brer Fox,' sezee, 'but don't fling me in dat brier-patch,' sezee.

" 'Hit's so much trouble fer ter kindle a fire,' sez Brer Fox, sezee, 'dat I speck I'll hatter hang you,' sezee.

" 'Hang me des ez high ez you please, Brer Fox,' sez Brer Rabbit, sezee, 'but do fer de Lord's sake don't fling me in that brier-patch,' sezee.

" 'I ain't got no string,' sez Brer Fox, sezee, 'en now I speck I'll hatter drown you,' sezee.

" 'Drown me des ez deep ez you please, Brer Fox,' sez Brer Rabbit, sezee, 'but do don't fling me in dat brier-patch,' sezee.

" 'Dey ain't no water nigh,' sez Brer Fox, sezee, 'en now I speck I'll hatter skin you,' sezee.

" 'Skin me, Brer Fox,' sez Brer Rabbit, sezee, 'snatch out my eyeballs, t'ar out my years by de roots, en cut off my legs,' sezee, 'but do please, Brer Fox, don't fling me in dat brier-patch,' sezee.

"Co'se Brer Fox wanter hurt Brer Rabbit bad ez he kin, so he cotch 'im by de behime legs en slung 'im right in de middle er de brier-patch. Dar was a considerbul flutter whar Brer Rabbit struck de bushes, en Brer Fox sorter hang 'roun' fer ter see w'at wuz gwineter happen. Bimeby he hear somebody call 'im, en way up de hill he see Brer Rabbit settin' cross-legged on a chinkapin log koamin' de pitch outen his har wid a chip. Den Brer Fox know dat he bin swop off mighty bad. Brer Rabbit wuz bleedzed fer ter fling back some er his sass, en he holler out:

" 'Bred en bawn in a brier-patch, Brer Fox—bred en bawn in a brier-patch!' en wid dat he skip out des ez lively ez a cricket in de embers."

V.
THE STORY OF THE DELUGE
AND HOW IT CAME ABOUT.

"One time," said Uncle Remus—adjusting his spectacles so as to be able to see how to thread a large darning-needle with which he was patching his coat—"one time, way back yander, 'fo' you wuz borned, honey, en 'fo' Mars John er Miss Sally wuz borned— way back yander 'fo' enny un us wuz borned, de anemils en de beasteses sorter 'lecshuneer roun' 'mong dey-selves, twel at las' dey 'greed fer ter have a 'sembly. In dem days," continued the old man, observing a look of incredulity on the little boy's face, "in dem days creeturs had lots mo' sense dan dey got now; let 'lone dat, dey had sense same like folks. Hit was tech en go wid um, too, mon, en w'en dey make up dere mines w'at hatter be done, 'twant mo'n menshun'd 'fo' hit wuz done. Well, dey 'lected dat dey hatter hole er 'sembly fer ter sorter straighten out marters en yer de complaints, en w'en de day come dey wuz on han'. De Lion, he wuz dere, kaze he wuz de king, en he hatter be dere. De Rhynossyhoss, he wuz dere, en de Elephent, he wuz dere, en de Cammils, en de Cows, en plum down ter de Crawfishes, dey wuz dere. Dey wuz all dere. En w'en de Lion shuck his mane, en tuck his seat in de big cheer, den de sesshun begun fer ter commence."

"What did they do, Uncle Remus?" asked the little boy.

"I kin skacely call to mine 'zackly wa't dey did do, but dey spoke speeches, en hollered, en cusst, en flung der langwidge 'roun' des like w'en yo' daddy wuz gwineter run fer de legislater en got lef'. Howsomever, dey 'ranged der 'fairs, en splained der bizness. Bimeby, w'ile dey wuz 'sputin' 'longer wunner nudder, de Elephent tromped on wunner de Crawfishes. Co'se w'en dat creetur put his foot down, w'atsumever's under dere's bound fer ter be squshed, en dey wuzn't nuff er dat Crawfish lef' fer ter tell dat he'd bin dar.

"Dis make de udder Crawfishes mighty mad, en dey sorter swawmed tergedder en draw'd up a kinder peramble wid some wharfo'es in it, en read her out in de 'sembly. But, bless grashus! sech a racket wuz a gwine on dat nobody ain't hear it, 'ceppin may be de Mud Turkle en de Spring Lizzud, en dere enfloons wuz pow'ful lackin'.

"Bimeby, w'iles de Nunicorn wuz 'sputin' wid de Lion, en w'ile de Hyener wuz a laffin ter hisse'f, de Elephent squshed anudder one er de Crawfishes, en a little mo'n he'd er ruint de Mud Turkle. Den de Crawfishes, w'at dey wuz lef' un um, swawmed tergedder en draw'd up anudder peramble wid sum mo' wharfo'es; but dey might ez well er sung Ole Dan Tucker ter a harrycane. De udder creeturs wuz too bizzy wid der fussin' fer ter 'spon' unto de Crawfishes. So dar dey wuz, de Crawfishes, en dey didn't know w'at minnit wuz gwineter be de nex'; en key dep' on gittin madder en madder en skeerder en skeerder, twel bimeby dey gun de wink ter de Mud Turkle en de Spring Lizzud, en den dey bo'd little holes in de groun' en went down outer sight."

"Who did, Uncle Remus?" asked the little boy.

"De Crawfishes, honey. Dey bo'd inter de groun' en kep' on bo'in twel dey onloost de fountains er de earf; en de waters squirt out, en riz higher en higher twel de hills wuz kivvered, en de creeturs wuz all drownded; en all bekaze dey let on 'mong deyselves dat dey wuz bigger dan de Crawfishes."

Then the old man blew the ashes from a smoking yam, and proceeded to remove the peeling.

"Where was the ark, Uncle Remus?" the little boy inquired, presently.

"W'ich ark's dat?" asked the old man, in a tone of well-feigned curiosity.

"Noah's ark," replied the child.

"Don't you pester wid ole man Noah, honey. I boun' he tuck keer er dat ark. Dat's w'at he wuz dere fer, en dat's w'at he done. Leas'ways, dat's w'at dey tells me. But don't you bodder longer dat ark, 'ceppin' your mammy fetches it up. Dey mout er bin two deloojes, en den agin dey moutent. Ef dey wuz enny ark in dish yer w'at de Crawfishes brung on, I ain't heern tell un it, en w'en dey ain't no arks 'roun, I ain't got no time fer ter make um en put um in dere. Hit's gittin' yo' bedtime, honey."

VI.
MR. RABBIT GROSSLY DECEIVES MR. FOX.

One evening when the little boy, whose nights with Uncle Remus are as entertaining as those Arabian ones of blessed memory, had finished supper and hurried out to sit with his venerable patron, he found the old man in great glee. Indeed, Uncle Remus was talking and laughing to himself at such a rate that the little boy was afraid he had company. The truth is, Uncle Remus had heard the child coming, and, when the rosy-cheeked chap put his head in at the door, was engaged in a monologue, the burden of which seemed to be—

> "Ole Molly Har',
>   W'at you doin' dar,
>   Settin' in de cornder
>   Smokin' yo' seegyar?"

As a matter of course this vague allusion reminded the little boy of the fact that the wicked Fox was still in pursuit of the Rabbit, and he immediately put his curiosity in the shape of a question.

"Uncle Remus, did the Rabbit have to go clean away when he got loose from the Tar-Baby?"

"Bless grashus, honey, dat he didn't. Who? Him? You dunno nuthin' 'tall 'bout Brer Rabbit ef dat's de way you puttin' 'im down. W'at he gwine 'way fer? He mouter stayed sorter close twel de pitch rub off'n his ha'r, but twern't menny days 'fo' he wuz lopin' up en down de naberhood same ez ever, en I dunno ef he wern't mo' sassier dan befo'.

"Seem like dat de tale 'bout how he got mixt up wid de Tar-Baby got 'roun' 'mongst de nabers. Leas'ways, Miss Meadows en de gals got win' un' it, en de nex' time Brer Rabbit paid um a visit Miss Meadows tackled 'im 'bout it, en de gals sot up a monstus gigglement. Brer Rabbit, he sot up des ez cool ez a cowcumber, he did, en let 'em run on."

"Who was Miss Meadows, Uncle Remus?" inquired the little boy.

"Don't ax me, honey. She wuz in de tale, Miss Meadows en de gals wuz, en de tale I give you like hi't wer' gun ter me. Brer Rabbit, he sot dar, he did, sorter lam' like, en den bimeby he cross his legs, he did, and wink his eye slow, en up en say, sezee:

" 'Ladies, Brer Fox wuz my daddy's ridin'-hoss fer thirty year; maybe mo', but thirty year dat I knows un,' sezee; en den he paid um his 'specks, en tip his beaver, en march off, he did, des ez stiff en ez stuck up ez a fire-stick.

"Nex' day, Brer Fox cum a callin', and w'en he gun fer ter laff 'bout Brer Rabbit, Miss Meadows en de gals, dey ups en tells 'im 'bout w'at Brer Rabbit say. Den Brer Fox grit his toof sho' nuff, he did, en he look mighty dumpy, but w'en he riz fer ter go he up en say, sezee:

" 'Ladies, I ain't 'sputin' w'at you say, but I'll make Brer Rabbit chaw up his words en spit um out right yer whar you kin see 'im,' sezee, en wid dat off Brer Fox marcht.

"En w'en he got in de big road, he shuck de dew off'n his tail, en made a straight shoot for Brer Rabbit's house. W'en he got dar, Brer Rabbit wuz spectin' un 'im, en de do' wuz shet fas'. Brer Fox knock. Nobody ain't ans'er. Brer Fox knock. Nobody ans'er. Den he knock agin—blam! blam! Den Brer Rabbit holler out mighty weak:

" 'Is dat you, Brer Fox? I want you ter run en fetch de doctor. Dat bait er pusly w'at I e't dis mawnin' is git-tin' 'way wid me. Do, please, Brer Fox, run quick,' sez Brer Rabbit, sezee.

" 'I come after you, Brer Rabbit,' sez Brer Fox, sezee. 'Dere's gwineter be a party up at Miss Mead-ows's,' sezee. 'All de gals 'll be dere, en I promus' dat I'd fetch you. De gals, dey 'lowed dat hit wouldn't be no party 'ceppin' I fotch you,' sez Brer Fox, sezee.

"Den Brer Rabbit say he wuz too sick, en Brer Fox say he wuzzent, en dar dey had it up and down, 'sputin' en contendin'. Brer Rabbit say he can't walk. Brer Fox say he tote 'im. Brer Rabbit say how? Brer Fox say in his arms. Brer Rabbit say he drap 'im. Brer Fox 'low he won't. Bimeby Brer Rabbit say he go ef Brer Fox tote 'im on his back. Brer Fox say he would. Brer Rabbit say he can't ride widout a saddle. Brer Fox say he git de saddle. Brer Rabbit say he can't set in saddle less he have bridle fer ter hol' by. Brer Fox say he git de bridle. Brer Rabbit say he can't ride widout bline bridle, kaze Brer Fox be shyin' at stumps 'long de road, en fling 'im off. Brer Fox say he git bline bridle. Den Brer Rabbit say he go. Den Brer Fox say he ride Brer Rabbit mos' up ter Miss Meadows's, en den he could git down en walk de balance er de way. Brer Rabbit 'greed, en den Brer Fox lipt out atter de saddle en de bridle.

"Co'se Brer Rabbit know de game dat Brer Fox wuz fixin' fer ter play, en he 'termin' fer ter outdo 'im, en by de time he koam his ha'r en twis' his mustarsh, en sorter rig up, yer come Brer Fox, saddle en bridle on, en lookin' ez peart ez a circus pony. He trot up ter de do' en stan' dar pawin' de ground en chompin' de bit same like sho 'nuff hoss, en Brer Rabbit he mount, he did, en dey amble off. Brer Fox can't see behime wid de bline bridle on, but bimeby he feel Brer Rabbit raise one er his foots.

" 'W'at you doin' now, Brer Rabbit?' sezee.

" 'Short'nin' de lef stir'p, Brer Fox,' sezee.

"Bimeby Brer Rabbit raise up de udder foot.

" 'W'at you doin' now, Brer Rabbit?' sezee.

" 'Pullin' down my pants, Brer Fox,' sezee.

"All de time, bless grashus, honey, Brer Rabbit wer puttin' on his spurrers, en w'en dey got close to Miss Meadows's, whar Brer Rabbit wuz to git off, en Brer Fox made a motion fer ter stan' still, Brer Rabbit slap de spurrers into Brer Fox flanks, en you better b'leeve he got over groun'. W'en dey got ter de house, Miss Meadows en all de gals wuz settin' on de peazzer, en stidder stoppin' at de gate, Brer Rabbit rid on by, he did, en den come gallopin' down de road en up ter de hoss-rack, w'ich he hitch Brer Fox at, en den he santer into de house, he did, en shake han's wid de gals, en set dar, smokin' his seegyar same ez a town man. Bimeby he draw in long puff, en den let hit out in a cloud, en squar hisse'f back en holler out, he did:

"'Ladies, ain't I done tell you Brer Fox wuz de ridin'-hoss fer our fambly? He sorter losin' his gait' now, but I speck I kin fetch 'im all right in a mont' er so,' sezee.

"En den Brer Rabbit sorter grin, he did, en de gals giggle, en Miss Meadows, she praise up de pony, en dar wuz Brer Fox hitch fas' ter de rack, en couldn't he'p hisse'f."

"Is that all, Uncle Remus?" asked the little boy as the old man paused.

"Dat ain't all, honey, but 'twon't do fer ter give out too much cloff fer ter cut one pa'r pants," replied the old man sententiously.

VII.
MR. FOX IS
AGAIN VICTIMIZED.

When "Miss Sally's" little boy went to Uncle Remus the next night to hear the conclusion of the adventure in which the Rabbit made a riding-horse of the Fox to the great enjoyment and gratification of Miss Meadows and the girls, he found the old man in a bad humor.

"I ain't tellin' no tales ter bad chilluns," said Uncle Remus curtly.

"But, Uncle Remus, I ain't bad," said the little boy plaintively.

"Who dat chunkin' dem chickens dis mawnin'? Who dat knockin' out fokes's eyes wid dat Yallerbammer sling des 'fo' dinner? Who dat sickin' dat pinter puppy atter my pig? Who dat scatterin' my ingun sets? Who dat flingin' rocks on top er my house, w'ich a little mo' en one un em would er drap spang on my head?"

"Well, now, Uncle Remus, I didn't go to do it. I won't do so any more. Please, Uncle Remus, if you will tell me, I'll run to the house and bring you some tea-cakes."

"Seein' um's better'n hearin' tell un um," replied the old man, the severity of his countenance relaxing some-what; but the little boy darted out, and in a few minutes came running back with his pockets full and his hands full.

"I lay yo' mammy 'll 'spishun dat de rats' stummucks is widenin' in dis naberhood w'en she come fer ter count up 'er cakes," said Uncle Remus, with a chuckle. "Deze," he continued, dividing the cakes into two equal parts—"deze I'll tackle now, en deze I'll lay by fer Sun-day.

"Lemme see. I mos' dis'member wharbouts Brer Fox en Brer Rabbit wuz."

"The rabbit rode the fox to Miss Meadows's, and hitched him to the horse-rack," said the little boy.

"W'y co'se he did," said Uncle Remus. "Co'se he did. Well, Brer Rabbit rid Brer Fox up, he did, en tied 'im to de rack, en den sot out in de peazzer wid de gals a smokin' er his seegyar wid mo' proudness dan wa't you mos' ever see. Dey talk, en dey sing, en dey play on de peanner, de gals did, twel bimeby hit come time fer Brer Rabbit fer to be gwine, en he tell um all good-by, en strut out to de hoss-rack same's ef he wuz de king er de patter-rollers,* en den he mount Brer Fox en ride off.

"Brer Fox ain't sayin' nuthin 'tall. He des rack off, he did, en keep his mouf shet, en Brer Rabbit know'd der

---

* Patrols. In the country districts, order was kept on the planta-tions at night by the knowledge that they were liable to be visited at any moment by the patrols. Hence a song current among the negroes, the chorus of which was:

> "Run, nigger, run; patter-roller ketch you—
> Run, nigger, run; hit's almos' day."

wuz bizness cookin' up fer him, en he feel monstus skittish. Brer Fox amble on twel he git in de long lane, outer sight er Miss Meadows's house, en den he tu'n loose, he did. He rip en he r'ar, en he cuss, en he swar; he snort en he cavort."

"What was he doing that for, Uncle Remus?" the little boy inquired.

"He wuz tryin' fer ter fling Brer Rabbit off'n his back, bless yo' soul! But he des might ez well er rastle wid his own shadder. Every time he hump hisse'f Brer Rabbit slap de spurrers in 'im, en dar dey had it, up en down. Brer Fox fa'rly to' up de groun', he did, en he jump so high en he jump so quick dat he mighty nigh snatch his own tail off. Dey kep' on gwine on dis way twel bimeby Brer Fox lay down en roll over, he did, en dis sorter onsettle Brer Rabbit, but by de time Brer Fox got back on his footses agin, Brer Rabbit wuz gwine thoo de underbresh mo' samer dan a race-hoss. Brer Fox he lit out atter 'im, he did, en he push Brer Rabbit so close dat it wuz 'bout all he could do fer ter git in a holler tree. Hole too little fer Brer Fox fer ter git in, en he hatter lay down en res' en gedder his mine tergedder.

"While he wuz layin' dar, Mr. Buzzard come floppin' long, en seein' Brer Fox stretch out on de groun', he lit en view de premusses. Den Mr. Buzzard sorter shake his wing, en put his head on one side, en say to hisse'f like, sezee:

" 'Brer Fox dead, en I so sorry,' sezee.

" 'No I ain't dead, nudder,' sez Brer Fox, sezee. 'I got ole man Rabbit pent up in yer,' sezee, 'en I'm a gwineter git 'im dis time ef it take twel Chris'mus,' sezee.

"Den, atter some mo' palaver, Brer Fox make a bargain dat Mr. Buzzard wuz ter watch de hole, en keep Brer Rabbit dar wiles Brer Fox went atter his axe. Den Brer Fox, he lope off, he did, en Mr. Buzzard, he tuck up his stan' at de hole. Bimeby, w'en all git still, Brer

Rabbit sorter scramble down close ter de hole, he did, en holler out:

" 'Brer Fox! Oh! Brer Fox!'

"Brer Fox done gone, en nobody say nuthin'. Den Brer Rabbit squall out like he wuz mad; sezee:

" 'You needn't talk less you wanter,' sezee; 'I knows youer dar, en I ain't keerin',' sezee. 'I des wanter tell you dat I wish mighty bad Brer Tukkey Buzzard wuz here,' sezee.

"Den Mr. Buzzard try ter talk like Brer Fox:

" 'W'at you want wid Mr. Buzzard?' sezee.

" 'Oh, nuthin' in 'tickler, 'cep' dere's de fattes' gray squir'l in yer dat ever I see,' sezee, 'en ef Brer Tukkey Buzzard wuz 'roun' he'd be mighty glad fer ter git 'im,' sezee.

" 'How Mr. Buzzard gwine ter git 'im?' sez de Buzzard, sezee.

" 'Well, dars a little hole roun' on de udder side er de tree,' sez Brer Rabbit, sezee, 'en ef Brer Tukkey Buzzard wuz here so he could take up his stan' dar,' sezee, 'I'd drive dat squir'l out,' sezee.

" 'Drive 'im out, den,' sez Mr. Buzzard, sezee, 'en I'll see dat Brer Tukkey Buzzard gits 'im,' sezee.

"Den Brer Rabbit kick up a racket, like he wer' drivin' sumpin' out, en Mr. Buzzard he rush 'roun' fer ter ketch de squir'l, en Brer Rabbit, he dash out, he did, en he des fly fer home."

At this point Uncle Remus took one of the tea-cakes, held his head back, opened his mouth, dropped the cake in with a sudden motion, looked at the little boy with an expression of astonishment, and then closed his eyes, and began to chew, mumbling as an accompaniment the plaintive tune of "Don't you Grieve atter Me."

The *séance* was over; but, before the little boy went into the "big house," Uncle Remus laid his rough hand tenderly on the child's shoulder, and remarked, in a confidential tone:

"Honey, you mus' git up soon Chris'mus mawnin' en open de do'; kase I'm gwineter bounce in on Marse John en Miss Sally, en holler Chris'mus gif' des like I useter endurin' de fahmin' days fo' de war, w'en old Miss wuz 'live. I boun' dey don't fergit de ole nigger, nudder. W'en you hear me callin' de pigs, honey, you des hop up en onfassen de do'. I lay I'll give Marse John wunner deze yer 'sprize parties."

VIII.
MR. FOX IS "OUTDONE" BY MR. BUZZARD.

"Ef I don't run inter no mistakes," remarked Uncle Remus, as the little boy came tripping in to see him after supper, "Mr. Tukkey Buzzard wuz gyardin' de holler whar Brer Rabbit went in at, en w'ich he come out un."

The silence of the little boy verified the old man's recollection.

"Well, Mr. Buzzard, he feel mighty lonesome, he did, but he done prommust Brer Fox dat he'd stay, en he 'termin' fer ter sorter hang 'roun' en jine in de joke. En he ain't hatter wait long, nudder, kase bimeby yer come Brer Fox gallopin' thoo de woods wid his axe on his shoulder.

" 'How you speck Brer Rabbit gittin' on, Brer Buzzard?' sez Brer Fox, sezee.

" 'Oh, he in dar,' sez Brer Buzzard, sezee. 'He mighty still, dough. I speck he takin' a nap,' sezee.

" 'Den I'm des in time fer ter wake 'im up,' sez Brer Fox, sezee. En wid dat he fling off his coat, en spit in his han's, en grab de axe. Den he draw back en come down on de tree—pow! En eve'y time he come down wid de axe—pow!—Mr. Buzzard, he step high, he did, en holler out:

"'Oh, he in dar, Brer Fox. He in dar, sho.'

"En eve'y time a chip ud fly off, Mr. Buzzard, he'd jump, en dodge, en hole his head sideways, he would, en holler:

"'He in dar, Brer Fox. I done heerd 'im. He in dar, sho.'

"En Brer Fox, he lammed away at dat holler tree, he did, like a man maulin' rails, twel bimeby, atter he done got de tree mos' cut thoo, he stop fer ter ketch his bref, en he seed Mr. Buzzard laffin' behime his back, he did, en right den en dar, widout gwine enny fudder, Brer Fox, he smelt a rat. But Mr. Buzzard, he keep on holler'n:

"'He in dar, Brer Fox. He in dar, sho. I done seed 'im.'

"Den Brer Fox, he make like he peepin' up de holler, en he say, sezee:

"'Run yer, Brer Buzzard, en look ef dis ain't Brer Rabbit's foot hanging down yer.'

"En Mr. Buzzard, he come steppin' up, he did, same ez ef he wer treddin' on kurkle-burrs, en he stick his head in de hole; en no sooner did he done dat dan Brer Fox grab 'im. Mr. Buzzard flap his wings, en scramble 'roun' right smartually, he did, but 'twant no use. Brer Fox had de 'vantage er de grip, he did, en he hilt 'im right down ter de groun'. Den Mr. Buzzard squall out, sezee:

"'Lemme 'lone, Brer Fox. Tu'n me loose,' sezee; 'Brer Rabbit'll git out. Youer gittin' close at 'im,' sezee, 'en leb'm mo 'licks'll fetch 'im,' sezee.

"'I'm nigher ter you, Brer Buzzard,' sez Brer Fox, sezee, 'dan I'll be ter Brer Rabbit dis day,' sezee. 'W'at you fool me fer?' sezee.

" 'Lemme 'lone, Brer Fox,' sez Mr. Buzzard, sezee; 'my ole 'oman waitin' fer me. Brer Rabbit in dar,' sezee.

" 'Dar's a bunch er his fur on dat black-be'y bush,' sez Brer Fox, sezee, 'en dat ain't de way he come,' sezee.

"Den Mr. Buzzard up'n tell Brer Fox how 'twuz, en he low'd, Mr. Buzzard did, dat Brer Rabbit wuz de low-downest w'atsizname w'at he ever run up wid. Den Brer Fox say, sezee:

" 'Dat's needer here ner dar, Brer Buzzard,' sezee. 'I lef' you yer fer ter watch dish yer hole, en I lef' Brer Rabbit in dar. I comes back en I fines you at de hole en Brer Rabbit ain't in dar,' sezee. 'I'm gwineter make you pay fer't. I done bin tampered wid twel plum' down ter de sap sucker'll set on a log en sassy me. I'm gwineter fling you in a bresh-heap en burn you up,' sezee.

" 'Ef you fling me on der fier, Brer Fox, I'll fly 'way,' sez Mr. Buzzard, sezee.

" 'Well, den, I'll settle yo' hash right now,' sez Brer Fox, sezee, en wid dat he grab Mr. Buzzard by de tail, he did, en make fer ter dash 'im 'gin de groun', but des 'bout dat time de tail fedders come out, en Mr. Buzzard sail off like wunner dese yer berloons; en ez he riz, he holler back:

" 'You gimme good start, Brer Fox,' sezee, en Brer Fox sot dar en watch 'im fly outer sight.''

"But what became of the Rabbit, Uncle Remus?" asked the little boy.

"Don't you pester 'longer Brer Rabbit, honey, en don't you fret 'bout 'im. You'll year whar he went en how he come out. Dish yer cole snap rastles wid my bones, now," continued the old man, putting on his hat and picking up his walking-stick. "Hit rastles wid me monstus, en I gotter rack 'roun' en see if I kin run up agin some Chris'mus leavin's."

IX.
MISS COW FALLS
A VICTIM TO MR. RABBIT.

"Uncle Remus," said the little boy, "what became of the Rabbit after he fooled the Buzzard, and got out of the hollow tree?"

"Who? Brer Rabbit? Bless yo' soul, honey, Brer Rabbit went skippin' 'long home, he did, des ez sassy ez a jay-bird at a sparrer's nes'. He went gallopin' 'long, he did, but he feel mighty tired out, en stiff in his jints, en he wuz mighty nigh dead for sumpin fer ter drink, en bimeby, wen he got mos' home, he spied ole Miss Cow feedin' roun' in a fiel', he did, en he 'termin' fer ter try his han' wid 'er. Brer Rabbit know mighty well dat Miss Cow won't give 'im no milk, kaze she done 'fuse 'im mo'n once, en w'en his ole 'oman wuz sick, at dat. But never mind dat. Brer Rabbit sorter dance up 'long side er de fence, he did, en holler out:

" 'Howdy, Sis Cow,' sez Brer Rabbit, sezee.

" 'W'y, howdy, Brer Rabbit,' sez Miss Cow, sez she.

" 'How you fine yo'se'f deze days, Sis Cow?' sez Brer Rabbit, sezee.

" 'I'm sorter toler'ble, Brer Rabbit; how you come on?' sez Miss Cow, sez she.

" 'Oh, I'm des toler'ble myse'f, Sis Cow; sorter linger'n' twix' a bauk en a break-down,' sez Brer Rabbit, sezee.

" 'How yo' fokes, Brer Rabbit?' sez Miss Cow, sez she.

" 'Dey er des middlin', Sis Cow; how Brer Bull gittin' on?' sez Brer Rabbit, sezee.

" 'Sorter so-so,' sez Miss Cow, sez she.

" 'Dey er some mighty nice 'simmons up dis tree, Sis

Cow,' sez Brer Rabbit, sezee, 'en I'd like mighty well fer ter have some un um,' sezee.

" 'How you gwineter git um, Brer Rabbit?' sez she.

" 'I 'low'd maybe dat I might ax you fer ter butt 'gin de tree, en shake some down, Sis Cow,' sez Brer Rabbit, sezee.

"C'ose Miss Cow don't wanter diskommerdate Brer Rabbit, en she march up ter de 'simmon tree, she did, en hit it a rap wid 'er hawns—blam! Now, den," continued Uncle Remus, tearing off the corner of a plug of tobacco and cramming it into his mouth—"now, den, dem 'simmons wuz green ez grass, en na'er one never drap. Den Miss Cow butt de tree—blim! Na'er 'simmon drap. Den Miss Cow sorter back off little, en run agin de tree—blip! No 'simmons never drap. Den Miss Cow back off little fudder, she did, en hi'st her tail on 'er back, en come agin de tree, kerblam! en she come so fas', en she come so hard, twel wunner her hawns went spang thoo de tree, en dar she wuz. She can't go forreds, en she can't go backerds. Dis zackly w'at Brer Rabbit waitin' fer, en he no sooner seed ole Miss Cow all fas'en'd up dan he jump up, he did, en cut de pidjin-wing.

" 'Come he'p me out, Brer Rabbit,' sez Miss Cow, sez she.

" 'I can't clime, Sis Cow,' sez Brer Rabbit, sezee, 'but I'll run'n tell Brer Bull,' sezee; en wid dat Brer Rabbit put out fer home, en 'twan't long 'fo here he come wid his ole 'oman en all his chilluns, en de las' wunner de fambly wuz totin' a pail. De big uns had big pails, en de little uns had little pails. En dey all s'roundid ole Miss Cow, dey did, en you hear me, honey, dey milk't 'er dry. De ole uns milk't en de young uns milk't, en den w'en dey done got nuff, Brer Rabbit, he up'n say, sezee:

" 'I wish you mighty well, Sis Cow. I 'low'd bein's how dat you'd hatter sorter camp out all night dat I'd better come en swaje yo' bag,' sezee."

"Do which, Uncle Remus?" asked the little boy.

"Go 'long, honey! Swaje 'er bag. W'en cows don't git milk't, der bag swells, en youk'n hear um a moanin' en a beller'n des like dey wuz gittin' hurtid. Dat's w'at Brer Rabbit done. He 'sembled his fambly, he did, en he swaje ole Miss Cow's bag.

"Miss Cow, she stood dar, she did, en she study en study, and strive fer ter break loose, but de hawn done bin jam in de tree so tight dat twuz way 'fo day in de mornin' 'fo she loose it. Ennyhow hit wuz endurin' er de night, en atter she git loose she sorter graze 'roun', she did, fer ter jestify 'er stummuck. She 'low'd, ole Miss Cow did, dat Brer Rabbit be hoppin' 'long dat way fer ter see how she gittin' on, en she tuck'n lay er trap fer 'im; en des 'bout sunrise wat'd ole Miss Cow do but march up ter de 'simmon tree en stick er hawn back in de hole? But, bless yo' soul, honey, w'ile she wuz croppin' de grass, she tuck one moufull too menny, kaze w'en she hitch on ter de 'simmon tree agin, Brer Rabbit wuz settin' in de fence cornder a watchin' un 'er. Den Brer Rabbit he say ter hisse'f:

" 'Heyo,' sezee, 'w'at dis yer gwine on now? Hole yo' hosses, Sis Cow, twel you hear me comin',' sezee.

"En den he crope off down de fence, Brer Rabbit did, en bimeby here he come—lippity-clippity, clippity-lippity—des a sailin' down de big road.

" 'Mawnin', Sis Cow,' sez Brer Rabbit, sezee, 'how you come on dis mawnin'?' sezee.

" 'Po'ly, Brer Rabbit, po'ly,' sez Miss Cow, sez she. 'I ain't had no res' all night,' sez she. 'I can't pull loose,' sez she, 'but ef you'll come en ketch holt er my tail, Brer Rabbit,' sez she, 'I reckin may be I kin fetch my hawn out,' sez she. Den Brer Rabbit, he come up little closer, but he ain't gittin' too close.

" 'I speck I'm nigh nuff, Sis Cow,' sez Brer Rabbit, sezee. 'I'm a mighty puny man, en I might git trompled,' sezee. 'You do de pullin', Sis Cow,' sezee, 'en I'll do de gruntin',' sezee.

Den Miss Cow, she pull out 'er hawn, she did, en tuck atter Brer Rabbit, en down de big road dey had it, Brer Rabbit wid his years laid back, en Miss Cow wid 'er head down en 'er tail curl. Brer Rabbit kep' on gainin', en bime-by he dart in a brier-patch, en by de time Miss Cow come 'long he had his head stickin' out, en his eyes look big ez Miss Sally's chany sassers.

" 'Heyo, Sis Cow! Whar you gwine?' sez Brer Rabbit, sezee.

" 'Howdy, Brer Big-Eyes,' sez Miss Cow, sez she. 'Is you seed Brer Rabbit go by?'

" 'He des dis minit pas',' sez Brer Rabbit, sezee, 'en he look mighty sick,' sezee.

"En wid dat, Miss Cow tuck down de road like de dogs wuz atter 'er, en Brer Rabbit, he des lay down dar in de brier-patch en roll en laff twel his sides hurtid 'im. He bleedzd ter laff. Fox atter 'im, Buzzard atter 'im, en Cow atter 'im, en dey ain't kotch 'im yit."

X.
MR. TERRAPIN APPEARS
UPON THE SCENE.

"Miss Sally's" little boy again occupying the anxious position of auditor, Uncle Remus took the shovel and "put de noses er de chunks tergedder," as he expressed it, and then began:

"One day, atter Sis Cow done run pas' 'er own shadder tryin' fer ter ketch 'im, Brer Rabbit tuck'n 'low dat he wuz gwineter drap in en see Miss Meadows en de gals, en he got out his piece er lookin'-glass en primp up, he did, en sot out. Gwine canterin' 'long de road, who should Brer Rabbit run up wid but ole Brer Tarrypin— de same ole one-en-sixpunce. Brer Rabbit stop, he did, en rap on de roof er Brer Tarrypin house."

"On the roof of his house, Uncle Remus?" interrupted the little boy.

"Co'se, honey, Brer Tarrypin kare his house wid 'im. Rain er shine, hot er cole, strike up wid ole Brer Tarrypin w'en you will en w'ilst you may, en whar you fine 'im, dar you'll fine his shanty. Hit's des like I tell you. So den! Brer Rabbit he rap on de roof er Brer Tarrypin's house, he did, en ax wuz he in, en Brer Tarrypin 'low dat he wuz, en den Brer Rabbit, he ax 'im howdy, en den Brer Tarrypin he likewise 'spon' howdy, en den Brer Rabbit he say whar wuz Brer Tarrypin gwine, en Brer Tarrypin, he say w'ich he wern't gwine nowhar skasely. Den Brer Rabbit 'low he wuz on his way fer ter see Miss Meadows en de gals, en he ax Brer Tarrypin ef he won't jine in en go long, en Brer Tarrypin 'spon' he don't keer ef he do, en den dey sot out. Dey had plenty er time fer confabbin' 'long de way, but bimeby dey got dar, en Miss Meadows en de gals dey come ter de do', dey did, en ax um in, en in dey went.

"W'en dey got in, Brer Tarrypin wuz so flat-footed dat he wuz too low on de flo', en he wern't high nuff in a cheer, but while they wuz all scramblin' 'roun' tryin' fer ter git Brer Tarrypin a cheer, Brer Rabbit, he pick 'im up en put 'im on de shelf whar de water-bucket sot, en ole Brer Tarrypin, he lay back up dar, he did, des es proud ez a nigger widder cook 'possum.

"Co'se de talk fell on Brer Fox, en Miss Meadows en de gals make a great 'miration 'bout w'at a gaily ridin'-hoss Brer Fox wuz, en dey make lots er fun, en laff en giggle same like gals duz deze days. Brer Rabbit, he sot dar in de cheer smokin' his seegyar, en he sorter kler up his th'oat, en say, sezee:

" 'I'd er rid 'im over dis mawnin', ladies,' sezee, 'but I rid 'im so hard yistiddy dat he went lame in de off fo' leg, en I speck I'll hatter swop 'im off yit,' sezee.

"Den Brer Tarrypin, he up'n say, sezee:

" 'Well, ef you gwineter sell 'im, Brer Rabbit,' sezee, 'sell him some'rs outen dis naberhood, kase he done bin yer too long now,' sezee. 'No longer'n day 'fo' yistiddy,' sezee, 'Brer Fox pass me on de road, en whatter you reckin he say?' sezee.

" 'Law, Brer Tarrypin,' sez Miss Meadows, sez she, 'you don't mean ter say he cust?' sez she, en den de gals hilt der fans up 'fo' der faces.

" 'Oh, no, ma'm,' sez Brer Tarrypin, sezee, 'he didn't cust, but he holler out—"Heyo Stinkin' Jim!" ' sezee.

" 'Oh, my! You hear dat, gals?' sez Miss Meadows, sez she; 'Brer Fox call Brer Tarrypin Stinkin' Jim,' sez she, en den Miss Meadows en de gals make great wonderment how Brer Fox kin talk dat a way 'bout nice man like Brer Tarrypin.

"But bless grashus, honey! w'ilst all dis gwine on, Brer Fox wuz stannin' at de back do' wid one year at de cat-hole lissenin'. Eave-drappers don't hear no good er deyse'f, en de way Brer Fox wuz 'bused dat day wuz a caution.

"Bimeby Brer Fox stick his head in de do', en holler out:

" 'Good evenin', fokes, I wish you mighty well,' sezee, en wid dat he make a dash fer Brer Rabbit, but Miss Meadows en de gals dey holler en squall, dey did, en Brer Tarrypin he got ter scramblin' roun' up dar on de shelf, en off he come, en blip he tuck Brer Fox on de back er de head. Dis sorter stunted Brer Fox, en w'en he gedder his 'membunce de mos' he seed wuz a pot er greens turnt over in de fireplace, en a broke cheer. Brer Rabbit wuz gone, en Brer Tarrypin wuz gone, en Miss Meadows en de gals wuz gone."

"Where did the Rabbit go, Uncle Remus?" the little boy asked, after a pause.

"Bless yo' soul, honey! Brer Rabbit he skint up de chimbly—dats w'at turnt de pot er greens over. Brer Tarrypin, he crope under de bed, he did, en got behime de cloze-chist, en Miss Meadows en de gals, dey run out in de yard.

"Brer Fox, he sorter look roun' en feel er de back er his head, whar Brer Tarrypin lit, but he don't see no sine er Brer Rabbit. But de smoke en de ashes gwine up de chimbly got de best er Brer Rabbit, en bimeby he sneeze—*huckychow!*

" 'Aha!' sez Brer Fox, sezee: 'youer dar, is you?' sezee. 'Well, I'm gwineter smoke you out, ef it takes a mont'. Youer mine dis time,' sezee. Brer Rabbit ain't sayin' nuthin'.

" 'Ain't you comin' down?' sez Brer Fox, sezee. Brer Rabbit ain't sayin' nuthin'. Den Brer Fox, he went out atter some wood, he did, en w'en he come back he hear Brer Rabbit laffin'.

" 'W'at you laffin' at, Brer Rabbit?' sez Brer Fox, sezee.

" 'Can't tell you, Brer Fox,' sez Brer Rabbit, sezee.

" 'Better tell, Brer Rabbit,' sez Brer Fox, sezee.

" ' 'Taint nuthin but a box er money somebody done gone en lef' up yer in de chink er de chimbly,' sez Brer Rabbit, sezee.

" 'Don't b'leeve you,' sez Brer Fox, sezee.

" 'Look up en see,' sez Brer Rabbit, sezee, en w'en Brer Fox look up, Brer Rabbit spit his eyes full er ter-barker joose, he did, en Brer Fox, he make a break fer de branch, en Brer Rabbit he come down en tole de ladies good-by.

" 'How you git 'im off, Brer Rabbit?' sez Miss Meadows, sez she.

" 'Who? me?' sez Brer Rabbit, sezee; 'w'y I des tuck en tole 'im dat ef he didn't go 'long home en stop playin' his pranks on spectubble fokes, dat I'd take 'im out and th'ash 'im,' sezee."

"And what became of the Terrapin?" asked the little boy.

"Oh, well den!" exclaimed the old man, "chilluns

can't speck ter know all 'bout eve'ything 'fo' dey git some res'. Dem eyeleds er yone wanter be propped wid straws dis minnit."

XI.
MR. WOLF MAKES
A FAILURE.

"I lay yo' ma got comp'ny," said Uncle Remus, as the little boy entered the old man's door with a huge piece of mince-pie in his hand, "en ef she aint got comp'ny, den she done gone en drap de cubberd key som'ers whar you done run up wid it."

"Well, I saw the pie lying there, Uncle Remus, and I just thought I'd fetch it out to you."

"Tooby sho, honey," replied the old man, regarding the child with admiration. "Tooby sho, honey; dat changes marters. Chrismus doin's is outer date, en dey aint got no bizness layin' roun' loose. Dish yer pie," Uncle Remus continued, holding it up and measuring it with an experienced eye, "will gimme strenk fer ter persoo on atter Brer Fox en Brer Rabbit en de udder beastesses w'at dey roped in 'long wid um."

Here the old man paused, and proceeded to demolish the pie—a feat accomplished in a very short time. Then he wiped the crumbs from his beard and began:

"Brer Fox feel so bad, en he git so mad 'bout Brer Rabbit, dat he dunno w'at ter do, en he look mighty downhearted. Bimeby, one day wiles he wuz gwine 'long de road, ole Brer Wolf come up wid 'im. W'en dey done howdyin' en axin' atter one nudder's fambly kunnexshun, Brer Wolf, he 'low, he did, dat der wuz sump'n wrong wid Brer Fox, en Brer Fox, he 'low'd der wern't, en he went on en laff en make great ter-do kaze Brer

Wolf look like he spishun sump'n. But Brer Wolf, he got mighty long head, en he sorter broach 'bout Brer Rabbit's kyar'ns on, kaze de way dat Brer Rabbit 'ceive Brer Fox done got ter be de talk er de naberhood. Den Brer Fox en Brer Wolf dey sorter palavered on, dey did, twel bimeby Brer Wolf he up'n say dat he done got plan fix fer ter trap Brer Rabbit. Den Brer Fox say how. Den Brer Wolf up'n tell 'im dat de way fer ter git de drap on Brer Rabbit wuz ter git 'im in Brer Fox house. Brer Fox dun know Brer Rabbit uv ole, en he know dat sorter game done wo' ter a frazzle, but Brer Wolf, he talk mighty 'swadin'.

" 'How you gwine git 'im dar?' sez Brer Fox, sezee.

" 'Fool 'im dar,' sez Brer Wolf, sezee.

" 'Who gwine do de foolin'?' sez Brer Fox, sezee.

" 'I'll do de foolin',' sez Brer Wolf, sezee, 'ef you'll do de gamin',' sezee.

" 'How you gwine do it?' sez Brer Fox, sezee.

" 'You run 'long home, en git on de bed, en make like you dead, en don't you say nuthin' twel Brer Rabbit come en put his han's onter you,' sez Brer Wolf, sezee, 'en ef we don't git 'im fer supper, Joe's dead en Sal's a widder,' sezee.

"Dis look like mighty nice game, en Brer Fox 'greed. So den he amble off home, en Brer Wolf, he march off ter Brer Rabbit house. W'en he got dar, hit look like nobody at home, but Brer Wolf he walk up en knock on de do'—blam! blam! Nobody come. Den he lam aloose en knock 'gin—blim! blim!

" 'Who dar?' sez Brer Rabbit, sezee.

" 'Fr'en',' sez Brer Wolf.

" 'Too menny fr'en's spiles de dinner,' sez Brer Rabbit, sezee; 'w'ich un's dis?' sezee.

" 'I fetch bad news, Brer Rabbit,' sez Brer Wolf, sezee.

" 'Bad news is soon tole,' sez Brer Rabbit, sezee.

"By dis time Brer Rabbit done come ter de do', wid his head tied up in a red hankcher.

" 'Brer Fox died dis mawnin',' sez Brer Wolf, sezee.

" 'Whar yo' mo'nin' gown, Brer Wolf?' sez Brer Rabbit, sezee.

" 'Gwine atter it now,' sez Brer Wolf, sezee. 'I des call by fer ter bring de news. I went down ter Brer Fox house little bit 'go, en dar I foun' 'im stiff,' sezee.

"Den Brer Wolf lope off. Brer Rabbit sot down en scratch his head, he did, en bimeby he say ter hisse'f dat he b'leeve he sorter drap 'roun' by Brer Fox house fer ter see how de lan' lay. No sooner said'n done. Up he jump, en out he went. W'en Brer Rabbit got close ter Brer Fox house, all look lonesome. Den he went up nigher. Nobody stirrin'. Den he look in, en dar lay Brer Fox stretch out on de bed des ez big ez life. Den Brer Rabbit make like he talkin' to hisse'f.

" 'Nobody 'roun' fer ter look atter Brer Fox—not even Brer Tukkey Buzzard ain't come ter de funer'l,' sezee. 'I hope Brer Fox ain't dead, but I speck he is,' sezee. 'Even down ter Brer Wolf done gone en lef' 'im. Hit's de busy season wid me, but I'll set up wid 'im. He seem like he dead, yit he mayn't be,' sez Brer Rabbit, sezee. 'W'en a man go ter see dead fokes, dead fokes allers raises up der behime leg en hollers, *wahoo!*' sezee.

"Brer Fox he stay still. Den Brer Rabbit he talk little louder:

" 'Mighty funny. Brer Fox look like he dead, yit he don't do like he dead. Dead fokes hists der behime leg en hollers *wahoo!* w'en a man come ter see um,' sez Brer Rabbit, sezee.

"Sho' nuff, Brer Fox lif' up his foot en holler *wahoo!* en Brer Rabbit he tear out de house like de dogs wuz atter 'im.' Brer Wolf mighty smart, but nex' time you hear fum 'im, honey, he'll be in trouble. You des hole yo' breff'n wait."

XII.
MR. FOX TACKLES
OLD MAN TARRYPIN.

"One day," said Uncle Remus, sharpening his knife on the palm of his hand—"one day Brer Fox strike up wid Brer Tarrypin right in de middle er de big road. Brer Tarrypin done heerd 'im comin', en he 'low ter hissef dat he'd sorter keep one eye open; but Brer Fox wuz monstus perlite, en he open up de confab, he did, like he ain't see Brer Tarrypin sence de las' freshit.

" 'Heyo, Brer Tarrypin, whar you bin dis long-come-short?' sez Brer Fox, sezee.

" 'Lounjun 'roun', Brer Fox, lounjun 'roun',' sez Brer Tarrypin.

" 'You don't look sprucy like you did, Brer Tarrypin,' sez Brer Fox, sezee.

" 'Lounjun 'roun' en suffer'n',' sez Brer Tarrypin, sezee.

"Den de talk sorter run on like dis:

" 'W'at ail you, Brer Tarrypin? Yo' eye look mighty red,' sez Brer Fox, sezee.

" 'Lor', Brer Fox, you dunner w'at trubble is. You ain't bin lounjun 'roun' en suffer'n',' sez Brer Tarrypin, sezee.

" 'Bofe eyes red, en you look like you mighty weak, Brer Tarrypin,' sez Brer Fox, sezee.

" 'Lor', Brer Fox, you dunner w'at trubble is,' sez Brer Tarrypin, sezee.

" 'W'at ail you now, Brer Tarrypin?' sez Brer Fox, sezee.

" 'Tuck a walk de udder day, en man come 'long en sot de fiel' a-fier. Lor', Brer Fox, you dunner w'at trubble is,' sez Brer Tarrypin, sezee.

" 'How you git out de fier, Brer Tarrypin?' sez Brer Fox, sezee.

" 'Sot en tuck it, Brer Fox,' sez Brer Tarrypin, sezee. 'Sot en tuck it, en de smoke sif' in my eye, en de fier scorch my back,' sez Brer Tarrypin, sezee.

" 'Likewise hit bu'n yo' tail off,' sez Brer Fox, sezee.

" 'Oh, no, dar's de tail, Brer Fox,' sez Brer Tarrypin, sezee, en wid dat he oncurl his tail fum under de shell, en no sooner did he do dat dan Brer Fox grab it, en holler out:

" 'Oh, yes, Brer Tarrypin! Oh, yes! En so youer de man w'at lam me on de head at Miss Meadows's, is you? Youer in wid Brer Rabbit, is you? Well, I'm gwineter out you.'

"Brer Tarrypin beg en beg, but 'twan't no use. Brer Fox done bin fool so much dat he look like he 'termin' fer ter have Brer Tarrypin haslett. Den Brer Tarrypin beg Brer Fox not fer ter drown 'im, but Brer Fox ain't makin' no prommus, en den he beg Brer Fox fer ter bu'n' im, kaze he done useter fier, but Brer Fox don't say nuthin'. Bimeby Brer Fox drag Brer Tarrypin off little ways b'low de spring-'ouse, en souze 'im under de water. Den Brer Tarrypin begin fer ter holler:

" 'Tu'n loose dat stump root en ketch holt er me— tu'n loose dat stump root en ketch holt er me.'

"Brer Fox he holler back:

" 'I ain't got holt er no stump root, en I is got holt er you.'

"Brer Tarrypin he keep on holler'n:

" 'Ketch holt er me—I'm a drownin'—I'm a drownin'—tu'n loose de stump root en ketch holt er me.'

"Sho nuff, Brer Fox tu'n loose de tail, en Brer Tarrypin, he went down ter de bottom—kerblunkity-blink!"

No typographical combination or description could do justice to the guttural sonorousness—the peculiar intonation—which Uncle Remus imparted to this combination. It was so peculiar, indeed, that the little boy asked:

"How did he go to the bottom, Uncle Remus?"

"Kerblunkity-blink!"

"Was he drowned, Uncle Remus?"

"Who? Ole man Tarrypin? Is you drowndid w'en yo' ma tucks you in de bed?"

"Well, no," replied the little boy, dubiously.

"Ole man Tarrypin wuz at home I tell you, honey. Kerblinkity-blunk!"

XIII.
THE AWFUL FATE OF
MR. WOLF.

Uncle Remus was half-soling one of his shoes, and his Miss Sally's little boy had been handling his awls, his hammers, and his knives to such an extent that the old man was compelled to assume a threatening attitude; but peace reigned again, and the little boy perched himself on a chair, watching Uncle Remus driving in pegs.

"Folks w'at's allers pesterin' people, en bodderin' 'longer dat w'at ain't dern, don't never come ter no good eend. Dar wuz Brer Wolf; stidder mindin' un his own bizness, he hatter take en go in pardnerships wid Brer Fox, en dey want skacely a minnit in de day dat he want atter Brer Rabbit, en he kep' on en kep' on twel fus' news you knowed he got kotch up wid—en he got kotch up wid monstus bad."

"Goodness, Uncle Remus! I thought the Wolf let the Rabbit alone, after he tried to fool him about the Fox being dead."

"Better lemme tell dish yer my way. Bimeby hit'll be yo' bed time, en Miss Sally'll be a hollerin' atter you, en you'll be a whimplin' roun', en den Mars John'll fetch up de re'r wid dat ar strop w'at I made fer 'im."

The child laughed, and playfully shook his fist in the

simple, serious face of the venerable old darkey, but said no more. Uncle Remus waited awhile to be sure there was to be no other demonstration, and then proceeded:

"Brer Rabbit ain't see no peace w'atsumever. He can't leave home 'cep' Brer Wolf 'ud make a raid en tote off some er de fambly. Brer Rabbit b'ilt 'im a straw house, en hit wuz tored down; den he made a house outen pine-tops, en dat went de same way; den he made 'im a bark house, en dat wuz raided on, en eve'y time he los' a house he los' wunner his chilluns. Las' Brer Rabbit got mad, he did, en cust, en den he went off, he did, en got some kyarpinters, en dey b'ilt 'im a plank house wid rock foundashuns. Atter dat he could have some peace en quietness. He could go out en pass de time er day wid his nabers, en come back en set by de fier, en smoke his pipe, en read de newspapers same like enny man w'at got a fambly. He made a hole, he did, in de cellar whar de little Rabbits could hide out w'en dar wuz much uv a racket in de naberhood, en de latch er de front do' kotch on de inside. Brer Wolf, he see how de lan' lay, he did, en he lay low. De little Rabbits wuz mighty skittish, but hit got so dat cole chills ain't run up Brer Rabbit's back no mo' w'en he heerd Brer Wolf go gallopin' by.

"Bimeby, one day w'en Brer Rabbit wuz fixin' fer ter call on Miss Coon, he heerd a monstus fuss en clatter up de big road, en 'mos' 'fo' he could fix his years fer ter lissen, Brer Wolf run in de do'. De little Rabbits dey went inter dere hole in de cellar, dey did, like blowin' out a cannle. Brer Wolf wuz far'ly kivver'd wid mud, en mighty nigh outer win'.

" 'Oh, do pray save me, Brer Rabbit!' sez Brer Wolf, sezee. 'Do please, Brer Rabbit! de dogs is atter me, en dey'll t'ar me up. Don't you year um comin'? Oh, do please save me, Brer Rabbit! Hide me some'rs whar de dogs won't git me.'

"No quicker sed dan done.

" 'Jump in dat big chist dar, Brer Wolf,' sez Brer

Rabbit, sezee; 'jump in dar en make yo'se'f at home.'

"In jump Brer Wolf, down come de led, en inter de hasp went de hook, en dar Mr. Wolf wuz. Den Brer Rabbit went ter de lookin'-glass, he did, en wink at hisse'f, en den he drawd de rockin'-cheer in front er de fier, he did, en tuck a big chaw terbarker."

"Tobacco, Uncle Remus?" asked the little boy, incredulously.

"Rabbit terbarker, honey. You know dis yer life ev'lastin' w'at Miss Sally puts 'mong de cloze in de trunk; well, dat's rabbit terbarker. Den Brer Rabbit sot dar long time, he did, turnin' his mine over en wukken his thinkin' masheen. Bimeby he got up, en sorter stir 'roun'. Den Brer Wolf open up:

" 'Is de dogs all gone, Brer Rabbit?'

" 'Seem like I hear one un um smellin' roun' de chimbly-cornder des now.'

"Den Brer Rabbit git de kittle en fill it full er water, en put it on de fier.

" 'W'at you doin' now, Brer Rabbit?'

" 'I'm fixin' fer ter make you a nice cup er tea, Brer Wolf.'

"Den Brer Rabbit went ter de cubberd en git de gimlet, en commence fer ter bo' little holes in de chist-led.

" 'W'at you doin' now, Brer Rabbit?'

" 'I'm a bo'in' little holes so you kin get bref, Brer Wolf.'

"Den Brer Rabbit went out en git some mo' wood, en fling it on de fier.

" 'W'at you doin' now, Brer Rabbit?'

" 'I'm a chunkin' up de fier so you won't git cole, Brer Wolf.'

"Den Brer Rabbit went down inter de cellar en fotch out all his chilluns.

" 'W'at you doin' now, Brer Rabbit?'

" 'I'm a tellin' my chilluns w'at a nice man you is, Brer Wolf.'

"En de chilluns, dey had ter put der han's on der moufs fer ter keep fum laffin'. Den Brer Rabbit he got de kittle en commenced fer ter po' de hot water on de chist-lid.

" 'W'at dat I hear, Brer Rabbit?'

" 'You hear de win' a blowin', Brer Wolf.'

"Den de water begin fer ter sif' thoo.

" 'W'at dat I feel, Brer Rabbit?'

" 'You feels de fleas a bitin', Brer Wolf.'

" 'Dey er bitin' mighty hard, Brer Rabbit.'

" 'Tu'n over on de udder side, Brer Wolf.'

" 'W'at dat I feel now, Brer Rabbit?'

" 'Still you feels de fleas, Brer Wolf.'

" 'Dey er eatin' me up, Brer Rabbit,' en dem wuz de las' words er Brer Wolf, kase de scaldin' water done de bizness.

"Den Brer Rabbit call in his nabers, he did, en dey hilt a reg'lar juberlee; en ef you go ter Brer Rabbit's house right now, I dunno but w'at you'll fine Brer Wolf's hide hangin' in de back-po'ch, en all bekaze he wuz so bizzy wid udder fo'kses doin's."

XIV.
MR. FOX AND
THE DECEITFUL FROGS.

When the little boy ran in to see Uncle Remus the night after he had told him of the awful fate of Brer Wolf, the only response to his greeting was:

"I-doom-er-ker-kum-mer-ker!"

No explanation could convey an adequate idea of the intonation and pronunciation which Uncle Remus brought to bear upon this wonderful word. Those who can recall to mind the peculiar gurgling, jerking, liquid sound made by pouring water from a large jug, or the sound produced by throwing several stones in rapid succession into a pond of deep water, may be able to form a very faint idea of the sound, but it can not be reproduced in print. The little boy was astonished.

"What did you say, Uncle Remus?"

"I-doom-er-ker-kum-mer-ker! I-doom-er-ker-kum-mer-ker!"

"What is that?"

"Dat's Tarrypin talk, dat is. Bless yo' soul, honey," continued the old man, brightening up, "w'en you git ole ez me—w'en you see w'at I sees, en year w'at I years—de creeturs dat you can't talk wid 'll be mighty skase—dey will dat. W'y, ders er old gray rat w'at uses 'bout yer, en time atter time he comes out w'en you all done gone ter bed en sets up dar in de cornder en dozes, en me en him talks by de 'our; en w'at dat ole rat dunno ain't down in de spellin' book. Des now, w'en you run in and broke me up, I wuz fetchin' inter my mine w'at Brer Tarrypin say ter Brer Fox w'en he turn 'im loose in de branch."

"What did he say, Uncle Remus?"

"Dat w'at he said—I-doom-er-ker-kum-mer-ker! Brer Tarrypin wuz at de bottom er de pon', en he talk back, he did, in bubbles—I-doom-er-ker-kum-mer-ker! Brer Fox, he ain't sayin' nuthin', but Brer Bull-Frog, settin' on de bank, he hear Brer Tarrypin, he did, en he holler back:

" 'Jug-er-rum-kum-dum! Jug-er-rum-kum-dum!'

"Den n'er Frog holler out:

" 'Knee-deep! Knee-deep!'

"Den ole Brer Bull-Frog, he holler back:

" 'Don't-you-berlieve-'im! Don't-you-berlieve-'im!'

"Den de bubbles come up fum Brer Tarrypin:

" 'I-doom-er-ker-kum-mer-ker!'

"Den n'er Frog sing out:

" 'Wade in! Wade in!'

"Den ole Brer Bull-Frog talk thoo his ho'seness:

" 'Dar-you'll-fine-yo'-brudder!   Dar-you'll-fine-yo'-brudder!'

"Sho nuff, Brer Fox look over de bank, he did, en dar wuz n'er Fox lookin' at 'im outer de water. Den he retch out fer ter shake han's, en in he went, heels over head, en Brer Tarrypin bubble out:

" 'I-doom-er-ker-kum-mer-ker!' "

"Was the Fox drowned, Uncle Remus?" asked the little boy.

"He wern't zackly drowndid, honey," replied the old man, with an air of cautious reserve. "He did manage fer ter scramble out, but a little mo' en de Mud Turkle would er got 'im, en den he'd er bin made hash un worril widout een'."

XV.
MR. FOX GOES A-HUNTING,
BUT MR. RABBIT BAGS THE GAME.

"Atter Brer Fox hear 'bout how Brer Rabbit done Brer Wolf," said Uncle Remus, scratching his head with the point of his awl, "he 'low, he did, dat he better not be so brash, en he sorter let Brer Rabbit 'lone. Dey wuz all time seein' one nudder, en 'bunnunce er times Brer Fox could er nab Brer Rabbit, but eve'y time he got de chance, his mine 'ud sorter rezume 'bout Brer Wolf, en he let Brer Rabbit 'lone. Bimeby dey 'gun ter git kinder familious wid wunner nudder like dey useter, en it got so Brer Fox'd call on Brer Rabbit, en dey'd set up en smoke der pipes, dey would, like no ha'sh feelin's 'd ever rested 'twixt um.

"Las', one day Brer Fox come 'long all rig out, en ax Brer Rabbit fer ter go huntin' wid 'im, but Brer Rabbit, he sorter feel lazy, en he tell Brer Fox dat he got some udder fish fer ter fry. Brer Fox feel mighty sorry, he did, but he say he b'leeve he try his han' enny how, en off he put. He wuz gone all day, en he had a monstus streak er luck, Brer Fox did, en he bagged a sight er game. Bimeby, to'rds de shank er de evenin', Brer Rabbit sorter stretch hisse'f, he did, en 'low hit's mos' time fer Brer Fox fer ter git 'long home. Den Brer Rabbit, he went'n mounted a stump fer ter see ef he could year Brer Fox comin'. He ain't bin dar long, twel sho' nuff, yer come Brer Fox thoo de woods, singing like a nigger at a frolic. Brer Rabbit, he lipt down off'n de stump, he did, en lay down in de road en make like he dead. Brer Fox he come 'long, he did, en see Brer Rabbit layin' dar. He tu'n 'im over, he did, en 'zamine 'im, en say, sezee:

" 'Dish yer rabbit dead. He look like he bin dead long time. He dead, but he mighty fat. He de fattes' rabbit w'at I ever see, but he bin dead too long. I feard ter take 'im home,' sezee.

"Brer Rabbit ain't sayin' nuthin'. Brer Fox, he sorter lick his chops, but he went on en lef' Brer Rabbit layin' in de road. Dreckly he wuz outer sight, Brer Rabbit, he jump up, he did, en run roun' thoo de woods en git befo Brer Fox agin. Brer Fox, he come up, en dar lay Brer Rabbit, periently cole en stiff. Brer Fox, he look at Brer Rabbit, en he sorter study. Atter while he onslung his game-bag, en say ter hisse'f, sezee:

" 'Deze yer rabbits gwine ter was'e. I'll des 'bout leave my game yer, en I'll go back'n git dat udder rab- bit, en I'll make fokes b'leeve dat I'm ole man Hunter fum Huntsville,' sezee.

"En wid dat he drapt his game en loped back up de road atter de udder rabbit, en w'en he got outer sight, ole Brer Rabbit, he snatch up Brer Fox game en put out fer home. Nex' time he see Brer Fox, he holler out:

" 'What you kill de udder day, Brer Fox?' sezee.

"Den Brer Fox, he sorter koam his flank wid his tongue, en holler back:

" 'I kotch a han'ful er hard sense, Brer Rabbit,' sezee.

"Den ole Brer Rabbit, he laff, he did, en up en 'spon,' sezee:

" 'Ef I'd a know'd you wuz atter dat, Brer Fox, I'd a loant you some er mine,' sezee."

XVI.
OLD MR. RABBIT,
HE'S A GOOD FISHERMAN.

"Brer Rabbit en Brer Fox wuz like some chilluns w'at I knows un," said Uncle Remus, regarding the little boy, who had come to hear another story, with an affectation of great solemnity. "Bofe un um wuz allers atter wunner nudder, a prankin' en a pester'n 'roun', but Brer Rabbit did had some peace, kaze Brer Fox done got skittish 'bout puttin' de clamps on Brer Rabbit.

"One day, w'en Brer Rabbit, en Brer Fox, en Brer Coon, en Brer B'ar, en a whole lot un um wuz clearin' up a new groun' fer ter plant a roas'n'year patch, de sun 'gun ter git sorter hot, en Brer Rabbit he got tired; but he didn't let on, kaze he 'fear'd de balance un um'd call 'im lazy, en he keep on totin' off trash en pilin' up bresh, twel bimeby he holler out dat he gotter brier in his han', en den he take'n slip off, en hunt fer cool place fer ter res'. Atter w'ile he come 'crosst a well wid a bucket hangin' in it.

" 'Dat look cool,' sez Brer Rabbit, sezee, 'en cool I speck she is. I'll des 'bout git in dar en take a nap,' en wid dat in he jump, he did, en he ain't no sooner fix hisse'f dan de bucket 'gun ter go down."

"Wasn't the Rabbit scared, Uncle Remus?" asked the little boy.

"Honey, dey ain't bin no wusser skeer'd beas' sence de worril begin dan dish yer same Brer Rabbit. He far'ly had a ager. He know whar he cum fum, but he dunner whar he gwine. Dreckly he feel de bucket hit de water, en dar she sot, but Brer Rabbit he keep mighty still, kaze he dunner w'at minnit gwineter be de nex'. He des lay dar en shuck en shiver.

"Brer Fox allers got one eye on Brer Rabbit, en w'en he slip off fum de new groun', Brer Fox he sneak atter 'im. He know Brer Rabbit wuz atter some projick er nudder, en he tuck'n crope off, he did, en watch 'im. Brer Fox see Brer Rabbit come to de well en stop, en den he see 'im jump in de bucket, en den, lo en beholes, he see 'im go down outer sight. Brer Fox wuz de mos' 'stonish Fox dat you ever laid eyes on. He sot off dar in de bushes en study en study, but he don't make no head ner tails ter dis kinder bizness. Den he say ter hisse'f, sezee:

" 'Well, ef dis don't bang my times,' sezee, 'den Joe's dead en Sal's a widder. Right down dar in dat well Brer Rabbit keep his money hid, en ef 'tain't dat den he done gone en 'skiver'd a gole-mine, en ef 'tain't dat, den I'm a gwineter see w'at's in dar,' sezee.

"Brer Fox crope up little nigher, he did, en lissen, but he don't year no fuss, en he keep on gittin' nigher, en yit he don't year nuthin'. Bimeby he git up close en peep down, but he don't see nuthin' en he don't year nuthin'. All dis time Brer Rabbit mighty nigh skeer'd outen his skin, en he fear'd fer ter move kaze de bucket might keel over en spill him out in de water. W'ile he sayin' his pra'rs over like a train er kyars runnin', ole Brer Fox holler out:

" 'Heyo, Brer Rabbit! Who you wizzitin' down dar?' sezee.

" 'Who? Me? Oh, I'm des a fishin', Brer Fox,' sez Brer Rabbit, sezee. 'I des say ter myse'f dat I'd sorter sprize you all wid a mess er fishes fer dinner, en so here I is, en dar's de fishes. I'm a fishin' fer suckers, Brer Fox,' sez Brer Rabbit, sezee.

" 'Is dey many un um down dar, Brer Rabbit?' sez Brer Fox, sezee.

" 'Lot's un um, Brer Fox; scoze en scoze un um. De water is natally live wid um. Come down en he'p me haul um in, Brer Fox,' sez Brer Rabbit, sezee.

" 'How I gwineter git down, Brer Rabbit?'

" 'Jump inter de bucket, Brer Fox. Hit'll fetch you down all safe en soun'.'

"Brer Rabbit talk so happy en talk so sweet dat Brer Fox he jump in de bucket, he did, en, ez he went down, co'se his weight pull Brer Rabbit up. W'en dey pass one nudder on de half-way groun', Brer Rabbit he sing out:

> " 'Good-by, Brer Fox, take keer yo' cloze,
>   Fer dis is de way de worril goes;
>   Some goes up en some goes down,
>   You'll git ter de bottom all safe en soun'.'*

"W'en Brer Rabbit got out, he gallop off en tole de fokes w'at de well b'long ter dat Brer Fox wuz down in dar muddyin' up de drinkin' water, en den he gallop back ter de well, en holler down ter Brer Fox:

> " 'Yer come a man wid a great big gun—
>   W'en he haul you up, you jump en run.' "

"What then, Uncle Remus?" asked the little boy, as the old man paused.

"In des 'bout half n'our, honey, bofe un um wuz back in de new groun'. wukkin des like dey never heer'd er no well, ceppin' dat eve'y now'n den Brer Rabbit'd bust out in er laff, en ole Brer Fox, he'd git a spell er de dry grins."

---

* As a Northern friend suggests that this story may be somewhat obscure, it may be as well to state that the well is supposed to be supplied with a rope over a wheel, or pulley, with a bucket at each end

XVII.
MR. RABBIT NIBBLES
UP THE BUTTER.

"De animils en de beastesses," said Uncle Remus, shaking his coffee around in the bottom of his tin-cup, in order to gather up all the sugar, "dey kep' on gittin' mo' en mo' familious wid wunner nudder, twel bimeby, 'twan't long 'fo' Brer Rabbit, en Brer Fox, en Brer Possum got ter sorter bunchin' der perwishuns ter-gedder in de same shanty. Atter w'ile de roof sorter 'gun ter leak, en one day Brer Rabbit, en Brer Fox, en Brer Possum, 'semble fer ter see ef dey can't kinder patch her up. Dey had a big day's work in front un um, en dey fotch der dinner wid um. Dey lump de vittles up in one pile, en de butter w'at Brer Fox brung, dey goes en puts in de spring-'ouse fer ter keep cool, en den dey went ter wuk, en 'twan't long 'fo' Brer Rabbit stummuck 'gun ter sorter growl en pester 'im. Dat butter er Brer Fox sot heavy on his mine, en his mouf water eve'y time he 'member 'bout it. Present'y he say ter hisse'f dat he bleedzd ter have a nip at dat butter, en den he lay his plans, he did. Fus' news you know, w'ile dey wuz all wukkin' 'long, Brer Rabbit raise his head quick en fling his years forrerd en holler out:

" 'Here I is. W'at you want wid me?' en off he put like sump'n wuz atter 'im.

"He sallied 'roun', ole Brer Rabbit did, en atter he make sho dat nobody ain't foller'n un 'im, inter de spring-'ouse he bounces, en dar he stays twel he git a bait er butter. Den he santer on back en go to wuk.

" 'Whar you bin?' sez Brer Fox, sezee.

" 'I hear my chilluns callin' me,' sez Brer Rabbit, sezee, 'en I hatter go see w'at dey want. My ole 'oman done gone en tuck mighty sick,' sezee.

"Dey wuk on twel bimeby de butter tas'e so good dat ole Brer Rabbit want some mo'. Den he raise up his head, he did, en holler out:

" 'Heyo! Hole on! I'm a comin'!' en off he put.

"Dis time he stay right smart w'ile, en w'en he git back Brer Fox ax him whar he bin.

" 'I bin ter see my ole 'oman, en she's a sinkin,' sezee.

"Dreckly Brer Rabbit hear um callin' 'im ag'in en off he goes, en dis time, bless yo' soul, he gits de butter out so clean dat he kin see hisse'f in de bottom er de bucket. He scrape it clean en lick it dry, en den he go back ter wuk lookin' mo' samer dan a nigger w'at de patter-rollers bin had holt un.

" 'How's yo' ole 'oman dis time?' sez Brer Fox, sezee.

" 'I'm oblije ter you, Brer Fox,' sez Brer Rabbit, sezee, 'but I'm fear'd she's done gone by now,' en dat sorter make Brer Fox en Brer Possum feel in moanin' wid Brer Rabbit.

"Bimeby, w'en dinner-time come, dey all got out der vittles, but Brer Rabbit keep on lookin' lonesome, en Brer Fox en Brer Possum dey sorter rustle roun' fer ter see ef dey can't make Brer Rabbit feel sorter splimmy."

"What is that, Uncle Remus?" asked the little boy.

"Sorter splimmy-splammy, honey—sorter like he in a crowd—sorter like his ole 'oman ain't dead ez she mout be. You know how fokes duz w'en dey gits whar people's a moanin'.' "

The little boy didn't know, fortunately for him, and Uncle Remus went on:

"Brer Fox en Brer Possum rustle roun', dey did, gittin out de vittles, en bimeby Brer Fox, he say, sezee:

" 'Brer Possum, you run down ter de spring en fetch de butter, en I'll sail 'roun' yer en set de table,' sezee.

"Brer Possum, he lope off atter de butter, en dreckly here he come lopin' back wid his years a trimblin' en his tongue a hangin' out. Brer Fox, he holler out:

" 'W'at de matter now, Brer Possum?' sezee.

" 'You all better run yer, fokes,' sez Brer Possum, sezee. 'De las' drap er dat butter done gone!'

" 'Whar she gone?' sez Brer Fox, sezee.

" 'Look like she dry up,' sez Brer Possum, sezee.

"Den Brer Rabbit, he look sorter sollum, he did, en he up'n say, sezee:

" 'I speck dat butter melt in somebody mouf,' sezee.

"Den dey went down ter de spring wid Brer Possum, en sho nuff de butter done gone. W'iles dey wuz sputin' over der wunderment, Brer Rabbit say he see tracks all 'roun' dar, en he p'int out dat ef dey'll all go ter sleep, he kin ketch de chap w'at stole de butter. Den dey all lie down en Brer Fox en Brer Possum dey soon drapt off ter sleep, but Brer Rabbit he stay 'wake, en w'en de time come he raise up easy en smear Brer Possum mouf wid de butter on his paws, en den he run off en nibble up de bes' er de dinner w'at dey lef' layin' out, en den he come back en wake up Brer Fox, en show 'im de butter on Brer Possum mouf. Den dey wake up Brer Possum, en tell 'im 'bout it, but co'se Brer Possum 'ny it ter de las'. Brer Fox, dough, he's a kinder lawyer, en he argafy dis way—dat Brer Possum wuz de fus one at de butter, en de fus one fer ter miss it, en mo'n dat, dar hang de signs on his mouf. Brer Possum see dat dey got 'im jammed up in a cornder, en den he up en say dat de way fer ter ketch de man w'at stole de butter is ter b'il' a big bresh-heap en set her afier, en all han's try ter jump over, en de one w'at fall in, den he de chap w'at stole de butter. Brer Rabbit en Brer Fox dey bofe 'gree, dey did, en dey whirl in en b'il' de bresh-heap, en dey b'il' her high en dey b'il' her wide, en den dey totch her off. W'en she got ter blazin' up good, Brer Rabbit, he tuck de fus turn. He sorter step back, en look 'roun' en giggle, en over he went mo' samer dan a bird flyin'. Den come Brer Fox. He got back little fudder, en spit on his han's, en lit out en made de jump, en he come so nigh gittin' in dat de een' er his tail kotch afier. Ain't you never see no fox, honey?" inquired Uncle Remus, in a tone that implied both conciliation and information.

The little boy thought probably he had, but he wouldn't commit himself.

"Well, den," continued the old man, "nex' time you see one un um, you look right close en see ef de een' er his tail ain't w'ite. Hit's des like I tell you. Dey b'ars de skyar er dat bresh-heap down ter dis day. Dey er marked—dat's w'at dey is—dey er marked."

"And what about Brother Possum?" asked the little boy.

"Ole Brer Possum, he tuck a runnin' start, he did, en he come lumberin' 'long, en he lit—kerblam!—right in de middle er de fier, en dat wuz de las' er ole Brer Possum."

"But, Uncle Remus, Brother Possum didn't steal the butter after all," said the little boy, who was not at all satisfied with such summary injustice.

"Dat w'at make I say w'at I duz, honey. In dis worril, lots er fokes is gotter suffer fer udder fokes sins. Look like hit's mighty onwrong; but hit's des dat away. Tribbalashun seem like she's a waitin' roun' de cornder fer ter ketch one en all un us, honey."

XVIII.
MR. RABBIT FINDS HIS
MATCH AT LAST.

"Hit look like ter me dat I let on de udder night dat in dem days w'en de beastesses wuz santer'n 'roun' same like fokes, none un um wuz brash nuff fer ter ketch up wid Brer Rabbit," remarked Uncle Remus, reflectively.

"Yes," replied the little boy, "that's what you said."

"Well, den," continued the old man with unction, "dar's whar my 'membunce gin out, kaze Brer Rabbit did git kotched up wid, en hit cool 'im off like po'in' spring water on one er deze yer biggity fices."

"How was that, Uncle Remus?" asked the little boy.

"One day w'en Brer Rabbit wuz gwine lippity-clip-pitin' down de road, he meet up wid ole Brer Tarrypin, en atter dey pass de time er day wid wunner nudder, Brer Rabbit, he 'low dat he wuz much 'blije ter Brer Tarrypin fer de han' he tuck in de rumpus dat day down at Miss Meadows's."

"When he dropped off of the water-shelf on the Fox's head," suggested the little boy.

"Dat's de same time, honey. Den Brer Rabbit 'low dat Brer Fox run mighty fas' dat day, but dat ef he'd er bin atter 'im stidder Brer Rabbit, he'd er kotch 'im. Brer Rabbit say he could er kotch 'im hisse'f but he didn't keer 'bout leavin' de ladies. Dey keep on talkin', dey did, twel bimeby dey gotter 'sputin' 'bout w'ich wuz de swif'es'. Brer Rabbit, he say he kin outrun Brer Tarry-pin, en Brer Tarrypin, he des vow dat he kin outrun Brer Rabbit. Up en down dey had it, twel fus news you know Brer Tarrypin say he got a fifty-dollar bill in de chink er de chimbly at home, en dat bill done tole 'im dat he could beat Brer Rabbit in a fa'r race. Den Brer Rabbit say he got a fifty-dollar bill w'at say dat he kin leave Brer Tarrypin so fur behime, dat he could sow barley ez he went 'long en hit 'ud be ripe nuff fer ter cut by de time Brer Tarrypin pass dat way.

"Enny how dey make de bet en put up de money, en ole Brer Tukky Buzzard, he wuz summonzd fer ter be de jedge, en de stakeholder; en 'twan't long 'fo' all de 'rangements wuz made. De race wuz a five-mile heat, en de groun' wuz medjud off, en at de een' er ev'ey mile a pos' wuz stuck up. Brer Rabbit wuz ter run down de big road, en Brer Tarrypin, he say he'd gallup thoo de woods. Fokes tole 'im he could git long faster in de road, but ole Brer Tarrypin, he know w'at he doin'. Miss Meadows en de gals en mos' all de nabers got win' er de fun, en w'en de day wuz sot dey 'termin' fer ter be on han'. Brer Rabbit he train hisse'f ev'ey day, en he skip over de groun' des ez gayly ez a June cricket. Ole Brer Tarrypin, he lay low in de swamp. He had a wife en th'ee chilluns, ole Brer Tarrypin did, en dey wuz all de ve'y spit en image er de ole man. Ennybody w'at know one fum de udder gotter take a spy-glass, en den dey er li'ble fer ter git fooled.

"Dat's de way marters stan' twel de day er de race, en on dat day, ole Brer Tarrypin, en his ole 'oman, en his th'ee chilluns, dey got up 'fo' sun-up, en went ter de place. De ole 'oman, she tuck 'er stan' nigh de fus' mile-pos', she did, en de chilluns nigh de udders, up ter de las', en dar ole Brer Tarrypin, he tuck his stan'. Bimeby, here come de fokes: Jedge Buzzard, he come, en Miss Meadows en de gals, dey come, en den yer come Brer Rabbit wid ribbins tied 'roun' his neck en streamin' fum his years. De fokes all went ter de udder een' er de track fer ter see how dey come out. W'en de time come Jedge Buzzard strut 'roun' en pull out his watch, en holler out:

" 'Gents, is you ready?'

"Brer Rabbit, he say 'yes,' en ole Miss Tarrypin holler 'go' fum de aidge er de woods. Brer Rabbit, he lit out on de race, en ole Miss Tarrypin, she put out for home. Jedge Buzzard, he riz en skimmed 'long fer ter see dat de race wuz runned fa'r. W'en Brer Rabbit got ter de fus' mile-pos' wunner de Tarrypin chilluns crawl out de woods, he did, en make fer de place. Brer Rabbit, he holler out:

" 'Whar is you, Brer Tarrypin?'

" 'Yer I come a bulgin',' sez de Tarrypin, sezee.

"Brer Rabbit so glad he's ahead dat he put out harder dan ever, en de Tarrypin, he make fer home. W'en he come ter de nex' pos', nudder Tarrypin crawl out er de woods.

" 'Whar is you, Brer Tarrypin?' sez Brer Rabbit, sezee.

" 'Yer I come a bilin',' sez de Tarrypin, sezee.

"Brer Rabbit, he lit out, he did, en come ter nex' pos', en dar wuz de Tarrypin. Den he come ter nex', en dar wuz de Tarrypin. Den he had one mo' mile fer ter run, en he feel like he gittin' bellust. Bimeby, ole Brer Tarrypin look way off down de road en he see Jedge Buzzard sailin' 'long en he know hit's time fer 'im fer ter be up. So he scramble outen de woods, en roll 'cross de ditch, en shuffle thoo de crowd er folks en git ter de mile-pos' en crawl behime it. Bimeby, fus' news you know, yer come Brer Rabbit. He look 'roun' en he don't see Brer Tarrypin, en den he squall out:

" 'Gimme de money, Brer Buzzard! Gimme de money!'

"Den Miss Meadows en de gals, dey holler and laff fit ter kill deyse'f, en ole Brer Tarrypin, he raise up from behime de pos' en sez, sezee:

" 'Ef you'll gimme time fer ter ketch my breff, gents en ladies, one en all, I speck I'll finger dat money myse'f,' sezee, en sho nuff, Brer Tarrypin tie de pu's 'roun' his neck en skaddle* off home."

"But, Uncle Remus," said the little boy, dolefully, "that was cheating."

"Co'se, honey. De beastesses 'gun ter cheat, en den fokes tuck it up, en hit keep on spreadin'. Hit mighty ketchin', en you mine yo' eye, honey, dat somebody don't cheat you 'fo' yo' ha'r git gray ez de ole nigger's."

---

* It may be interesting to note here that in all probability the word "skedaddle," about which there was some controversy during the war, came from the Virginia negro's use of "skaddle," which is a corruption of "scatter." The matter, however, is hardly worth referring to.

XIX.
THE FATE OF
MR. JACK SPARROW.

"You'll tromple on dat bark twel hit won't be fitten fer ter fling 'way, let 'lone make hoss-collars out'n," said Uncle Remus, as the little boy came running into his cabin out of the rain. All over the floor long strips of "wahoo" bark were spread, and these the old man was weaving into horse-collars.

"I'll sit down, Uncle Remus," said the little boy.

"Well, den, you better, honey," responded the old man, "kaze I 'spizes fer ter have my wahoo trompled on. Ef 'twuz shucks, now, hit mout be diffunt, but I'm a gittin' too ole fer ter be projickin' longer shuck collars."

For a few minutes the old man went on with his work, but with a solemn air altogether unusual. Once or twice he sighed deeply, and the sighs ended in a prolonged groan, that seemed to the little boy to be the result of the most unspeakable mental agony. He knew by experience that he had done something which failed to meet the approval of Uncle Remus, and he tried to remember what it was, so as to frame an excuse; but his memory failed him. He could think of nothing he had done calculated to stir Uncle Remus's grief. He was not exactly seized with remorse, but he was very uneasy. Presently Uncle Remus looked at him in a sad and hopeless way, and asked:

"W'at dat long rigmarole you bin tellin' Miss Sally 'bout yo' little brer dis mawnin?"

"Which, Uncle Remus?" asked the little boy, blushing guiltily.

"Dat des w'at I'm a axin' un you now. I hear Miss

Sally say she's a gwineter stripe his jacket, en den I knowed you bin tellin' on 'im."

"Well, Uncle Remus, he was pulling up your onions, and then he went and flung a rock at me," said the child, plaintively.

"Lemme tell you dis," said the old man, laying down the section of horse-collar he had been plaiting, and looking hard at the little boy—"lemme tell you dis—der ain't no way fer ter make tattlers en tale-b'arers turn out good. No, dey ain't. I bin mixin' up wid fokes now gwine on eighty year, en I ain't seed no tattler come ter no good een'. Dat I ain't. En ef ole man M'thoozlum wuz livin' clean twel yit, he'd up'n tell you de same. Sho ez youer settin' dar. You 'member w'at 'come er de bird w'at went tattlin' 'roun' 'bout Brer Rabbit?"

The little boy didn't remember, but he was very anxious to know, and he also wanted to know what kind of a bird it was that so disgraced itself.

"Hit wuz wunner deze yer uppity little Jack Sparrers, I speck," said the old man; "dey wuz allers bodder'n' longer udder fokes's bizness, en dey keeps at it down ter dis day—peckin' yer, and pickin' dar, en scratchin' out yander. One day, atter he bin fool by ole Brer Tarrypin, Brer Rabbit wuz settin' down in de woods studdyin' how he wuz gwineter git even. He feel mighty lonesome, en he feel mighty mad, Brer Rabbit did. Tain't put down in de tale, but I speck he cusst en r'ar'd 'roun' considerbul. Leas'ways, he wuz settin' out dar by hisse'f, en dar he sot, en study en study, twel bimeby he jump up en holler out:

" 'Well, doggone my cats ef I can't gallop 'roun' ole Brer Fox, en I'm gwineter do it. I'll show Miss Meadows en de gals dat I'm de boss er Brer Fox,' sezee.

"Jack Sparrer up in de tree, he hear Brer Rabbit, he did, en he sing out:

" 'I'm gwine tell Brer Fox! I'm gwine tell Brer Fox!

Chick-a-biddy-win'-a-blowin'-acuns-fallin'! I'm gwine tell Brer Fox!' "

Uncle Remus accompanied the speech of the bird with a peculiar whistling sound in his throat, that was a marvelous imitation of a sparrow's chirp, and the little boy clapped his hands with delight, and insisted on a repetition.

"Dis kinder tarrify Brer Rabbit, en he skasely know w'at he gwine do; but bimeby he study ter hisse'f dat de man w'at see Brer Fox fus wuz boun' ter have de inturn, en den he go hoppin' off to'rds home. He didn't got fur w'en who should he meet but Brer Fox, en den Brer Rabbit, he open up:

" 'W'at dis twix' you en me, Brer Fox?' sez Brer Rabbit, sezee. 'I hear tell you gwine ter sen' me ter 'struckshun, en nab my fambly, en 'stroy my shanty,' sezee.

"Den Brer Fox he git mighty mad.

" 'Who bin tellin' you all dis?' sezee.

"Brer Rabbit make like he didn't want ter tell, but Brer Fox he 'sist en 'sist, twel at las' Brer Rabbit he up en tell Brer Fox dat he hear Jack Sparrer say all dis.

" 'Co'se,' sez Brer Rabbit, sezee, 'w'en Brer Jack Sparrer tell me dat I flew up, I did, en I use some langwidge w'ich I'm mighty glad dey wern't no ladies 'roun' nowhars so dey could hear me go on,' sezee.

"Brer Fox he sorter gap, he did, en say he speck he better be sa'nter'n on. But, bless yo' soul, honey, Brer Fox ain't sa'nter fur, 'fo' Jack Sparrer flipp down on a 'simmon-bush by de side er de road, en holler out:

" 'Brer Fox! Oh, Brer Fox!—Brer Fox!'

"Brer Fox he des sorter canter 'long, he did, en make like he don't hear 'im. Den Jack Sparrer up'n sing out agin:

" 'Brer Fox! Oh, Brer Fox! Hole on, Brer Fox! I got some news fer you. Wait, Brer Fox! Hit'll 'stonish you.'

"Brer Fox he make like he don't see Jack Sparrer, ner needer do he hear 'im, but bimeby he lay down by de road, en sorter stretch hisse'f like he fixin' fer ter nap. De tattlin' Jack Sparrer he flew'd 'long, en keep on callin' Brer Fox, but Brer Fox, he ain't sayin' nuthin'. Den little Jack Sparrer, he hop down on de groun' en flutter 'roun' 'mongst de trash. Dis sorter 'track Brer Fox 'tenshun, en he look at de tattlin' bird, en de bird he keep on callin':

" 'I got sump'n fer ter tell you, Brer Fox.'

" 'Git on my tail, little Jack Sparrer,' sez Brer Fox, sezee, 'kaze I'm de'f in one year, en I can't hear out'n de udder. Git on my tail,' sezee.

"Den de little bird he up'n hop on Brer Fox's tail.

" 'Git on my back, little Jack Sparrer, kaze I'm de'f in one year en I can't hear out'n de udder.'

"Den de little bird hop on his back.

" 'Hop on my head, little Jack Sparrer, kaze I'm de'f in bofe years.'

"Up hop de little bird.

" 'Hop on my toof, little Jack Sparrer, kaze I'm de'f in one year en I can't hear out'n de udder.'

"De tattlin' little bird hop on Brer Fox's toof, en den—"

Here Uncle Remus paused, opened wide his mouth and closed it again in a way that told the whole story.[*]

"Did the Fox eat the bird all—all—up?" asked the little boy.

[*] An Atlanta friend heard this story in Florida, but an alligator was substituted for the fox, and a little boy for the rabbit. There is another version in which the impertinent gosling goes to tell the fox something her mother has said, and is caught; and there may be other versions. I have adhered to the middle Georgia version, which is characteristic enough. It may be well to state that there are different versions of all the stories—the shrewd narrators of the mythology of the old plantation adapting themselves with ready tact to the years, tastes, and expectations of their juvenile audiences.

"Jedge B'ar come 'long nex' day," replied Uncle Remus, "en he fine some fedders, en fum dat word went roun' dat ole man Squinch Owl done kotch nudder watz-izname."

XX.
HOW MR. RABBIT
SAVED HIS MEAT.

"One time," said Uncle Remus, whetting his knife slowly and thoughtfully on the palm of his hand, and gazing reflectively in the fire—"one time Brer Wolf—"

"Why, Uncle Remus!" the little boy broke in, "I thought you said the Rabbit scalded the Wolf to death a long time ago."

The old man was fairly caught and he knew it; but this made little difference to him. A frown gathered on his usually serene brow as he turned his gaze upon the child—a frown in which both scorn and indignation were visible. Then all at once he seemed to regain control of himself. The frown was chased away by a look of Christian resignation.

"Dar now! W'at I tell you?" he exclaimed as if addressing a witness concealed under the bed. "Ain't I done tole you so? Bless grashus! ef chilluns ain't gittin' so dey knows mo'n ole fokes, en dey'll spute longer you en spute longer you, ceppin der ma call um, w'ich I speck twon't be long 'fo' she will, en den I'll set yere by de chimbly-cornder en git some peace er mine. W'en ole Miss wuz livin'," continued the old man, still addressing some imaginary person, "hit 'uz mo'n enny her chilluns 'ud dast ter do ter come 'sputin' longer me, en Mars John'll tell you de same enny day you ax 'im."

"Well, Uncle Remus, you know you said the Rabbit

poured hot water on the Wolf and killed him," said the little boy.

The old man pretended not to hear. He was engaged in searching among some scraps of leather under his chair, and kept on talking to the imaginary person. Finally, he found and drew forth a nicely plaited whip-thong with a red snapper all waxed and knotted.

"I wuz fixin' up a w'ip fer a little chap," he continued, with a sigh, "but, bless grashus! 'fo' I kin git 'er done, de little chap done grow'd up twel he know mo'n I duz."

The child's eyes filled with tears and his lips began to quiver, but he said nothing; whereupon Uncle Remus immediately melted.

"I 'clar' to goodness," he said, reaching out and taking the little boy tenderly by the hand, 'ef you ain't de ve'y spit en image er ole Miss w'en I brung 'er de las' news er de war. Hit's des like skeerin' up a ghos' w'at you ain't fear'd un."

Then there was a pause, the old man patting the little child's hand caressingly.

"You ain't mad, is you, honey?" Uncle Remus asked finally, "kaze ef you is, I'm gwine out yere en butt my head 'gin de do' jam'."

But the little boy wasn't mad. Uncle Remus had conquered him and he had conquered Uncle Remus in pretty much the same way before. But it was some time before Uncle Remus would go on with the story. He had to be coaxed. At last, however, he settled himself back in the chair and began:

"Co'se, honey, hit mout er bin ole Brer Wolf, er hit mout er bin er n'er Brer Wolf; it mout er bin 'fo' he got kotch up wid, er it mout er bin atterwards. Ez de tale wer gun to me des dat away I gin it unter you. One time Brer Wolf wuz comin' 'long home fum a fishin' frolic. He s'anter 'long de road, he did, wid his string er fish 'cross his shoulder, wen fus news you know ole Miss Pa'tridge, she hop outer de bushes en flutter 'long right at Brer Wolf nose. Brer Wolf he say ter hisse'f dat old Miss Pa'tridge tryin' fer ter toll 'im 'way fum her nes', en wid dat he lay his fish down en put out inter de bushes whar ole Miss Pa'tridge come fum, en 'bout dat time Brer Rabbit, he happen 'long. Dar wuz de fishes, en dar wuz Brer Rabbit, en w'en dat de case w'at you speck a sorter innerpen'ent man like Brer Rabbit gwine do? I kin tell you dis, dat dem fishes ain't stay whar Brer Wolf put um at, en w'en Brer Wolf come back dey wuz gone.

"Brer Wolf, he sot down en scratch his head, he did, en study en study, en den hit sorter rush into his mine dat Brer Rabbit bin 'long dar, en den Brer Wolf, he put out fer Brer Rabbit house, en w'en he git dar he hail 'im. Brer Rabbit, he dunno nuthin' tall 'bout no fishes. Brer Wolf he up'n say he bleedzd ter b'leeve Brer Rabbit got dem fishes. Brer Rabbit 'ny it up en down, but Brer Wolf stan' too it dat Brer Rabbit got dem fishes. Brer Rabbit, he say dat if Brer Wolf b'leeve he got de fishes, den he give Brer Wolf lief fer ter kill de bes' cow he got. Brer Wolf, he tuck Brer Rabbit at his word, en go off ter de pastur' en drive up de cattle en kill Brer Rabbit bes' cow.

"Brer Rabbit, he hate mighty bad fer ter lose his cow, but he lay his plans, en he tell his chilluns dat he gwine-ter have dat beef yit. Brer Wolf, he bin tuck up by de patter-rollers 'fo' now, en he mighty skeerd un um, en fus news you know, yer come Brer Rabbit hollerin' en tellin' Brer Wolf dat de patter-rollers comin'.

" 'You run en hide, Brer Wolf,' sez Brer Rabbit, sezee, 'en I'll stay yer en take keer er de cow twel you gits back,' sezee.

"Soon's Brer Wolf hear talk er de patter-rollers, he scramble off inter de underbresh like he bin shot out'n a gun. En he want mo'n gone 'fo' Brer Rabbit, he whirl in en skunt de cow en salt de hide down, en den he tuck'n cut up de kyarkiss en stow it 'way in de smoke-'ouse, en

den he tuck'n stick de een' er de cow-tail in de groun'.
Atter he gone en done all dis, den Brer Rabbit he squall
out fer Brer Wolf:

" 'Run yer, Brer Wolf! Run yer! Yo' cow gwine in de
groun'! Run yer!'

"W'en ole Brer Wolf got dar, w'ich he come er scootin', dar wuz Brer Rabbit hol'in' on ter de cow-tail, fer
ter keep it fum gwine in de groun'. Brer Wolf, he kotch
holt, en dey 'gin a pull er two en up come de tail. Den
Brer Rabbit, he wink his off eye en say, sezee:

" 'Dar! de tail done pull out en de cow gone,' sezee.

"But Brer Wolf he wer'n't de man fer ter give it up
dat away, en he got 'im a spade, en a pick-axe, en a
shovel, en he dig en dig fer dat cow twel diggin' wuz
pas' all endu'unce, en ole Brer Rabbit he sot up dar in
his front po'ch en smoke his seegyar. Eve'y time ole
Brer Wolf stuck de pick-axe in de clay, Brer Rabbit, he
giggle ter his chilluns:

" 'He diggy, diggy, diggy, but no meat dar! He
diggy, diggy, diggy, but no meat dar!'

"Kaze all de time de cow wuz layin' pile up in his
smoke-'ouse, en him en his chilluns wuz eatin' fried beef
en inguns eve'y time dey mouf water.

"Now den, honey, you take dis yer w'ip," continued
the old man, twining the leather thong around the little
boy's neck, "en scamper up ter de big 'ouse en tell Miss
Sally fer ter gin you some un it de nex' time she fine yo'
tracks in de sugar-bairl."

XXI.
MR. RABBIT MEETS
HIS MATCH AGAIN.

"Dere wuz nudder man dat sorter play it sharp on
Brer Rabbit," said Uncle Remus, as, by some
mysterious process, he twisted a hog's bristle into the

end of a piece of thread—an operation which the little boy watched with great interest. "In dem days," continued the old man, "de beastesses kyar'd on marters same ez fokes. Dey went inter fahmin', en I speck ef de troof wuz ter come out, dey kep' sto', en had der camp-meetin' times en der bobbycues w'en de wedder wuz 'greeble."

Uncle Remus evidently thought that the little boy wouldn't like to hear of any further discomfiture of Brer Rabbit, who had come to be a sort of hero, and he was not mistaken.

"I thought the Terrapin was the only one that fooled the Rabbit," said the little boy, dismally.

"Hit's des like I tell you, honey. Dey ain't no smart man, 'cep' w'at dey's a smarter. Ef ole Brer Rabbit hadn't er got kotch up wid, de nabers 'ud er tuck 'im for a h'ant, en in dem times dey bu'nt witches 'fo' you could squinch yo' eyeballs. Dey did dat."

"Who fooled the Rabbit this time?" the little boy asked.

When Uncle Remus had the bristle "sot" in the thread, he proceeded with the story:

"One time Brer Rabbit en ole Brer Buzzard 'cluded dey'd sorter go snacks, en crap tergedder. Hit wuz a mighty good year, en de truck tu'n out monstus well, but bimeby, w'en de time come fer dividjun, hit come ter light dat ole Brer Buzzard ain't got nuthin'. De crap wuz all gone, en dey want nuthin' dar fer ter show fer it. Brer Rabbit, he make like he in a wuss fix'n Brer Buzzard, en he mope 'roun', he did, like he fear'd dey gwineter sell 'im out.

"Brer Buzzard, he ain't sayin' nuthin', but he keep up a monstus thinkin', en one day he come 'long en holler en tell Brer Rabbit dat he done fine rich gole-mine des 'cross de river.

" 'You come en go 'longer me, Brer Rabbit,' sez Brer

Tukky Buzzard, sezee. 'I'll scratch en you kin grabble, en 'tween de two un us we'll make short wuk er dat gole-mine,' sezee.

"Brer Rabbit, he wuz high up fer de job, but he study en study, he did, how he gwineter git 'cross de water, kaze ev'y time he git his foot wet all de fambly kotch cole. Den he up'n ax Brer Buzzard how he gwine do, en Brer Buzzard he up'n say dat he kyar Brer Rabbit 'cross, en wid dat ole Brer Buzzard, he squot down, he did, en spread his wings, en Brer Rabbit, he mounted, en up dey riz." There was a pause.

"What did the Buzzard do then?" asked the little boy.

"Dey riz," continued Uncle Remus, "en w'en dey lit, dey lit in de top er de highest sorter pine, en de pine w'at dey lit in wuz growin' on er ilun, en de ilun wuz in de middle er de river, wid de deep water runnin' all 'roun'. Dey ain't mo'n lit 'fo' Brer Rabbit, he know w'ich way de win' 'uz blowin', en by de time ole Brer Buzzard got hisse'f ballunce on a lim', Brer Rabbit, he up'n say, sezee:

" 'W'iles we er res'n here, Brer Buzzard, en bein's you bin so good, I got sump'n fer ter tell you,' sezee. 'I got a gole-mine er my own, one w'at I make myse'f, en I speck we better go back ter mine 'fo' we bodder 'longer yone,' sezee.

"Den ole Brer Buzzard, he laff, he did, twel he shake, en Brer Rabbit, he sing out:

" 'Hole on, Brer Buzzard! Don't flop yo' wings w'en you laff, kaze den ef you duz, sump'n 'ill drap fum up yer, en my gole-mine won't do you no good, en needer will yone do me no good.'

"But 'fo' dey got down fum dar, Brer Rabbit done tole all 'bout de crap, en he hatter promus fer ter 'vide fa'r en squar. So Brer Buzzard, he kyar 'im back, en Brer Rabbit he walk weak in de knees a mont' atterwuds."

XXII.
A STORY ABOUT THE
LITTLE RABBITS.

"Fine um whar you will en w'en you may," remarked Uncle Remus with emphasis, "good chilluns allers gits tuck keer on. Dar wuz Brer Rabbit's chilluns; dey minded der daddy en mammy fum day's een' ter day's een' W'en ole man Rabbit say 'scoot,' dey scooted, en w'en ole Miss Rabbit say 'scat,' dey scatted. Dey did dat. En dey kep der cloze clean, en dey ain't had no smut on der nose nudder."

Involuntarily the hand of the little boy went up to his face, and he scrubbed the end of his nose with his coat-sleeve.

"Dey wuz good chilluns," continued the old man, heartily, "en ef dey hadn't er bin, der wuz one time w'en dey wouldn't er bin no little rabbits—na'er one. Dat's w'at."

"What time was that, Uncle Remus?" the little boy asked.

"De time w'en Brer Fox drapt in at Brer Rabbit house, en didn't foun' nobody dar ceppin' de little Rabbits. Ole Brer Rabbit, he wuz off some'rs raiding on a collard patch, en ole Miss Rabbit she wuz tendin' on a quiltin' in de naberhood, en wiles de little Rabbits wuz playin' hidin'-switch, in drapt Brer Fox. De little Rabbits wuz so fat dat dey fa'rly make his mouf water, but he 'member 'bout Brer Wolf, en he skeered fer ter gobble um up ceppin' he got some skuse. De little Rabbits, dey mighty skittish, en dey sorter huddle deyse'f up ter-gedder en watch Brer Fox motions. Brer Fox, he sot dar en study w'at sorter skuse he gwineter make up. Bimeby he see a great big stalk er sugar-cane stan'in' up in de cornder, en he cle'r up his th'oat en talk biggity:

" 'Yer! you young Rabs dar, sail 'roun' yer en broke me a piece er dat sweetnin'-tree,' sezee, en den he koff.

De little Rabbits, dey got out de sugar-cane, dey did, en dey rastle wid it, en sweat over it, but twan't no use. Dey couldn't broke it. Brer Fox, he make like he ain't watchin', but he keep on holler'n:

" 'Hurry up dar, Rabs! I'm a waitin' on you.'

"En de little Rabbits, dey hustle 'roun' en rastle wid it, but dey couldn't broke it. Bimeby dey hear little bird singin' on top er de house, en de song w'at de little bird sing wuz dish yer:

> " 'Take yo' toofies en gnyaw it,
>   Take yo' toofies en saw it,
>   Saw it en yoke it,
>   En den you kin broke it.'

"Den de little Rabbits, dey git mighty glad, en dey gnyawed de cane mos' 'fo' ole Brer Fox could git his legs oncrosst, en w'en dey kyard 'im de cane, Brer Fox, he sot dar en study how he gwineter make some mo' skuse fer nabbin' un um, en bimeby he git up en git down de sifter w'at wuz hangin' on de wall, en holler out:

" 'Come yer, Rabs! Take dish yer sifter, en run down't de spring en fetch me some fresh water.'

"De little Rabbits, dey run down't de spring, en try ter dip up de water wid de sifter, but co'se hit all run out, en hit keep on runnin' out, twell bimeby de little Rabbits sot down en 'gun ter cry. Den de little bird settin' up in de tree he begin fer ter sing, en dish yer's de song wa't he sing:

> " 'Sifter hole water same ez a tray,
>   Ef you fill it wid moss en dob it wid clay;
>   De Fox git madder de longer you stay—
>   Fill it wid moss en dob it wid clay.'

"Up dey jump, de little Rabbits did, en dey fix de sifter so 'twon't leak, en den dey kyar de water ter ole Brer Fox. Den Brer Fox he git mighty mad, en p'int out a great big stick er wood, en tell de little Rabbits fer ter put dat on de fier. De little chaps dey got 'roun' de wood, dey did, en dey lif' at it so hard twel dey could see der own sins, but de wood ain't budge. Den dey hear de little bird singin', en dish yer's de song w'at he sing:

> " 'Spit in yo' han's en tug it en toll it,
>   En git behine it, en push it, en pole it;
>   Spit in yo' han's en r'ar back en roll it.'

"En des 'bout de time dey got de wood on de fier, der daddy, he come skippin' in, en de little bird, he flew'd away. Brer Fox, he seed his game wuz up, en 'twan't long 'fo' he make his skuse en start fer ter go.

" 'You better stay en take a snack wid me, Brer Fox,' sez Brer Rabbit, sezee. 'Sence Brer Wolf done quit comin' en settin' up wid me, I gittin' so I feels right lonesome dese long nights,' sezee.

"But Brer Fox, he button up his coat-collar tight en des put out fer home. En dat w'at you better do, honey, kaze I see Miss Sally's shadder sailin' backerds en for'ds 'fo' de winder, en de fus' news you know she'll be spectin' un you."

XXIII.
MR. RABBIT AND MR. BEAR.

"Dar wuz one season," said Uncle Remus, pulling thoughtfully at his whiskers, "w'en Brer Fox say to hisse'f dat he speck he better whirl in en plant a goober-patch, en in dem days, mon, hit wuz tech en go. De wud wern't mo'n out'n his mouf 'fo' de groun' 'uz brok'd up en de goobers 'uz planted. Ole Brer Rabbit, he sot off en watch de motions, he did, en he sorter shet one eye en sing to his chilluns:

" 'Ti-yi!   Tungalee!
  I eat um pea, I pick um pea.
  Hit grow in de groun', hit grow so free;
  Ti-yi! dem goober pea.'

"Sho' 'nuff w'en de goobers 'gun ter ripen up, eve'y time Brer Fox go down ter his patch, he fine whar somebody bin grabblin' 'mongst de vines, en he git mighty mad. He sorter speck who de somebody is, but ole Brer Rabbit he cover his tracks so cute dat Brer Fox dunner how ter ketch 'im. Bimeby, one day Brer Fox take a walk all roun' de groun'-pea patch, en 'twan't long 'fo' he fine a crack in de fence whar de rail done bin rub right smoove, en right dar he sot 'im a trap. He tuck'n ben' down a hick'ry saplin', growin' in de fence-cornder, en tie one een' un a plow-line on de top, en in de udder een' he fix a loop-knot, en dat he fasten wid a trigger right in de crack. Nex' mawnin' w'en ole Brer Rabbit come slippin' 'long en crope thoo de crack, de loop-knot kotch 'im behime de fo' legs, en de saplin' flew'd up, en dar he wuz 'twix' de heavens en de yeth. Dar he swung, en he fear'd he gwineter fall, en he fear'd he wer'n't gwineter fall. W'ile he wuz a fixin' up a tale for Brer Fox, he hear a lumberin' down de road, en present'y yer cum ole Brer B'ar amblin' 'long fum whar he bin takin' a bee-tree. Brer Rabbit, he hail 'im:

" 'Howdy, Brer B'ar!'

"Brer B'ar, he look 'roun en bimeby he see Brer Rabbit swingin' fum de saplin', en he holler out:

" 'Heyo, Brer Rabbit! How you come on dis mawnin'?'

" 'Much oblije, I'm middlin', Brer B'ar,' sez Brer Rabbit, sezee.

"Den Brer B'ar, he ax Brer Rabbit w'at he doin' up

dar in de elements, en Brer Rabbit, he up'n say he makin' dollar minnit. Brer B'ar, he say how. Brer Rabbit say he keepin' crows out'n Brer Fox's groun'-pea patch, en den he ax Brer B'ar ef he don't wanter make dollar minnit, kaze he got big fambly er chilluns fer ter take keer un, en den he make sech nice skeer-crow. Brer B'ar 'low dat he take de job, en den Brer Rabbit show 'im how ter ben' down de saplin', en twan't long 'fo' Brer B'ar wuz swingin' up dar in Brer Rabbit place. Den Brer Rabbit, he put out fer Brer Fox house, en w'en he got dar he sing out:

" 'Brer Fox! Oh, Brer Fox! Come out yer, Brer Fox, en I'll show you de man w'at bin stealin' yo' goobers.'

"Brer Fox, he grab up his walkin'-stick, en bofe un um went runnin' back down ter der goober-patch, en w'en dey got dar, sho 'nuff, dar wuz ole Brer B'ar.

" 'Oh, yes! youer kotch, is you?' sez Brer Fox, en 'fo' Brer B'ar could 'splain, Brer Rabbit he jump up en down, en holler out:

" 'Hit 'im in de mouf, Brer Fox; hit 'im in de mouf'; en Brer Fox, he draw back wid de walkin'-cane, en blip he tuck 'im, en eve'y time Brer B'ar'd try ter 'splain, Brer Fox'd shower down on him.

"W'iles all dis 'uz gwine on, Brer Rabbit, he slip off en git in a mud-hole en des lef' his eyes stickin' out, kaze he know'd dat Brer B'ar'd be a comin' atter 'im. Sho 'nuff, bimeby here come Brer B'ar down de road, en w'en he git ter de mud-hole, he say:

" 'Howdy, Brer Frog; is you seed Brer Rabbit go by yer?'

" 'He des gone by,' sez Brer Rabbit, en ole man B'ar tuck off down de road like a skeer'd mule, en Brer Rabbit, he come out en dry hisse'f in de sun, en go home ter his fambly same ez enny udder man."

"The Bear didn't catch the Rabbit, then?" inquired the little boy, sleepily.

"Jump up fum dar, honey!" exclaimed Uncle Remus, by way of reply. "I ain't got no time fer ter be settin' yer proppin' yo' eyeleds open."

XXIV.
MR. BEAR CATCHES
OLD MR. BULL-FROG.

"Well, Uncle Remus," said the little boy, counting to see if he hadn't lost a marble somewhere, "the Bear didn't catch the Rabbit after all, did he?"

"Now you talkin', honey," replied the old man, his earnest face breaking up into little eddies of smiles—"now you talkin' sho. 'Tain't bin proned inter no Brer B'ar fer ter kotch Brer Rabbit. Hit sorter like settin' a mule fer ter trap a hummin'-bird. But Brer B'ar, he tuck'n got hisse'f inter some mo' trubble, w'ich it look like it mighty easy. Ef folks could make der livin' longer gittin' inter trubble," continued the old man, looking curiously at the little boy, "ole Miss Favers wouldn't be bodder'n yo' ma fer ter borry a cup full er sugar eve'y now en den; en it look like ter me dat I knows a nigger dat wouldn't be squattin' 'roun' yer makin' dese yer fish-baskits."

"How did the Bear get into more trouble, Uncle Remus?" asked the little boy.

"Natchul, honey. Brer B'ar, he tuck a notion dat ole Brer Bull-frog wuz de man wa't fool 'im, en he say dat he'd come up wid 'im ef 'twuz a year atterwuds. But 'twan't no year, an 'twan't no mont', en mo'n dat, hit wan't skasely a week, w'en bimeby one day Brer B'ar wuz gwine home fum de takin' un a bee-tree, en lo en beholes, who should he see but ole Brer Bull-frog settin' out on de aidge er de mud-puddle fas' 'sleep! Brer B'ar drap his axe, he did, en crope up, en retch out wid his paw, en scoop ole Brer Bull-frog in des dis away." Here the old man used his hand ladle-fashion, by way of illustration. "He scoop 'im in, en dar he wuz. W'en Brer B'ar got his clampers on 'im good, he sot down en talk at 'im.

" 'Howdy, Brer Bull-frog, howdy! En how yo' fambly? I hope deyer well, Brer Bull-frog, kaze dis day you got some bizness wid me w'at'll las' you a mighty long time.'

"Brer Bull-frog, he dunner w'at ter say. He dunner wat's up, en he don't say nuthin'. Ole Brer B'ar he keep runnin' on:

" 'Youer de man w'at tuck en fool me 'bout Brer Rabbit t'er day. You had yo' fun, Brer Bull-frog, en now I'll git mine.'

"Den Brer Bull-frog, he gin ter git skeerd, he did, en he up'n say:

" 'W'at I bin doin', Brer B'ar? How I bin foolin' you?'

"Den Brer B'ar laff, en make like he dunno, but he keep on talkin'.

" 'Oh, no, Brer Bull-frog! You ain't de man w'at stick yo' head up out'n de water en tell me Brer Rabbit done gone on by. Oh, no! you ain't de man. I boun' you ain't. 'Bout dat time, you wuz at home wid yo' fambly, whar you allers is. I dunner whar you wuz, but I knows whar you is, Brer Bull-frog, en hit's you en me fer it. Atter de sun goes down dis day you don't fool no mo' folks gwine 'long dis road.'

"Co'se, Brer Bull-frog dunner w'at Brer B'ar drivin' at, but he know sump'n hatter be done, en dat mighty soon, kaze Brer B'ar 'gun to snap his jaws tergedder en foam at de mouf, en Brer Bull-frog holler out:

" 'Oh, pray, Brer B'ar! Lemme off dis time, en I won't never do so no mo'. Oh, pray, Brer B'ar! do lemme off dis time, en I'll show you de fattes' bee-tree in de woods.'

"Ole Brer B'ar, he chomp his toofies en foam at de mouf. Brer Bull-frog he des up'n squall:

" 'Oh, pray, Brer B'ar! I won't never do so no mo'! Oh, pray, Brer B'ar! lemme off dis time!'

"But ole Brer B'ar say he gwineter make way wid 'im, en den he sot en study, ole Brer B'ar did, how he gwineter squench Brer Bull-frog. He know he can't drown 'im, en he ain't got no fier fer ter bu'n 'im, en he git mighty pestered. Bimeby ole Brer Bull-frog, he sorter stop his cryin' en his boo-hooin', en he up'n say:

" 'Ef you gwineter kill me, Brer B'ar, kyar me ter dat big flat rock out dar on de aidge er de mill-pon', whar I kin see my fambly, en atter I see um, den you kin take you axe en sqush me.'

"Dis look so fa'r and squar' dat Brer B'ar he 'gree, en he take ole Brer Bull-frog by wunner his behime legs, en sling his axe on his shoulder, en off he put fer de big flat rock. When he git dar he lay Brer Bull-frog down on de rock, en Brer Bull-frog make like he lookin' 'roun' fer his folks. Den Brer B'ar, he draw long breff en pick up his axe. Den he spit in his han's en draw back en come down on de rock—pow!"

"Did he kill the Frog, Uncle Remus?" asked the little boy, as the old man paused to scoop up a thimbleful of glowing embers in his pipe.

" 'Deed, en dat he didn't, honey. 'Twix' de time w'en Brer B'ar raise up wid his axe en w'en he come down wid it, ole Brer Bull-frog he lipt up en dove down in de mill-pon', kerblink-kerblunk! En w'en he riz way out in de pon' he riz a singin', en dish yer's de song w'at he sing:

> " 'Ingle-go-jang, my joy, my joy—
> Ingle-go-jang, my joy!
> I'm right at home, my joy, my joy—
> Ingle-go-jang, my joy!' "

"That's a mighty funny song," said the little boy.

"Funny now, I speck," said the old man, "but 'twern't funny in dem days, en 'twouldn't be funny now ef folks know'd much 'bout de Bull-frog langwidge ez dey useter. Dat's w'at."

XXV.
HOW MR. RABBIT LOST
HIS FINE BUSHY TAIL.

"**O**ne time," said Uncle Remus, sighing heavily and settling himself back in his seat with an air of melancholy resignation—"one time Brer Rabbit wuz gwine 'long down de road shakin' his big bushy tail, en feelin' des ez scrumpshus ez a bee-martin wid a fresh bug." Here the old man paused and glanced at the little boy, but it was evident that the youngster had become so accustomed to the marvelous developments of Uncle Remus's stories, that the extraordinary statement made no unusual impression upon him. Therefore the old man began again, and this time in a louder and more insinuating tone:

"One time ole man Rabbit, he wuz gwine 'long down de road shakin' his long, bushy tail, en feelin' mighty biggity."

This was effective.

"Great goodness, Uncle Remus!" exclaimed the little boy in open-eyed wonder, "everybody knows that rabbits haven't got long, bushy tails."

The old man shifted his position in his chair and allowed his venerable head to drop forward until his whole appearance was suggestive of the deepest dejection; and this was intensified by a groan that seemed to be the result of great mental agony. Finally he spoke, but not as addressing himself to the little boy.

"I notices dat dem fokes w'at makes a great 'miration 'bout w'at dey knows is des de folks w'ich you can't put no 'pennunce in w'en de 'cashun come up. Yer one un um now, en he done come en excuse me er 'lowin' dat rabbits is got long, bushy tails, w'ich goodness knows ef I'd a dremp' it, I'd a whirl in en ondremp it."

"Well, but Uncle Remus, you said rabbits had long, bushy tails," replied the little boy. "Now you know you did."

"Ef I ain't fergit it off'n my mine, I say dat ole Brer Rabbit wuz gwine down de big road shakin' his long, bushy tail. Dat w'at I say, en dat I stan's by."

The little boy looked puzzled, but he didn't say anything. After a while the old man continued:

"Now, den, ef dat's 'greed ter, I'm gwine on, en ef tain't 'greed ter, den I'm gwineter pick up my cane en look atter my own intrust. I got wuk lyin' roun' yer dat's des natally gittin' moldy."

The little boy still remained quiet, and Uncle Remus proceeded:

"One day Brer Rabbit wuz gwine down de road shakin' his long, bushy tail, w'en who should he strike up wid but ole Brer Fox gwine amblin' long wid a big string er fish! W'en dey pass de time er day wid wunner nudder, Brer Rabbit, he open up de confab, he did, en he ax Brer Fox whar he git dat nice string er fish, en Brer Fox, he up'n 'spon' dat he kotch um, en Brer Rabbit, he say whar'bouts, en Brer Fox, he say down at de babtizin' creek, en Brer Rabbit he ax how, kaze in dem days dey wuz monstus fon' er minners, en Brer Fox, he sot down on a log, he did, en he up'n tell Brer Rabbit dat all he gotter do fer ter git er big mess er minners is ter go ter de creek atter sun down, en drap his tail in de water en set dar twel daylight, en den draw up a whole armful er fishes, en dem w'at he don't want, he kin fling back. Right dar's whar Brer Rabbit drap his watermillion, kaze he tuck'n sot out dat night en went a fishin'. De wedder wuz sorter cole, en Brer Rabbit, he got 'im a bottle er dram en put out fer de creek, en w'en he git dar he pick out a good place, en he sorter squot down, he did, en let his tail hang in de water. He sot dar, en he sot dar, en he drunk his dram, en he think he gwineter freeze, but bimeby day come, en dar he wuz. He make a pull, en he feel like he comin' in two, en he fetch nudder jerk, en lo en beholes, whar wuz his tail?"

There was a long pause.

"Did it come off, Uncle Remus?" asked the little boy, presently.

"She did dat!" replied the old man with unction. "She did dat, and dat w'at make all deze yer bob-tail rabbits w'at you see hoppin' en skaddlin thoo de woods."

"Are they all that way just because the old Rabbit lost his tail in the creek?" asked the little boy.

"Dat's it, honey," replied the old man. "Dat's w'at dey tells me. Look like dey er bleedzd ter take atter der pa."

XXVI.
MR. TERRAPIN SHOWS
HIS STRENGTH.

"Brer Tarrrypin wuz de out'nes' man," said Uncle Remus, rubbing his hands together contemplatively, and chuckling to himself in a very significant manner; "he wuz de out'nes' man er de whole gang. He wuz dat."

The little boy sat perfectly quiet, betraying no impatience when Uncle Remus paused to hunt, first in one pocket and then in another, for enough crumbs of tobacco to replenish his pipe. Presently the old man proceeded:

"One night Miss Meadows en de gals dey gun a

candy-pullin', en so many er de nabers come in 'sponse ter de invite dat dey hatter put de 'lasses in de wash pot en b'il' de fier in de yard. Brer B'ar, he hope* Miss Meadows bring de wood, Brer Fox, he men' de fier, Brer Wolf, he kep' de dogs off, Brer Rabbit, he grease de bottom er de plates fer ter keep de candy fum stickin', en Brer Tarrypin, he klum up in a cheer, en say he'd watch en see dat de 'lasses didn't bile over. Dey wuz all dere, en dey wern't cuttin' up no didos, nudder, kase Miss Meadows, she done put her foot down, she did, en say dat w'en dey come ter her place dey hatter hang up a flag er truce at de front gate en 'bide by it.

"Well, den, w'iles dey wuz all a settin' dar en de 'lasses wuz a bilin' en a blubberin', dey got ter runnin' on talkin' mighty biggity. Brer Rabbit, he say he de swiffes'; but Brer Tarrypin, he rock 'long in de cheer en watch de 'lasses. Brer Fox, he say he de sharpes', but Brer Tarrypin he rock 'long. Brer Wolf, he say he de mos' suvvigus, but Brer Tarrypin, he rock en he rock 'long. Brer B'ar, he say he de mos' stronges', but Brer Tarrypin he rock, en he keep on rockin'. Bimeby he sorter shet one eye, en say, sezee:

" 'Hit look like 'periently dat de ole hardshell ain't nowhars 'longside er dis crowd, yit yer I is, en I'm de same man w'at show Brer Rabbit dat he ain't de swiffes'; en I'm de same man w'at kin show Brer B'ar dat he ain't de stronges',' sezee.

"Den dey all laff en holler, kaze it look like Brer B'ar mo' stronger dan a steer. Bimeby, Miss Meadows, she up'n ax, she did, how he gwine do it.

" 'Gimme a good strong rope,' sez Brer Tarrypin, sezee, 'en lemme git in er puddle er water, en den let Brer B'ar see ef he kin pull me out,' sezee.

"Den dey all laff g'in, en Brer B'ar, he ups en sez, sezee: 'We ain't got no rope,' sezee.

* Holp; helped.

" 'No,' sez Brer Tarrypin, sezee, 'en needer is you got de strenk,' sezee, en den Brer Tarrypin, he rock en rock 'long, en watch de 'lasses a bilin' en a blubberin'.

"Atter w'ile Miss Meadows, she up en say, she did, dat she'd take'n loan de young men her bed-cord, en w'iles de candy wuz a coolin' in de plates, dey could all go ter de branch en see Brer Tarrypin kyar out his projick. Brer Tarrypin," continued Uncle Remus, in a tone at once confidential and argumentative, "wern't much bigger'n de pa'm er my han', en it look mighty funny fer ter year 'im braggin' 'bout how he kin outpull Brer B'ar. But dey got de bed-cord atter w'ile, en den dey all put out ter de branch. W'en Brer Tarrypin fine de place he wanter, he tuck one een' er de bed-cord, en gun de yuther een' to Brer B'ar.

" 'Now den, ladies en gents,' sez Brer Tarrypin, sezee, 'you all go wid Brer B'ar up dar in de woods en I'll stay yer, en w'en you year me holler, den's de time fer Brer B'ar fer ter see ef he kin haul in de slack er de rope. You all take keer er dat ar een',' sezee, 'en I'll take keer er dish yer een',' sezee.

"Den dey all put out en lef' Brer Tarrypin at de branch, en w'en dey got good en gone, he dove down inter de water, he did, en tie de bed-cord hard en fas' ter wunner deze yer big clay-roots, en den he riz up en gin a whoop.

"Brer B'ar he wrop de bed-cord roun' his han', en wink at de gals, en wid dat he gin a big juk, but Brer Tarrypin ain't budge. Den he take bofe han's en gin a big pull, but, all de same, Brer Tarrypin ain't budge. Den he tu'n 'roun,' he did, en put de rope cross his shoulders en try ter walk off wid Brer Tarrypin, but Brer Tarrypin look like he don't feel like walkin'. Den Brer Wolf, he put in en hope Brer B'ar pull, but dez like he didn't, en den dey all hope 'im, en, bless grashus! w'iles dey wuz all a pullin', Brer Tarrypin, he holler, en

ax um w'y dey don't take up de slack. Den w'en Brer
Tarrypin feel um quit pullin', he dove down, he did, en
ontie de rope, en by de time dey got ter de branch, Brer
Tarrypin, he wuz settin' in de aidge er de water des ez
natchul ez de nex' un, en he up'n say, sezee:

" 'Dat las' pull er yone wuz a mighty stiff un, en a
leetle mo'n you'd er had me,' sezee. 'Youer monstus
stout, Brer B'ar,' sezee, 'en you pulls like a yoke er
steers, but I sorter had de purchis on you,' sezee.

"Den Brer B'ar, bein's his mouf 'gun ter water atter
de sweetnin', he up'n say he speck de candy's ripe, en off
dey put atter it!"

"It's a wonder," said the little boy, after a while, "that
the rope didn't break."

"Break who?" exclaimed Uncle Remus, with a touch
of indignation in his tone—"break who? In dem days,
Miss Meadows's bed-cord would a hilt a mule."

This put an end to whatever doubts the child might
have entertained.

XXVII.
WHY MR. POSSUM HAS NO
HAIR ON HIS TAIL.

"Hit look like ter me," said Uncle Remus, frown-
ing, as the little boy came hopping and skipping
into the old man's cabin, "dat I see a young un 'bout yo'
size playin' en makin' free wid dem ar chilluns er ole
Miss Favers's yistiddy, en w'en I seed dat, I drap my
axe, en I come in yer en sot flat down right whar youer
settin' now, en I say ter myse'f dat it's 'bout time fer ole
Remus fer ter hang up en quit. Dat's des zackly w'at I
say."

"Well, Uncle Remus, they called me," said the

little boy, in a penitent tone. "They come and called me, and said they had a pistol and some powder over there."

"Dar now!" exclaimed the old man, indignantly. "Dar now! w'at I bin sayin'? Hit's des a born blessin' dat you wa'n't brung home on a litter wid bofe eyeballs hangin' out en one year clean gone; dat's w'at 'tis! Hit's des a born blessin'. Hit hope me up might'ly de udder day w'en I hear Miss Sally layin' down de law 'bout you en dem Favers chillun, yit, lo en beholes, de fus news I knows yer you is han'-in-glove wid um. Hit's nuff fer ter fetch ole Miss right up out'n dat berryin'-groun' fum down dar in Putmon County, en w'at yo' gran'ma wouldn't er stood me en yo' ma ain't gwineter stan' nudder, en de nex' time I hear 'bout sech a come off az dis, right den en dar I'm boun' ter lay de case 'fo' Miss Sally. Dem Favers's wa'n't no 'count 'fo' de war, en dey wa'n't no 'count endurin' er de war, en dey ain't no 'count atterwards, en w'iles my head's hot you ain't gwineter go mixin' up yo'se'f wid de riff-raff er crea-shun."

The little boy made no further attempt to justify his conduct. He was a very wise little boy, and he knew that, in Uncle Remus's eyes, he had been guilty of a flagrant violation of the family code. Therefore, instead of attempting to justify himself, he pleaded guilty, and promised that he would never do so any more. After this there was a long period of silence, broken only by the vigorous style in which Uncle Remus puffed away at his pipe. This was the invariable result. Whenever the old man had occasion to reprimand the little boy—and the occasions were frequent—he would relapse into a dignified but stubborn silence. Presently the youngster drew forth from his pocket a long piece of candle. The sharp eyes of the old man saw it at once.

"Don't you come a tellin' me dat Miss Sally gun you dat," he exclaimed, "kaze she didn't. En I lay you hatter be monstus sly 'fo' you gotter chance fer ter snatch up dat piece er cannle."

"Well, Uncle Remus," the little boy explained, "it was lying there all by itself, and I just thought I'd fetch it out to you."

"Dat's so, honey," said Uncle Remus, greatly mollified; "dat's so, kaze by now some er dem yuther niggers 'ud er done had her light up. Dey er mighty biggity, dem house niggers is, but I notices dat dey don't let nuthin' pass. Dey goes 'long wid der han's en der mouf open, en w'at one don't ketch de tother one do."

There was another pause, and finally the little boy said:

"Uncle Remus, you know you promised to-day to tell me why the 'Possum has no hair on his tail."

"Law, honey! ain't you done gone en fergot dat off'n yo' mine yit? Hit look like ter me," continued the old man, leisurely refilling his pipe, "dat she sorter run like dis: One time ole Brer Possum, he git so hongry, he did; dat he bleedzd fer ter have a mess er 'simmons. He monstus lazy man, ole Brer Possum wuz, but bimeby his stummuck 'gun ter growl en holler at 'im so dat he des hatter rack 'roun' en hunt up sump'n; en w'iles he wuz rackin' 'roun', who sh'd he run up wid but Brer Rabbit, en dey wuz hail-fellers, kaze Brer Possum, he ain't bin bodder'n Brer Rabbit like dem yuther beas's. Dey sot down by de side er de big road, en dar dey jabber en confab 'mong wunner nudder, twel bimeby old Brer Possum, he take 'n tell Brer Rabbit dat he mos' pe'sh out, en Brer Rabbit, he lip up in a de a'r, he did, en smack his han's tergedder, en say dat he know right whar Brer Possum kin git a bait er 'simmons. Den Brer Possum, he say whar, en Brer Rabbit, he say w'ich 'twuz over at Brer B'ar's 'simmon orchard."

"Did the Bear have a 'simmon orchard, Uncle Remus?" the little boy asked.

"Co'se, honey, kase in dem days Brer B'ar wuz a

bee-hunter. He make his livin' findin' bee trees, en de way he fine um he plant 'im some 'simmon-trees, w'ich de bees dey'd come ter suck de 'simmons en den ole Brer B'ar he'd watch um whar dey'd go, en den he'd be mighty ap' fer ter come up wid um. No matter 'bout dat, de 'simmon patch 'uz dar des like I tell you, en ole Brer Possum mouf 'gun ter water soon's he year talk un um, en mos' 'fo' Brer Rabbit done tellin' 'im de news, Brer Possum, he put out, he did, en 'twa'n't long 'fo' he wuz perch up in de highes' tree in Brer B'ar 'simmon patch. But Brer Rabbit, he done 'termin' fer ter see some fun, en w'iles all dis 'uz gwine on, he run 'roun' ter Brer B'ar house, en holler en tell 'im w'ich dey wuz somebody 'stroyin' un his 'simmons, en Brer B'ar, he hustle off fer ter ketch 'im.

"Eve'y now en den Brer Possum think he year Brer B'ar comin', but he keep on sayin', sezee:

"'I'll des git one mo' 'simmon en den I'll go; one 'simmon 'mo en den I'll go.'

"Las' he year Brer B'ar comin' sho nuff, but 'twuz de same ole chune—'One 'simmon mo' en den I'll go'—en des 'bout dat time Brer B'ar busted inter de patch, en gin de tree a shake, en Brer Possum, he drapt out longer de yuther ripe 'simmons, but time he totch de groun' he got his foots tergedder, en he lit out fer de fence same ez a race-hoss, en 'cross dat patch him en Brer B'ar had it, en Brer B'ar gain' eve'y jump, twel time Brer Possum make de fence Brer B'ar grab 'im by de tail, en Brer Possum, he went out 'tween de rails en gin a powerful juk en pull his tail out 'twix Brer B'ar tushes; en, lo en beholes, Brer B'ar hole so tight en Brer Possum pull so hard dat all de ha'r come off in Brer B'ar's mouf, w'ich, ef Brer Rabbit hadn't er happen up wid a go'd er water, Brer B'ar'd er got strankle.

"Fum dat day ter dis," said Uncle Remus, knocking the ashes carefully out of his pipe, "Brer Possum ain't had no ha'r on his tail, en needer do his chilluns."

XXVIII.
THE END OF MR. BEAR.

The next time the little boy sought Uncle Remus out, he found the old man unusually cheerful and good-humored. His rheumatism had ceased to trouble him, and he was even disposed to be boisterous. He was singing when the little boy got near the cabin, and the child paused on the outside to listen to the vigorous but mellow voice of the old man, as it rose and fell with the burden of the curiously plaintive song—a senseless affair so far as the words were concerned, but sung to a melody almost thrilling in its sweetness:

> "Han' me down my walkin'-cane
>   (Hey my Lily! go down de road!),
> Yo' true lover gone down de lane
>   (Hey my Lily! go down de road!)."

The quick ear of Uncle Remus, however, had detected the presence of the little boy, and he allowed his song to run into a recitation of nonsense, of which the following, if it be rapidly spoken, will give a faint idea:
"Ole M'er Jackson, fines' confraction, fell down sta'rs fer to git satisfaction; big Bill Fray, he rule de day, eve'ything he call fer come one, two by three. Gwine 'long one day, met Johnny Huby, ax him grine nine yards er steel fer me, tole me w'ich he couldn't; den I hist 'im over Hickerson Dickerson's barn-doors; knock 'im ninety-nine miles under water, w'en he rise, he rise in Pike straddle un a hanspike, en I lef' 'im dar smokin' er de hornpipe, Juba reda seda breda. Aunt Kate at de gate; I want to eat, she fry de meat en gimme skin, w'ich I fling it back agin. Juba!"
All this, rattled off at a rapid rate and with apparent seriousness, was calculated to puzzle the little boy, and

he slipped into his accustomed seat with an expression of awed bewilderment upon his face.

"Hit's all des dat away, honey," continued the old man, with the air of one who had just given an important piece of information. "En w'en you bin cas'n shadders long ez de ole nigger, den you'll fine out who's w'ich, en w'ich's who."

The little boy made no response. He was in thorough sympathy with all the whims and humors of the old man, and his capacity for enjoying them was large enough to include even those he could not understand. Uncle Remus was finishing an axe-handle, and upon these occasions it was his custom to allow the child to hold one end while he applied sand-paper to the other. These relations were pretty soon established, to the mutual satisfaction of the parties most interested, and the old man continued his remarks, but this time not at random:

"W'en I see deze yer swell-head folks like dat 'oman w'at come en tell yo' ma 'bout you chunkin' at her chilluns, w'ich yo' ma make Mars John strop you, hit make my mine run back to ole Brer B'ar. Ole Brer B'ar, he got de swell-headedness hisse'f, en ef der wuz enny swinkin', hit swunk too late fer ter he'p ole Brer B'ar. Leas'ways dat's w'at dey tells me, en I ain't never yearn it 'sputed."

"Was the Bear's head sure enough swelled, Uncle Remus?"

"Now you talkin', honey!" exclaimed the old man.

"Goodness! what made it swell?"

This was Uncle Remus's cue. Applying the sand-paper to the axe-helve with gentle vigor, he began:

"One time when Brer Rabbit wuz gwine lopin' home fum a frolic w'at dey bin havin' up at Miss Meadows's, who should he happin up wid but ole Brer B'ar. Co'se, atter w'at done pass 'twix um dey wa'n't no good feelin's 'tween Brer Rabbit en ole Brer B'ar, but Brer Rabbit, he wanter save his manners, en so he holler out:

" 'Heyo, Brer B'ar! how you come on? I aint seed you in a coon's age. How all down at yo' house? How Miss Brune en Miss Brindle?' "

"Who was that, Uncle Remus?" the little boy interrupted.

"Miss Brune en Miss Brindle? Miss Brune wuz Brer B'ar's ole 'oman, en Miss Brindle wuz his gal. Dat w'at dey call um in dem days. So den Brer Rabbit, he ax him howdy, he did, en Brer B'ar, he 'spon' dat he wuz mighty po'ly, en dey amble 'long, dey did, sorter familious like, but Brer Rabbit, he keep one eye on Brer B'ar, en Brer B'ar, he study how he gwine nab Brer Rabbit. Las' Brer Rabbit, he up'n say, sezee:

" 'Brer B'ar, I speck I got some bizness cut out fer you,' sezee.

" 'Wat dat, Brer Rabbit?' sez Brer B'ar, sezee.

" 'W'iles I wuz cleanin' up my new-groun' day 'fo' yistiddy,' sez Brer Rabbit, sezee, 'I come 'cross wunner deze yer ole time bee-trees. Hit start holler at de bottom, en stay holler plum ter de top, en de honey's des natally oozin' out, en ef you'll drap yo' 'gagements en go 'longer me,' sez Brer Rabbit, sezee, 'you'll git a bait dat'll las' you en yo' fambly twel de middle er nex' mont',' sezee.

"Brer B'ar say he much oblije en he b'leeve he'll go 'long, en wid dat dey put out fer Brer Rabbit's newgroun', w'ich twa'n't so mighty fur. Leas'ways, dey got dar atter w'ile. Ole Brer B'ar, he 'low dat he kin smell de honey. Brer Rabbit, he 'low dat he kin see de honeykoam. Brer B'ar, he 'low dat he kin hear de bees a zoonin'. Dey stan' 'roun' en talk biggity, dey did, twel bimeby Brer Rabbit, he up'n say, sezee:

" 'You do de clim'in', Brer B'ar, en I'll do de rushin' 'roun'; you clime up ter de hole, en I'll take dis yer pine pole en shove de honey up whar you kin git 'er,' sezee.

"Ole Brer B'ar, he spit on his han's en skint up de tree, en jam his head in de hole, en sho nuff, Brer Rabbit, he grab de pine pole, en de way he stir up dem bees wuz sinful—dat's w'at it wuz. Hit wuz sinful. En de bees dey swawm'd on Brer B'ar's head, twel 'fo' he could take it out'n de hole hit wuz done swell up bigger dan dat dinnerpot, en dar he swung, en ole Brer Rabbit, he dance 'roun' en sing:

" 'Tree stan' high, but honey mighty sweet—
    Watch dem bees wid stingers on der feet.'

"But dar ole Brer B'ar hung, en ef his head ain't swunk, I speck he hangin' dar yit—dat w'at I speck."

XXIX.
MR. FOX GETS INTO
SERIOUS BUSINESS.

"Hit turn out one time," said Uncle Remus, grinding some crumbs of tobacco between the palms of his hands, preparatory to enjoying his usual smoke after supper—"hit turn out one time dat Brer Rabbit make so free wid de man's collard-patch dat de man he tuck'n sot a trap fer ole Brer Rabbit."

"Which man was that, Uncle Remus?" asked the little boy.

"Des a man, honey. Dat's all. Dat's all I knows—des wunner dese yer mans w'at you see trollopin 'roun' eve'y day. Nobody ain't never year w'at his name is, en ef dey did dey kep' de news mighty close fum me. Ef dish yer man is bleedzd fer ter have a name, den I'm done, kaze you'll hatter go fudder dan me. Ef you bleedzd ter know mo' dan w'at I duz, den you'll hatter hunt up some er deze yer niggers w'at's sprung up sence I commence fer ter shed my ha'r."

"Well, I just thought, Uncle Remus," said the little

boy, in a tone remarkable for self-depreciation, "that the man had a name."

"Tooby sho," replied the old man, with unction, puffing away at his pipe. "Co'se. Dat w'at make I say w'at I duz. Dish yer man mout a had a name, en den ag'in he moutn't. He mout er bin name Slip-shot Sam, en he mouter bin name ole One-eye Riley, w'ich ef 'twuz hit ain't bin handed roun' ter me. But dis yer man, he in de tale, en w'at we gwine do wid 'im? Dat's de p'int, kase w'en I git ter huntin' 'roun' 'mong my 'membunce atter dish yer Mister W'atyoumaycollum's name, she ain't dar. Now den, less des call 'im Mr. Man en let 'im go at dat."

The silence of the little boy gave consent.

"One time," said Uncle Remus, carefully taking up the thread of the story where it had been dropped, "hit turn out dat Brer Rabbit bin makin' so free wid Mr. Man's greens en truck dat Mr. Man, he tuck'n sot a trap fer Brer Rabbit, en Brer Rabbit he so greedy dat he tuck'n walk right spang in it 'fo' he know hisse'f. Well, 'twa'n't long 'fo' yer come Mr. Man, broozin' 'roun', en he ain't no sooner see ole Brer Rabbit dan he smack his han's tergedder en holler out:

" 'Youer nice feller, you is! Yer you bin gobblin' up my green truck, en now you tryin' ter tote off my trap. Youer mighty nice chap—dat's w'at you is! But now dat I got you, I'll des 'bout settle wid you fer de ole en de new.'

"En wid dat, Mr. Man, he go off, he did, down in de bushes atter han'ful er switches. Ole Brer Rabbit he ain't sayin' nuthin', but he feelin' mighty lonesome, en he sot dar lookin' like eve'y minnit wuz gwineter be de nex'. En w'iles Mr. Man wuz off prepa'r'n his bresh-broom, who should come p'radin' 'long but Brer Fox? Brer Fox make a great 'miration, he did, 'bout de fix w'at he fine Brer Rabbit in, but Brer Rabbit he make like he fit ter kill hisse'f laffin', en he up'n tell Brer Fox, he did, dat Miss Meadows's fokes want 'im ter go down ter der house in 'tennunce on a weddin', en he 'low w'ich he couldn't, en dey 'low how he could, en den bimeby dey take'n tie 'im dar w'iles dey go atter de preacher, so he be dar w'en dey come back. En mo'n dat, Brer Rabbit up'n tell Brer Fox dat his chillun's mighty low wid de fever, en he bleedzd ter go atter some pills fer'm, en he ax Brer Fox fer ter take his place en go down ter Miss Meadows's en have nice time wid de gals. Brer Fox, he in fer dem kinder pranks, en 'twa'n't no time 'fo' Brer Rabbit had ole Brer Fox harness up dar in his place, en den he make like he got ter make 'as'e en git de pills fer dem sick chilluns. Brer Rabbit wa'n't mo'n out er sight 'fo' yer come Mr. Man wid a han'ful er hick'ries, but w'en he see Brer Fox tied up dar, he look like he 'stonished.

" 'Heyo!' sez Mr. Man, sezee, 'you done change color, en you done got bigger, en yo' tail done grow out. W'at kin'er w'atzyname is you, ennyhow?' sezee.

"Brer Fox, he stay still, en Mr. Man, he talk on:

" 'Hit's mighty big luck,' sezee, 'ef w'en I ketch de chap w'at nibble my greens, likewise I ketch de feller w'at gnyaw my goose,' sezee, en wid dat he let inter Brer Fox wid de hick'ries, en de way he play rap-jacket wuz a caution ter de naberhood. Brer Fox, he juk en he jump, en he squeal en he squall, but Mr. Man, he shower down on 'im, he did, like fightin' a red was'-nes'."

The little boy laughed, and Uncle Remus supplemented this endorsement of his descriptive powers with a most infectious chuckle.

"Bimeby," continued the old man, "de switches, dey got frazzle out, en Mr. Man, he put out atter mo', en w'en he done got fa'rly outer yearin', Brer Rabbit, he show'd up, he did, kaze he des bin hidin' out in de bushes lis'nin' at de racket, en he 'low hit mighty funny dat Miss Meadows ain't come 'long, kaze he done bin down ter de doctor house, en dat's fudder dan de preacher, yit. Brer Rabbit make like he hurr'in' on home, but Brer Fox, he open up, he did, en he say:

"'I thank you fer ter tu'n me loose, Brer Rabbit, en I'll be 'blije,' sezee, 'kaze you done tie me up so tight dat it make my head swim, en I don't speck I'd las' fer ter git ter Miss Meadows's,' sezee.

"Brer Rabbit, he sot down sorter keerless like, en begin fer ter scratch one year like a man studyin' 'bout sump'n.

"'Dat's so, Brer Fox,' sezee, 'you duz look sorter stove up. Look like sump'n bin onkoamin' yo' ha'rs,' sezee.

"Brer Fox ain't sayin' nothin', but Brer Rabbit, he keep on talkin':

"'Dey ain't no bad feelin's 'twix' us, is dey, Brer Fox? Kaze ef dey is, I ain't got no time fer ter be tarryin' 'roun' yer.'

"Brer Fox say w'ich he don't have no onfrennelness, en wid dat Brer Rabbit cut Brer Fox loose des in time fer ter hear Mr. Man w'isserlin up his dogs, en one went one way en de udder went nudder."

XXX.
HOW MR. RABBIT SUCCEEDED
IN RAISING A DUST.

"In dem times," said Uncle Remus, gazing admiringly at himself in a fragment of looking-glass, "Brer Rabbit, en Brer Fox, en Brer Coon, en dem yuther beas's go co'tin' en sparklin' 'roun' de naberhood mo' samer dan folks. 'Twan't no 'Lemme a hoss,' ner 'Fetch me my buggy,' but dey des up'n lit out en tote deyse'f. Dar's ole Brer Fox, he des wheel 'roun' en fetch his flank one swipe wid 'is tongue en he'd be koam up;

en Brer Rabbit, he des spit on his han' en twis' it 'roun'
'mongst de roots un his years en his ha'r'd be roach. Dey
wuz dat flirtashus," continued the old man, closing one
eye at his image in the glass, "dat Miss Meadows en de
gals don't see no peace fum one week een' ter de udder.
Chuseday wuz same as Sunday, en Friday wuz same as
Chuseday, en hit come down ter dat pass dat w'en Miss
Meadows 'ud have chicken-fixins fer dinner, in 'ud drap
Brer Fox en Brer Possum, en w'en she'd have fried
greens in 'ud pop ole Brer Rabbit, twel 'las' Miss Meadows, she tuck'n tell de gals dat she be dad-blame ef she
gwineter keep no tavvun. So dey fix it up 'mong deyse'f,
Miss Meadows en de gals did, dat de nex' time de gents
call dey'd gin um a game. De gents, dey wuz a co'tin,
but Miss Meadows, she don't wanter marry none un
um, en needer duz de gals, en likewise dey don't wanter
have um pester'n 'roun'. Las', one Chuseday, Miss
Meadows, she tole um dat ef dey come down ter her
house de nex' Sat'day evenin', de whole caboodle un um
'ud go down de road a piece, whar der wuz a big flint
rock, en de man w'at could take a sludge-hammer en
knock de dus' out'n dat rock, he wuz de man w'at 'ud git
de pick er de gals. Dey all say dey gwine do it, but ole
Brer Rabbit, he crope off whar der wuz a cool place
under some jimson weeds, en dar he sot wukkin his mind
how he gwineter git dus' out'n dat rock. Bimeby, w'ile
he wuz a settin' dar, up he jump en crack his heels tergedder en sing out:

" 'Make a bow ter de Buzzard en den ter de Crow,
    Takes a limber-toe gemmun fer ter jump Jim Crow,'

en wid dat he put out for Brer Coon house en borrer his
slippers. W'en Sat'day evenin' come, dey wuz all dere.
Miss Meadows en de gals, dey wuz dere; en Brer Coon,
en Brer Fox, en Brer Possum, en Brer Tarrypin, dey
wuz dere."

"Where was the Rabbit?" the little boy asked.

"Youk'n put yo' 'pennunce in ole Brer Rabbit," the old man replied, with a chuckle. "He wuz dere, but he shuffle up kinder late, kaze w'en Miss Meadows en de ballunce un um done gone down ter de place, Brer Rabbit, he crope 'roun' ter de ash-hopper, en fill Brer Coon slippers full er ashes, en den he tuck'n put um on en march off. He got dar atter 'w'ile, en soon's Miss Meadows en de gals seed 'im, dey up'n giggle, en make a great 'miration kaze Brer Rabbit got on slippers. Brer Fox, he so smart, he holler out, he did, en say he lay Brer Rabbit got de groun'-eatch, but Brer Rabbit, he sorter shet one eye, he did, en say, sezee:

" 'I bin so useter ridin' hoss-back, ez deze ladies knows, dat I'm gittin' sorter tender-footed;' en dey don't hear much mo' fum Brer Fox dat day, kaze he 'member how Brer Rabbit done bin en rid him; en hit 'uz des 'bout much ez Miss Meadows en de gals could do fer ter keep der snickers fum gittin' up a 'sturbance 'mong de congergashun. But, never mine dat, old Brer Rabbit, he wuz dar, en he so brash dat leetle mo' en he'd er grab up de sludge-hammer en er open up de racket 'fo' ennybody gun de word; but Brer Fox, he shove Brer Rabbit out'n de way en pick up de sludge hisse'f. Now den," continued the old man, with pretty much the air of one who had been the master of similar ceremonies, "de progance wuz dish yer: Eve'y gent wer ter have th'ee licks at de rock, en de gent w'at fetch de dus' he wer de one w'at gwineter take de pick er de gals. Ole Brer Fox, he grab de sludge-hammer, he did, en he come down on de rock—blim! No dus' ain't come. Den he draw back en down he come ag'in—blam! No dus' ain't come. Den he spit in his han's, en give 'er a big swing en down she come—ker-blap! En yit no dus' ain't flew'd. Den Brer Possum he make triul, en Brer Coon, en all de ballunce un um 'cep' Brer Tarrypin, en he 'low dat he got a crick in his neck. Den Brer Rabbit, he grab holt er de sludge, en he lipt up in de a'r en come down on de rock all at de same time—*pow!*—en de ashes, dey flew'd up so, dey did, dat Brer Fox, he tuck'n had a sneezin' spell, en Miss Meadows en de gals dey up'n koff. Th'ee times Brer Rabbit jump up en crack his heels tergedder en come down wid de sludge-hammer—*ker-blam!*—en eve'y time he jump up, he holler out:

" 'Stan' fudder, ladies! Yer come de dus'!' en sho nuff, de dus' come.

"Leas'ways," continued Uncle Remus, "Brer Rabbit got one er de gals, en dey had a weddin' en a big infa'r."

"Which of the girls did the Rabbit marry?" asked the little boy, dubiously.

"I did year tell un 'er name," replied the old man, with a great affectation of interest, "but look like I done gone en fergit it off'n my mine. Ef I don't disremember," he continued, "hit wuz Miss Molly Cottontail, en I speck we better let it go at dat."

XXXI.
A PLANTATION WITCH.

The next time the little boy got permission to call upon Uncle Remus, the old man was sitting in his door, with his elbows on his knees and his face buried in his hands, and he appeared to be in great trouble.

"What's the matter, Uncle Remus?" the youngster asked.

"Nuff de matter, honey—mo' dan dey's enny kyo fer. Ef dey ain't some quare gwines on 'roun' dis place I ain't name Remus."

The serious tone of the old man caused the little boy to open his eyes. The moon, just at its full, cast long, vague, wavering shadows in front of the cabin. A colony of tree-frogs somewhere in the distance were treating their neighbors to a serenade, but to the little boy it sounded like a chorus of lost and long-forgotten whistlers. The sound was wherever the imagination chose to locate it—to the right, to the left, in the air, on the ground, far away or near at hand, but always dim and always indistinct. Something in Uncle Remus's tone exactly fitted all these surroundings, and the child nestled closer to the old man.

"Yasser," continued Uncle Remus, with an ominous sigh and a mysterious shake of the head, "ef dey ain't some quare gwines on in dish yer naberhood, den I'm de ball-headest creetur 'twix' dis en nex' Jinawerry wus a year 'go, w'ich I knows I ain't. Dat's what."

"What is it, Uncle Remus?"

"I know Mars John bin drivin' Cholly sorter hard terday, en I say ter myse'f dat I'd drap 'roun' 'bout dus' en fling nudder year er corn in de troff en kinder gin 'im a techin' up wid de kurrier-koam; en bless grashus! I ain't bin in de lot mo'n a minnit 'fo' I seed sump'n wuz wrong wid de hoss, and sho' nuff dar wuz his mane full er witch-stirrups."

"Full of what, Uncle Remus?"

"Full er witch-stirrups, honey. Ain't you seed no witch-stirrups? Well, w'en you see two stran' er ha'r tied tergedder in a hoss' mane, dar you see a witch-stirrup, en, mo'n dat, dat hoss done bin rid by um."

"Do you reckon they have been riding Charley?" inquired the little boy.

"Co'se, honey. Tooby sho dey is. W'at else dey bin doin'?"

"Did you ever see a witch, Uncle Remus?"

"Dat ain't needer yer ner dar. W'en I see coon track in de branch, I know de coon bin 'long dar."

The argument seemed unanswerable, and the little boy asked, in a confidential tone:

"Uncle Remus, what are witches like?"

"Dey comes diffunt," responded the cautious old darkey. "Dey comes en dey cunjus fokes. Squinch-owl holler eve'y time he see a witch, en w'en you hear de dog howlin' in de middle er de night, one un um's mighty ap' ter be prowlin' 'roun'. Cunjun fokes kin tell a witch de minnit dey lays der eyes on it, but dem w'at ain't cunjun, hit's mighty hard ter tell w'en dey see one, kase dey might come in de 'pearunce un a cow en all kinder beas's. I ain't bin useter no cunjun myse'f, but I bin livin' long nuff fer ter know w'en you meets up wid a big black cat in de middle er de road, wid yaller eyeballs, dars yo' witch fresh fum de Ole Boy. En, fuddermo', I know dat 'tain't proned inter no dogs fer ter ketch de rabbit w'at use in a berryin'-groun'. Dey er de mos' ongodlies' creeturs w'at you ever laid eyes on," continued Uncle Remus, with unction. "Down dar in Putmon County yo' Unk Jeems, he make like he gwineter ketch wunner dem dar graveyard rabbits. Sho nuff, out he goes, en de dogs ain't no mo'n got ter de place fo' up jump de ole rabbit right 'mong um, en atter runnin' 'roun' a time or two, she skip right up ter Mars Jeems, en Mars Jeems, he des put de gun-bairl right on 'er en lammed aloose. Hit tored up de groun' all 'roun', en de dogs, dey rush up, but dey wan't no rabbit dar; but bimeby Mars Jeems, he seed de dogs tuckin' der tails 'tween der legs, en he look up, en dar wuz de rabbit caperin' 'roun' on a toomstone, en wid dat Mars Jeems say he sorter feel like de time done come w'en yo' gran'ma was 'specktin' un him home, en he call off de dogs en put out. But dem wuz ha'nts. Witches is deze yer kinder fokes wat kin drap der body en change inter a cat en a wolf en all kinder creeturs."

"Papa says there ain't any witches," the little boy interrupted.

"Mars John ain't live long ez I is," said Uncle Remus, by way of comment. "He ain't bin broozin' 'roun' all hours er de night en day. I know'd a nigger w'ich his brer wuz a witch, kaze he up'n tole me how he tuck'n kyo'd 'im; en he kyo'd 'im good, mon."

"How was that?" inquired the little boy.

"Hit seem like," continued Uncle Remus, "dat witch fokes is got a slit in de back er de neck, en w'en dey wanter change derse'f, dey des pull de hide over der head same ez if 'twuz a shut, en dar dey is."

"Do they get out of their skins?" asked the little boy, in an awed tone.

"Tooby sho, honey. You see yo' pa pull his shut off? Well, dat des 'zackly de way dey duz. But dish yere nigger w'at I'm tellin' you 'bout, he kyo'd his brer de ve'y fus pass he made at him. Hit got so dat fokes in de settlement didn't have no peace. De chilluns 'ud wake up in de mawnins wid der ha'r tangle up, en wid scratches on um like dey bin thoo a brier-patch, twel bimeby one day de nigger he 'low dat he'd set up dat night en keep one eye on his brer; en sho' nuff dat night, des ez de chickens wuz crowin' fer twelve, up jump de brer an pull off his skin en sail out'n de house in de shape un a bat, en w'at duz de nigger do but grab up de hide, en turn it wrongsudout'ards en sprinkle it wid salt. Den he lay down en watch fer ter see w'at de news wuz gwineter be. Des 'fo' day yer come a big black cat in de do', en de nigger git up, he did, en druv her away. Bimeby, yer come a big black dog snuffin' roun', en de nigger up wid a chunk en lammed 'im side er de head. Den a squinch-owl lit on de koam er de house, en de nigger jam de shovel in de fier en make 'im flew away. Las', yer come a great big black wolf wid his eyes shinin' like fier coals, en he grab de hide and rush out. 'Twa'n't long 'fo' de nigger year his brer holler'n en squallin', en he tuck a light, he did, en went out, en dar wuz his brer des a waller'n on de groun' en squirmin' 'roun', kaze de salt on de skin wuz stingin' wuss'n ef he had his britches lineded wid yaller-jackets. By nex' mawnin' he got so he could sorter shuffle 'long, but he gun up cunjun, en

ef dere wuz enny mo' witches in dat settlement dey kep'
mighty close, en dat nigger he ain't skunt hisse'f no mo'
not endurin' er my 'membunce."

The result of this was that Uncle Remus had to take
the little boy by the hand and go with him to the "big
house," which the old man was not loath to do; and,
when the child went to bed, he lay awake a long time
expecting an unseemly visitation from some mysterious
source. It soothed him, however, to hear the strong,
musical voice of his sable patron, not very far away, tenderly contending with a lusty tune; and to this accompaniment the little boy dropped asleep:

> "Hit's eighteen hunder'd, forty-en-eight,
>   Christ done made dat crooked way straight—
>   En I don't wanter stay here no longer;
>   Hit's eighteen hunder'd, forty-en-nine,
>   Christ done turn dat water inter wine—
>   En I don't wanter stay here no longer."

XXXII.
"JACKY-MY-LANTERN."*

Upon his next visit to Uncle Remus, the little boy
was exceedingly anxious to know more about
witches, but the old man prudently refrained from excit-
ing the youngster's imagination any further in that direction. Uncle Remus had a board across his lap, and,
armed with a mallet and a shoe-knife, was engaged in
making shoe-pegs.

* This story is popular on the coast and among the rice-plantations,
and, since the publication of some of the animal-myths in the newspapers, I have received a version of it from a planter in southwest
Georgia; but it seems to me to be an intruder among the genuine
myth stories of the negroes. It is a trifle too elaborate. Nevertheless,
it is told upon the plantations with great gusto, and there are several
versions in circulation.

"W'iles I wuz crossin' de branch des now," he said, endeavoring to change the subject, "I come up wid a Jacky-my-lantern, en she wuz bu'nin' wuss'n a bunch er lightnin'-bugs, mon. I know'd she wuz a fixin' fer ter lead me inter dat quogmire down in de swamp, en I steer'd cle'r un 'er. Yasser. I did dat. You ain't never seed no Jacky-my-lantuns, is you, honey?"

The little boy never had, but he had heard of them, and he wanted to know what they were, and thereupon Uncle Remus proceeded to tell him.

"One time," said the old darkey, transferring his spectacles from his nose to the top of his head and leaning his elbows upon his peg-board, "dere wuz a blacksmif man, en dish yer blacksmif man, he tuck'n stuck closer by his dram dan he did by his bellus. Monday mawnin' he'd git on a spree, en all dat week he'd be on a spree, en de nex' Monday mawnin' he'd take a fresh start. Bimeby, one dat, atter der blacksmif bin spreein' 'roun' en cussin' might'ly, he hear a sorter rustlin' fuss at de do', en in walk de Bad Man."

"Who, Uncle Remus?" the little boy asked.

"De Bad Man, honey; de Ole Boy hisse'f right fresh from de ridjun w'at you year Miss Sally readin' 'bout. He done hide his hawns, en his tail, en his hoof, en he come dress up like w'ite fokes. He tuck off his hat en he bow, en den he tell de blacksmif who he is, en dat he done come atter 'im. Den de blacksmif, he gun ter cry en beg, en he beg so hard en he cry so loud dat de Bad Man say he make a trade wid 'im. At de een' er one year de sperit er de blacksmif wuz to be his'n, en endurin' er dat time de blacksmif mus' put in his hottes' licks in de intruss er de Bad Man, en den he put a spell on de cheer de blacksmif was settin' in, en on his sludge-hammer. De man w'at sot in de cheer couldn't git up less'n de blacksmif let 'im, en de man w'at pick up de sludge 'ud hatter keep on knockin' wid it twel de blacksmif say quit; en den he gun 'im money plenty, en off he put.

"De blacksmif, he sail in fer ter have his fun, en he have so much dat he done clean forgot 'bout his contrack, but bimeby, one day he look down de road, en dar he see de Bad Man comin', en den he know'd de year wuz out. W'en de Bad Man got in de do', de blacksmif wuz poundin' 'way at a hoss-shoe, but he wa'n't so bizzy dat he didn't ax 'im in. De Bad Man sorter do like he ain't got no time fer ter tarry, but de blacksmif say he got some little jobs dat he bleedzd ter finish up, en den he ax de Bad Man fer ter set down a minnit; en de Bad Man, he tuck'n sot down, en he sot in dat cheer w'at he done conju'd, en, co'se, dar he wuz. Den de blacksmif, he 'gun ter poke fun at de Bad Man, en he ax him don't he want a dram, en won't he hitch his cheer up little nigher de fier, en de Bad Man, he beg en he beg, but 'twan't doin' no good, kase de blacksmif 'low dat he gwineteer keep 'im dar twel he promus dat he let 'im off one year mo', en, sho nuff, de Bad Man promus dat ef de blacksmif let 'im up he give 'im a n'er showin'. So den de blacksmif gun de wud, en de Bad Man sa'nter off down de big road, settin' traps en layin' his progance fer ter ketch mo' sinners.

"De nex' year hit pass same like t'er one. At de 'p'inted time yer come de Ole Boy atter de blacksmif, but still de blacksmif had some jobs dat he bleedzd ter finish up, en he ax de Bad Man fer ter take holt er de sludge en he'p 'im out; en de Bad Man, he 'low dat r'er'n be disperlite, he don't keer ef he do hit 'er a biff er two; en wid dat he grab up de sludge, en dar he wuz 'gin, kase he done conju'd de sludge so dat whosomedever tuck 'er up can't put 'er down less'n de blacksmif say de wud. Dey perlaver'd dar, dey did, twel bimeby de Bad Man up'n let 'im off n'er year.

"Well, den, dat year pass same ez t'er one. Mont' in en mont' out dat man wuz rollin' in dram, en bimeby yer come de Bad Man. De blacksmif cry en he holler, en he rip 'roun' en t'ar his ha'r, but hit des like he didn't, kase de Bad Man grab 'im up en cram 'im in a bag en tote 'im off. W'iles dey wuz gwine 'long dey come up wid a passel er fokes w'at wuz havin' wunner deze yer fote er July bobbycues, en de Ole Boy, he 'low dat maybe he kin git some mo' game, en w'at do he do but jine in wid um. He jines in en he talk politics same like t'er fokes, twel bimeby dinnertime come 'roun', en dey ax 'im up, w'ich 'greed wid his stummuck, en he pozzit his bag underneed de table 'longside de udder bags w'at de hongry fokes'd brung.

"No sooner did de blacksmif git back on de groun' dan he 'gun ter wuk his way outer de bag. He crope out, he did, en den he tuck'n change de bag. He tuck'n tuck a n'er bag en lay it down whar dish yer bag wuz, en den he crope outer de crowd en lay low in de underbresh.

"Las', w'en de time come fer ter go, de Ole Boy up wid his bag en slung her on his shoulder, en off he put fer de Bad Place. W'en he got dar he tuck'n drap de bag off'n his back en call up de imps, en dey des come a squallin' en a caperin', w'ich I speck dey mus' a bin hongry. Leas'ways dey des swawm'd 'roun', hollerin ou):

" 'Daddy, w'at you brung—daddy, w'at you brung?'

"So den dey open de bag, en lo en beholes, out jump a big bull-dog, en de way he shuck dem little imps wuz a caution, en he kep' on gnyawin' un um twel de Ole Boy open de gate en tu'n 'im out."

"And what became of the blacksmith?" the little boy asked, as Uncle Remus paused to snuff the candle with his fingers.

"I'm drivin' on 'roun', honey. Atter 'long time, de blacksmif he tuck'n die, en w'en he go ter de Good Place de man at de gate dunner who he is, en he can't squeeze in. Den he go down ter de Bad Place, en knock. De Ole Boy, he look out, he did, en he know'd de blacksmif de minnit he laid eyes on 'im; but he shake his head en say, sezee:

" 'You'll hatter skuze me, Brer Blacksmif, kase I dun had 'speunce 'longer you. You'll hatter go some'rs else ef you wanter raise enny racket,' sezee, en wid dat he shet de do'.

"En dey do say," continued Uncle Remus, with unction, "dat sence dat day de blacksmif bin sorter huv'rin' 'roun' 'twix' de heavens en de ye'th, en dark nights he shine out so fokes call 'im Jacky-my-lantun. Dat's w'at dey tells me. Hit may be wrong er't may be right, but dat's w'at I years."

XXXIII.
WHY THE NEGRO IS BLACK.

One night, while the little boy was watching Uncle Remus twisting and waxing some shoe-thread, he made what appeared to him to be a very curious discovery. He discovered that the palms of the old man's hands were as white as his own, and the fact was such a source of wonder that he at last made it the subject of remark. The response of Uncle Remus led to the earnest recital of a piece of unwritten history that must prove interesting to ethnologists.

"Tooby sho de pa'm er my han's w'ite, honey," he quietly remarked; "en, w'en it come ter dat, dey wuz a time w'en all de w'ite folks 'uz black—blacker dan me, kaze I done bin yer so long dat I bin sorter bleach out."

The little boy laughed. He thought Uncle Remus was making him the victim of one of his jokes; but the youngster was never more mistaken. The old man was serious. Nevertheless, he failed to rebuke the ill-timed mirth of the child, appearing to be altogether engrossed in his work. After a while he resumed:

"Yasser. Folks dunner w'at bin yit, let 'lone w'at gwineter be. Niggers is niggers now, but de time wuz w'en we 'uz all niggers tergedder."

"When was that, Uncle Remus?"

"Way back yander. In dem times we 'uz all un us black; we 'uz all niggers tergedder, en 'cordin' ter all de 'counts w'at I years fokes 'uz gittin 'long 'bout ez well in dem days ez dey is now. But atter 'w'ile de news come dat dere wuz a pon' er water some'rs in de naberhood, w'ich ef dey'd git inter dey'd be wash off nice en w'ite, en den one un um, he fine de place en make er splunge inter de pon', en come out w'ite ez a town gal. En den, bless grashus! w'en de fokes seed it, dey make a break fer de pon', en dem w'at wuz de soopless, dey got in fus' en dey come out w'ite; en dem w'at wuz de nex' soopless, dey got in nex', en dey come out merlatters; en dey wuz sech a crowd un um dat dey mighty nigh use de water up, w'ich w'en dem yuthers come 'long, de morest dey could do wuz ter paddle about wid der foots en dabble in it wid der han's. Dem wuz de niggers, en down ter dis day dey ain't no w'ite 'bout a nigger 'ceppin de pa'ms er der han's en de soles er der foot."

The little boy seemed to be very much interested in this new account of the origin of races, and he made some further inquiries, which elicited from Uncle Remus the following additional particulars:

"De Injun en de Chinee got ter be 'counted 'long er de merlatter. I ain't seed no Chinee dat I knows un, but dey tells me dey er sorter 'twix' a brown en a brindle. Dey er all merlatters."

"But mamma says the Chinese have straight hair," the little boy suggested.

"Co'se, honey," the old man unhesitatingly responded, "dem w'at git ter de pon' time nuff fer ter git der head in de water, de water hit onkink der ha'r. Hit bleedzd ter be dat away."

XXXIV.
THE SAD FATE OF MR. FOX.

"Now, den," said Uncle Remus, with unusual gravity, as soon as the little boy, by taking his seat, announced that he was ready for the evening's entertainment to begin; "now, den, dish yer tale w'at I'm agwine ter gin you is de las' row er stumps, sho. Dish yer's whar ole Brer Fox los' his breff, en he ain't fine it no mo' down ter dis day."

"Did he kill himself, Uncle Remus?" the little boy asked, with a curious air of concern.

"Hole on dar, honey!" the old man exclaimed, with a great affectation of alarm; "hole on dar! Wait! Gimme room! I don't wanter tell you no story, en ef you keep shovin' me forrerd, I mout git some er de facks mix up 'mong deyse'f. You gotter gimme room en you gotter gimme time."

The little boy had no other premature questions to ask, and, after a pause, Uncle Remus resumed:

"Well, den, one day Brer Rabbit go ter Brer Fox house, he did, en he put up mighty po' mouf. He say his ole 'oman sick, en his chilluns cole, en de fier done gone out. Brer Fox, he feel bad 'bout dis, en he tuck'n s'ply Brer Rabbit widder chunk er fier. Brer Rabbit see Brer Fox cookin' some nice beef, en his mouf gun ter water, but he take de fier, he did, en he put out to'rds home; but present'y yer he come back, en he say de fier done gone out. Brer Fox 'low dat he want er invite ter dinner, but he don't say nuthin', en bimeby Brer Rabbit he up'n say, sezee:

" 'Brer Fox, whar you git so much nice beef?' sezee, en den Brer Fox he up'n 'spon', sezee:

" 'You come ter my house ter-morrer ef yo' fokes ain't too sick, en I kin show you whar you kin git plenty beef mo' nicer dan dish yer,' sezee.

"Well, sho nuff, de nex' day fotch Brer Rabbit, en Brer Fox say, sezee:

" 'Dar's a man down yander by Miss Meadows's w'at got heap er fine cattle, en he gotter cow name Bookay,' sezee, 'en you des go en say *Bookay,* en she'll open her mouf, en you kin jump in en git des ez much meat ez you kin tote,' sez Brer Fox, sezee.

" 'Well, I'll go 'long,' sez Brer Rabbit, sezee, 'en you kin jump fus' en den I'll come follerin' atter,' sezee.

"Wid dat dey put out, en dey went promernadin' 'roun' 'mong de cattle, dey did, twel bimeby dey struck up wid de one dey wuz atter. Brer Fox, he up, he did, en holler *Bookay,* en de cow flung 'er mouf wide open. Sho nuff, in dey jump, en w'en dey got dar, Brer Fox, he say, sezee:

" 'You kin cut mos' ennywheres, Brer Rabbit, but don't cut 'roun' de haslett,' sezee.

"Den Brer Rabbit, he holler back, he did: 'I'm a gitten me out a roas'n-piece;' sezee.

" 'Roas'n, er bakin', er fryin',' sez Brer Fox, sezee, 'don't git too nigh de haslett,' sezee.

"Dey cut en dey kyarved, en dey kyarved en dey cut, en w'iles dey wuz cuttin' en kyarvin', en slashin' 'way, Brer Rabbit, he tuck'n hacked inter de haslett, en wid dat down fell de cow dead.

" 'Now, den,' sez Brer Fox, 'we er gone, sho', sezee.

" 'W'at we gwine do?' sez Brer Rabbit, sezee.

" 'I'll git in de maul,' sez Brer Fox, 'en you'll jump in de gall,' sezee.

"Nex' mawnin' yer cum de man w'at de cow b'long ter, an he ax who kill Bookay. Nobody don't say nuthin'. Den de man say he'll cut 'er open en see, en den he whirl in, en twan't no time 'fo' he had 'er intruls spread out. Brer Rabbit, he crope out'n de gall, en say, sezee:

" 'Mister Man! Oh, Mister Man! I'll tell you who kill yo' cow. You look in de maul, en dar you'll fine 'im,' sezee.

"Wid dat de man tuck a stick and lam down on de maul so hard dat he kill Brer Fox stone-dead. W'en Brer Rabbit see Brer Fox wuz laid out fer good, he make like he mighty sorry, en he up'n ax de man fer Brer Fox head. Man say he ain't keerin', en den Brer Rabbit tuck'n brung it ter Brer Fox house. Dar he see ole Miss Fox, en he tell 'er dat he done fotch her some nice beef w'at 'er ole man sont 'er, but she ain't gotter look at it twel she go ter eat it.

"Brer Fox son wuz name Tobe, en Brer Rabbit tell Tobe fer ter keep still w'iles his mammy cook de nice beef w'at his daddy sont 'im. Tobe he wuz mighty hongry, en he look in de pot he did w'iles de cookin' wuz gwine on, en dar he see his daddy head, en wid dat he sot up a howl en tole his mammy. Miss Fox, she git mighty mad w'en she fine she cookin' her ole man head, en she call up de dogs, she did, en sickt em on Brer Rabbit; en ole Miss Fox en Tobe en de dogs, dey push Brer Rabbit so close dat he hatter take a holler tree. Miss Fox, she tell Tobe fer ter stay dar en mine Brer Rabbit, w'ile she goes en git de axe, en w'en she gone, Brer Rabbit, he tole Tobe ef he go ter de branch en git 'im a drink er water dat he'll gin 'im a dollar. Tobe, he put out, he did, en bring some water in his hat, but by de time he got back Brer Rabbit done out en gone. Ole Miss Fox, she cut and cut twel down come de tree, but no Brer Rabbit dar. Den she lay de blame on Tobe, en she say she gwineter lash 'im, en Tobe, he put out en run, de ole 'oman atter 'im. Bimeby, he come up wid Brer Rabbit, en sot down fer to tell 'im how 'twuz, en w'iles dey wuz a settin' dar, yer come ole Miss Fox a slippin' up en grab um bofe. Den she tell um w'at she gwine do. Brer Rabbit she gwineter kill, en Tobe she gwineter lam ef its de las' ack. Den Brer Rabbit sez, sezee:

" 'Ef you please, ma'am, Miss Fox, lay me on de grindstone en groun' off my nose so I can't smell no mo' w'en I'm dead.'

"Miss Fox, she tuck dis ter be a good idee, en she fotch bofe un um ter de grindestone, en set um up on it so dat she could groun' off Brer Rabbit nose. Den Brer Rabbit, he up'n say, sezee:

" 'Ef you please, ma'am, Miss Fox, Tobe he kin turn de' handle w'iles you goes atter some water fer ter wet de grinestone,' sezee.

"Co'se, soon'z Brer Rabbit see Miss Fox go atter de water, he jump down en put out, en dis time he git clean away."

"And was that the last of the Rabbit, too, Uncle Remus?" the little boy asked, with something like a sigh.

"Don't push me too close, honey," responded the old man; "don't shove me up in no cornder. I don't wanter tell you no stories. Some say dat Brer Rabbit's ole 'oman died fum eatin' some pizen-weed, en dat Brer Rabbit married ole Miss Fox, en some say not. Some tells one tale en some tells nudder; some say dat fum dat time forrer'd de Rabbits en de Foxes make frien's en stay so; some say dey kep on quollin'. Hit look like it mixt. Let dem tell you w'at knows. Dat w'at I years you gits it straight like I yeard it."

There was a long pause, which was finally broken by the old man:

"Hit's 'gin de rules fer you ter be noddin' yer, honey. Bimeby you'll drap off en I'll hatter tote you up ter de big 'ouse. I hear dat baby cryin', en bimeby Miss Sally'll fly up en be a holler'n atter you."

"Oh, I wasn't asleep," the little boy replied. "I was just thinking."

"Well, dat's diffunt," said the old man. "Ef you'll clime up on my back," he continued, speaking softly, "I speck I ain't too ole fer ter be yo' hoss fum yer ter de house. Many en many's de time dat I toted yo' Unk Jeems dat away, en Mars Jeems wuz heavier sot dan w'at you is."

PLANTATION PROVERBS.

Big 'possum clime little tree.
Dem w'at eats kin say grace.
Ole man Know-All died las' year.
Better de gravy dan no grease 'tall.
Dram ain't good twel you git it.
Lazy fokes' stummucks don't git tired.
Rheumatiz don't he'p at de log-rollin'.
Mole don't see w'at his naber doin'.
Save de pacin' mar' fer Sunday.
Don't rain eve'y time de pig squeal.
Crow en corn can't grow in de same fiel'.
Tattlin' 'oman can't make de bread rise.
Rails split 'fo' bre'kfus' 'll season de dinner.
Dem w'at knows too much sleeps under de ash-
    hopper.
Ef you wanter see yo' own sins, clean up a new
    groun'.
Hog dunner w'ich part un 'im'll season de turnip
    salad.
Hit's a blessin' de w'ite sow don't shake de plum-tree.
Winter grape sour, whedder you kin reach 'im or not.
Mighty po' bee dat don't make mo' honey dan he
    want.
Kwishins on mule's foots done gone out er fashun.
Pigs dunno w'at a pen's fer.
Possum's tail good as a paw.
Dogs don't bite at de front gate.
Colt in de barley-patch kick high.
Jay-bird don't rob his own nes'.

Pullet can't roost too high for de owl.

Meat fried 'fo' day wont las' twel night.

Stump water won't kyo de gripes.

De howlin' dog know w'at he sees.

Bline hoss don't fall w'en he follers de bit.

Hongry nigger won't w'ar his maul out.

Don't fling away de empty wallet.

Black-snake know de way ter de hin nes'.

Looks won't do ter split rails wid.

Settin' hens don't hanker arter fresh aigs.

Tater-vine growin' w'ile you sleep.

Hit take two birds fer to make a nes'.

Ef you bleedzd ter eat dirt, eat clean dirt.

Tarrypin walk fast 'nuff fer to go visitin'

Empty smoke-house makes de pullet holler.

W'en coon take water he fixin' fer ter fight.

Corn makes mo' at de mill dan it does in de crib.

Good luck say: "Op'n yo' mouf en shet yo' eyes."

Nigger dat gets hurt wukkin oughter show de skyars.

Fiddlin' nigger say hit's long ways ter de dance.

Rooster makes mo' racket dan de hin w'at lay de aig.

Meller mush-million hollers at you fum over de fence.

Nigger wid a pocket-han'kcher better be looked atter.

Rain-crow don't sing no chune, but youk'n 'pen' on
    'im.

One-eyed mule can't be handled on de bline side.

Moon may shine, but a lightered knot's mighty
    handy.

Licker talks mighty loud w'en it git loose fum de jug.

De proudness un a man don't count w'en his head's
    cold.

Hongry rooster don't cackle w'en he fine a wum.

Some niggers mighty smart, but dey can't drive de
    pidgins ter roos'.

You may know de way, but better keep yo' eyes on de
    seven stairs.

All de buzzards in de settlement 'll come to de gray
mule's funer'l.

Youk'n hide de fier, but w'at you gwine do wid de
smoke?

Ter-morrow may be de carridge-driver's day for
ploughin'.

Hit's a mighty deaf nigger dat don't year de dinner-
ho'n.

Hit takes a bee fer ter git de sweetness out'n de hoar-
houn' blossom.

Ha'nts don't bodder longer hones' folks, but you better go 'roun' de grave-yard.

De pig dat runs off wid de year er corn gits little mo'
dan de cob.

Sleepin' in de fence-cornder don't fetch Chrismus in
de kitchen.

De spring-house may freeze, but de niggers'll keep de
shuck-pen warm.

'Twix' de bug en de bee-martin 'tain't hard ter tell
w'ich gwineter git kotch.

Don't 'spute wid de squinch-owl. Jam de shovel in de
fier.

You'd see mo' er de mink ef he know'd whar de yard
dog sleeps.

Troubles is seasonin'. 'Simmons ain't good twel dey
'er fros'-bit.

Watch out w'en you'er gittin all you want. Fattenin'
hogs ain't in luck.

HIS SONGS.

I.
REVIVAL HYMN.

Oh, whar shill we go w'en de great day comes,
Wid de blowin' er de trumpits en de bangin' er de
    drums?
How many po' sinners'll be kotched out late
En fine no latch ter de golden gate?
    No use fer ter wait twel ter-morrer!
    De sun musn't set on yo' sorrer,
    Sin's ez sharp ez a bamboo-brier—
    Oh, Lord! fetch de mo'ners up higher!

W'en de nashuns er de earf is a stan'in all aroun',
Who's a gwineter be choosen fer ter w'ar de glory-
    crown?
Who's a gwine fer ter stan' stiff-kneed en bol',
En answer to der name at de callin' er de roll?
    You better come now ef you comin'—
    Ole Satun is loose en a bummin'—
    De wheels er distruckshun is a hummin'—
    Oh, come 'long, sinner, ef you comin'!

De song er salvashun is a mighty sweet song,
En de Pairidise win' blow fur en blow strong,
En Aberham's bosom, hit's saft en hit's wide,
En right dar's de place whar de sinners oughter hide!
    Oh, you nee'nter be a stoppin' en a lookin';
    Ef you fool wid ole Satun you'll git took in;
    You'll hang on de aidge en get shook in,
    Ef you keep on a stoppin' en a lookin'.

De time is right now, en dish yer's de place—
Let de sun er salvashun shine squar' in yo' face;
Fight de battles er de Lord, fight soon en fight late,
En you'll allers fine a latch ter de golden gate.
      No use fer ter wait twel ter-morrer,
      De sun musn't set on yo' sorrer—
      Sin's ez sharp ez a bamboo-brier,
      Ax de Lord fer ter fetch you up higher!

II.
CAMP-MEETING SONG.*

Oh, de worril is roun' en de worril is wide—
      Lord! 'member deze chillun in de mornin'—
Hit's a mighty long ways up de mountain side,
En dey ain't no place fer dem sinners fer ter hide,
En dey ain't no place whar sin kin abide,
      W'en de Lord shill come in de mornin'!
            Look up en look aroun',
            Fling yo' burden on de groun',
         Hit's a gittin' mighty close on ter mornin'!
            Smoove away sin's frown—
            Retch up en git de crown,
         W'at de Lord will fetch in de mornin'!

De han' er ridem'shun, hit's hilt out ter you—
      Lord! 'member dem sinners in de mornin'!
Hit's a mighty pashent han', but de days is but few,
W'en Satun, he'll come a demandin' un his due,
En de stiff-neck sinners 'll be smotin' all fru—
      Oh, you better git ready fer de mornin'!

* In the days of slavery, the religious services held by the negroes
who accompanied their owners to the camp-meetings were marvels of
earnestness and devotion.

Look up en set yo' face
Todes de green hills er grace
'Fo' de sun rises up in de mornin'—
Oh, you better change yo' base,
Hit's yo' soul's las' race
Fer de glory dat's a comin' in de mornin'!

De farmer gits ready w'en de lan's all plowed
Fer ter sow dem seeds in de mornin'—
De sperrit may be puny en de flesh may be proud,
But you better cut loose fum de scoffin' crowd,
En jine dese Christuns w'at's a cryin' out loud
Fer de Lord fer ter come in de mornin'!
Shout loud en shout long,
Let de ekkoes ans'er strong,
W'en de sun rises up in de mornin'!
Oh, you allers will be wrong
Twel you choose ter belong
Ter de Marster w'at's a comin' in de mornin'!

III.
CORN-SHUCKING SONG.

Oh, de fus news you know de day'll be a breakin'—
(Hey O! Hi O! Up'n down de Bango!*)
An' de fier be a burnin' en' de ash-cake a bakin',
(Hey O! Hi O! Up'n down de Bango!)
An' de hen'll be a hollerin' en de boss'll be a wakin'—
(Hey O! Hi O! Up'n down de Bango!)
Better git up, nigger, en give yo'se'f a shakin'—
(Hi O, Miss Sindy Ann!)

* So far as I know, "Bango" is a meaningless term, introduced on account of its sonorous ruggedness.

Oh, honey! w'en you see dem ripe stars a fallin'—
      (Hey O! Hi O! Up'n down de Bango!)
Oh, honey! w'en you year de rain-crow a callin'—
      (Hey O! Hi O! Up'n down de Bango!)
Oh, honey! w'en you year dat red calf a bawlin'—
      (Hey O! Hi O! Up'n down de Bango!)
Den de day time's comin', a creepin' en a crawlin'—
      (Hi O, Miss Sindy Ann!)

Fer de los' ell en yard* is a huntin' fer de mornin',
      (Hi O! git 'long! go way!)
En she'll ketch up widdus 'fo' we ever git dis corn in—
      (Oh, go 'way, Sindy Ann!)

Oh, honey! w'en you year dat tin-horn a tootin'—
      (Hey O! Hi O! Up'n down de Bango!)
Oh, honey, w'en you year de squinch-owl a hootin'—
      (Hey O! Hi O! Up'n down de Bango!)
Oh, honey! w'en you year dem little pigs a rootin'—
      (Hey O! Hi O! Up'n down de Bango!)
Right den she's a comin' a skippin' en a scootin'—
      (Hi O, Miss Sindy Ann!)

Oh, honey, w'en you year dat roan mule whicker—
      (Hey O! Hi O! Up'n down de Bango!)
W'en you see Mister Moon turnin' pale en gittin'
    sicker—
      (Hey O! Hi O! Up'n down de Bango!)
Den hit's time fer ter handle dat corn a little quicker—
      (Hey O! Hi O! Up'n down de Bango!)
Ef you wanter git a smell er old Marster's jug er
    licker—
      (Hi O, Miss Sindy Ann!)

Fer de los' ell en yard is a huntin' fer de mornin,
      (Hi O! git 'long! go 'way!)

* The sword and belt in the constellation of Orion.

En she'll ketch up widdus 'fo' we ever git dis corn in—
    (Oh, go 'way, Sindy Ann!)

You niggers 'cross dar! you better stop your dancin'—
    (Hey O! Hi O! Up'n down de Bango!)
No use fer ter come a flingin' un yo' "sha'n'ts" in—
    (Hey O! Hi O! Up'n down de Bango!)
No use fer ter come a flingin' un yo' "can'ts" in—
    (Hey O! Hi O! Up'n down de Bango!)
Kaze dey ain't no time fer yo' pattin' ner yo' prancin'!
    (Hi O, Miss Sindy Ann!)

Mr. Rabbit see de Fox, en he sass um en jaws um—
    (Hey O! Hi O! Up'n down de Bango!)
Mr. Fox ketch de Rabbit, en he scratch um en he claws
    um—
    (Hey O! Hi O! Up'n down de Bango!)
En he tar off de hide, en he chaws um en he gnyaws
    um—
    (Hey O! Hi O! Up'n down de Bango!)
Same like gal chawin' sweet gum en rozzum—
    (Hi O, Miss Sindy Ann!)

Fer de los' ell en yard is a huntin' fer de mornin'
    (Hi O! git 'long! go 'way!)
En she'll ketch up widdus 'fo' we ever git dis corn in—
    (Oh, go 'way, Sindy Ann!)

Oh, work on, boys! give deze shucks a mighty wring-
    in'—
    (Hey O! Hi O! Up'n down de Bango!)
'Fo' de boss come aroun' a dangin' en a dingin'—
    (Hey O! Hi O! Up'n down de Bango!)
Git up en move aroun'! set dem big han's ter swingin'—
    (Hey O! Hi O! Up'n down de Bango!)
Git up'n shout loud! let de w'ite folks year you singin'!
    (Hi O, Miss Sindy Ann!)

Fer de los' ell en yard is a huntin' fer de mornin'
      (Hi O! git 'long! go 'way!)
En she'll ketch up widdus 'fo' we ever git dis corn in.
      (Oh, go 'way, Sindy Ann!)

IV.
THE PLOUGH-HANDS' SONG.

(JASPER COUNTY—1860.)

Nigger mighty happy w'en he layin' by co'n—
      Dat sun's a slantin';
Nigger mighty happy w'en he year de dinner-h'on—
      Dat sun's a slantin';
En he mo' happy still we'n de night draws on—
      Dat sun's a slantin';
Dat sun's a slantin' des ez sho's you bo'n!
      En it's rise up, Primus! fetch anudder yell:
      Dat old dun cow's des a shakin' up 'er bell,
      En de frogs chunin' up 'fo' de jew done fell:
      Good-night, Mr. Killdee! I wish you mighty well!
        —Mr. Killdee! I wish you mighty well!
          —I wish you mighty well!

De co'n 'll be ready 'g'inst dumplin day—
      Dat sun's a slantin';
But nigger gotter watch, en stick, en stay—
      Dat sun's a slantin';
Same ez de bee-martin watchin' un de jay—
      Dat sun's a slantin';
Dat sun's a slantin' en a slippin' away!
      Den it's rise up, Primus! en gin it t'um strong:
      De cow's gwine home wid der ding-dang-dong—

Sling in anudder tetch er de ole-time song:
Good-night, Mr. Whipperwill! don't stay long!
—Mr. Whipperwill! don't stay long!
—Don't stay long!

V.
CHRISTMAS PLAY-SONG.

(MYRICK PLACE, PUTNAM COUNTY—1858.)

Hi my rinktum!   Black gal sweet,
Same like goodies w'at de w'ite folks eat;
Ho my Riley! don't you take'n tell 'er name,
En den ef sumpin' happen you won't ketch de blame:
Hi my rinktum! better take'n hide yo' plum;
Joree don't holler eve'y time he fine a wum.
            Den it's hi my rinktum!
              Don't git no udder man;
            En it's ho my Riley!
              Fetch out Miss Dilsey Ann!

Ho my Riley!   Yaller gal fine;
She may be yone but she oughter be mine!
Hi my rinktum!   Lemme git by,
En see w'at she mean by de cut er dat eye!
Ho my Riley! better shet dat do'—
De w'ite folks 'll b'leeve we er t'arin up de flo'.
            Den it's ho my Riley!
              Come a siftin' up ter me!
            En it's hi my rinktum!
              Dis de way ter twis' yo' knee!

Hi my rinktum!   Aint de eas' gittin' red?
De squinch owl shiver like he wanter go ter bed;

Ho my Riley! but de gals en de boys,
Des now gittin' so dey kin sorter make a noise.
Hi my rinktum! let de yaller gal 'lone;
Niggers don't hanker arter sody in de pone.
        Den it's hi my rinktum!
            Better try anudder plan;
        An' it's ho my Riley!
            Trot out Miss Dilsey Ann!

Ho my Riley!   In de happy Chrismus' time
De niggers shake der cloze a huntin' fer a dime.
Hi my rinktum! En den dey shake der feet,
En greaze derse'f wid de good ham meat.
Ho my Riley! dey eat en dey cram,
En bimeby ole Miss 'll be a sendin' out de dram.
        Den it's ho my Riley!
            You hear dat, Sam!
        En it's hi my rinktum!
            Be a sendin' out de dram!

VI.
PLANTATION PLAY-SONG.

(PUTNAM COUNTY—1856.)

Hit's a gittin' mighty late, w'en de Guinny-hins squall,
En you better dance now, ef you gwineter dance a tall,
Fer by dis time ter-morrer night you can't hardly crawl,
Kaze you'll hatter take de hoe ag'in en likewise de
    maul—
Don't you hear dat bay colt a kickin' in his stall?
        Stop yo' humpin' up yo' sho'lders—
            Dat'll never do!
        Hop light, ladies,
            Oh, Miss Loo!

Hit takes a heap er scrougin'
        Fer ter git you thoo—

Hop light, ladies,
        Oh, Miss Loo!

Ef you niggers don't watch, you'll sing anudder chune,
Fer de sun'll rise'n ketch you ef you don't be mighty
        soon;
En de stars is gittin' paler, en de ole gray coon
Is a settin' in de grape-vine a watchin' fer de moon.
                W'en a feller comes a knockin'
                        Des holler—*Oh, shoo!*
                Hop light, ladies,
                        Oh, Miss Loo!
                Oh, swing dat yaller gal!
                        Do, boys, do!
                Hop light, ladies,
                        Oh, Miss Loo!

Oh, tu'n me loose! Lemme 'lone! Go way, now!
W'at you speck I come a dancin' fer ef I dunno how?
Deze de ve'y kinder footses w'at kicks up a row;
Can't you jump inter de middle en make yo' gal a bow?
                Look at dat merlatter man
                        A follerin' up Sue;
                Hop light, ladies,
                        Oh, Miss Loo!
                De boys ain't a gwine
                        W'en you cry *boo hoo*—
                Hop light, ladies,
                        Oh, Miss Loo!

VII.
TRANSCRIPTIONS.*

1.   A PLANTATION CHANT.

Hit's eighteen hunder'd forty-en-fo',
Christ done open dat He'v'mly do'—
　　An' I don't wanter stay yer no longer;
Hit's eighteen hunder'd forty-en-five,
Christ done made dat dead man alive—
　　An' I don't wanter stay yer no longer.
　　　　You ax me ter run home,
　　　　　　Little childun—
　　　　Run home, dat sun done roll—
　　　　　　An' I don't wanter stay yer no longer.

Hit's eighteen hunder'd forty-en-six,
Christ is got us a place done fix—
　　An' I don't wanter stay yer no longer;
Hit's eighteen hunder'd forty-en-sev'm
Christ done sot a table in Hev'm—
　　An' I don't wanter stay yer no longer.
　　　　You ax me ter run home,
　　　　　　Little childun—
　　　　Run home, dat sun done roll—
　　　　　　An' I don't wanter stay yer no longer.

Hit's eighteen hunder'd forty-en-eight,
Christ done make dat crooked way straight—
　　An' I don't wanter stay yer no longer;
Hit's eighteen hunder'd forty-en-nine,
Christ done tu'n dat water inter wine—
　　An' I don't wanter stay yer no longer.

* If these are adaptations from songs the negroes have caught from the whites, their origin is very remote. I have transcribed them literally, and I regard them as in the highest degree characteristic.

> You ax me ter run home,
>> Little childun—
> Run home, dat sun done roll—
>> An' I don't wanter stay yer no longer.

Hit's eighteen hunder'd forty-en-ten,
Christ is de mo'ner's onliest fr'en'—
    An' I don't wanter stay yer no longer;
Hit's eighteen hunder'd forty-en-'lev'm,
Christ'll be at de do' w'en we all git ter Hev'm—
    An' I don't wanter stay yer no longer.
> You ax me ter run home,
>> Little childun—
> Run home, dat sun done roll—
>> An' I don't wanter stay yer no longer.

2. A PLANTATION SERENADE.

De ole bee make de honey-comb,
    De young bee make de honey,
De niggers make de cotton en co'n,
    En de w'ite folks gits de money.
De raccoon he's a cu'us man,
    He never walk twel dark,
En nuthin' never 'sturbs his mine,
    Twel he hear ole Bringer bark.

De raccoon totes a bushy tail,
    De 'possum totes no ha'r,
Mr. Rabbit, he come skippin' by,
    He ain't got none ter spar'.

Monday mornin' break er day,
    W'ite folks got me gwine,
But Sat'dy night, w'en de sun goes down,
    Dat yaller gal's in my mine.

Fifteen poun' er meat a week,
    W'isky fer ter sell,
Oh, how can a young man stay at home,
    Dem gals dey look so well?

Met a 'possum in de road—
    Brer 'Possum, whar you gwine?
I thank my stars, I bless my life,
    I'm a huntin' fer de muscadine.

VIII.
THE BIG BETHEL CHURCH.

De big Bethel chu'ch! de Big Bethel chu'ch!
    Done put ole Satun behine um;
Ef a sinner git loose fum enny udder chu'ch,
    De Big Bethel chu'ch will fine um!

Hit's good ter be dere, en it's sweet ter be dere,
    Wid de sisterin' all aroun' you—
A shakin' dem shackles er mussy en' love
    Wharwid de Lord is boun' you.

Hit's sweet ter be dere en lissen ter de hymes,
    En hear dem mo'ners a shoutin'—
Dey done reach de place whar der ain't no room
    Fer enny mo' weepin' en doubtin'.

Hit's good ter be dere w'en de sinners all jine
    Wid de brudderin in dere singin',
En it look like Gaberl gwine ter rack up en blow
    En set dem heav'm bells ter ringin'!

Oh, de Big Bethel chu'ch! de Big Bethel chu'ch,
    Done put ole Satun behine um;

Ef a sinner git loose fum enny udder chu'ch
  De Big Bethel chu'ch will fine um!

IX.
TIME GOES BY TURNS.

Dar's a pow'ful rassle 'twix de Good en de Bad,
  En de Bad's got de all-under holt;
En w'en de wuss come, she come i'on-clad,
  En you hatter hole yo' bref fer de jolt.

But des todes de las' Good gits de knee-lock,
  En dey draps ter de groun'—*ker flop!*
Good had de inturn, en he stan' like a rock,
  En he bleedzd fer ter be on top.

De dry wedder breaks wid a big thunder-clap,
  Fer dey aint no drout' w'at kin las',
But de seasons wa't whoops up de cotton crap,
  Likewise dey freshens up de grass.

De rain fall so saf' in de long dark night,
  Twel you hatter hole yo' han' fer a sign,
But de drizzle wa't sets de tater-slips right
  Is de makin' er de May-pop vine.

In de mellerest groun' de clay root'll ketch
  En hole ter de tongue er de plow,
En a pine-pole gate at de gyardin-patch
  Never'll keep out de ole brindle cow.

One en all on us knows who's a pullin' at de bits
  Like de lead-mule dat g'ides by de rein,
En yit, somehow er nudder, de bestest un us gits
  Mighty sick er de tuggin' at de chain.

Hump yo'se'f ter de load en fergit de distress,
  En dem w'at stan's by ter scoff,
Fer de harder de pullin', de longer de res',
  En de bigger de feed in de troff.

A STORY OF
THE WAR.

A STORY OF THE WAR.

When Miss Theodosia Huntingdon, of Burlington, Vermont, concluded to come South in 1870, she was moved by three considerations. In the first place, her brother, John Huntingdon, had become a citizen of Georgia—having astonished his acquaintances by marrying a young lady, the male members of whose family had achieved considerable distinction in the Confederate army; in the second place, she was anxious to explore a region which she almost unconsciously pictured to herself as remote and semi-barbarous; and, in the third place, her friends had persuaded her that to some extent she was an invalid. It was in vain that she argued with herself as to the propriety of undertaking the journey alone and unprotected, and she finally put an end to inward and outward doubts by informing herself and her friends, including John Huntingdon, her brother, who was practicing law in Atlanta, that she had decided to visit the South.

When, therefore, on the 12th of October, 1870—the date is duly recorded in one of Miss Theodosia's letters—she alighted from the cars in Atlanta, in the midst of a great crowd, she fully expected to find her brother waiting to receive her. The bells of several locomotives were ringing, a number of trains were moving in and out, and the porters and baggage-men were screaming and bawling to such an extent that for several moments Miss Huntingdon was considerably confused; so much so that she paused in the hope that her brother would suddenly appear and rescue her from the smoke, and dust, and din. At that moment some one touched her on the arm, and she heard a strong, half-confident, half-apologetic voice exclaim:

"Ain't dish yer Miss Doshy?"

Turning, Miss Theodosia saw at her side a tall, gray-haired negro. Elaborating the incident afterward to her friends, she was pleased to say that the appearance of the old man was somewhat picturesque. He stood towering above her, his hat in one hand, a carriage-whip in the other, and an expectant smile lighting up his rugged face. She remembered a name her brother had often used in his letters, and, with a woman's tact, she held out her hand, and said:

"Is this Uncle Remus?"

"Law, Miss Doshy! how you know de ole nigger? I know'd you by de faver; but how you know me?" And then, without waiting for a reply: "Miss Sally, she sick in bed, en Mars John, he bleedzd ter go in de country, en dey tuck'n sont me. I know'd you de minnit I laid eyes on you. Time I seed you, I say ter myse'f, 'I lay dar's Miss Doshy,' en, sho nuff, dar you wuz. You ain't gun up yo' checks, is you? Kaze I'll git de trunk sont up by de 'spress waggin."

The next moment Uncle Remus was elbowing his way unceremoniously through the crowd, and in a very short time, seated in the carriage drive by the old man, Miss Huntingdon was whirling through the streets of Atlanta in the direction of her brother's home. She took advantage of the opportunity to study the old negro's face closely, her natural curiosity considerably sharpened by a knowledge of the fact that Uncle Remus had played an important part in her brother's history. The result of her observation must have been satisfactory, for presently she laughed, and said:

"Uncle Remus, you haven't told me how you knew me in that great crowd."

The old man chuckled, and gave the horses a gentle rap with the whip.

"Who? Me! I know'd you by de faver. Dat boy er Mars John's is de ve'y spit en immij un you. I'd a know'd you in New 'Leens, let 'lone down dar in de kyar-shed."

This was Miss Theodosia's introduction to Uncle Remus. One Sunday afternoon, a few weeks after her arrival, the family were assembled in the piazza enjoying the mild weather. Mr. Huntingdon was reading a newspaper; his wife was crooning softly as she rocked the baby to sleep; and the little boy was endeavoring to show his Aunt Dosia the outlines of Kennesaw Mountain through the purple haze that hung like a wonderfully fashioned curtain in the sky and almost obliterated the horizon. While they were thus engaged, Uncle Remus came round the corner of the house, talking to himself.

"Dey er too lazy ter wuk," he was saying, "en dey specks hones' fokes fer ter stan' up en s'port um. I'm gwine down ter Putmon County whar Mars Jeems is— dat's w'at I'm agwine ter do."

"What's the matter now, Uncle Remus?" inquired Mr. Huntingdon, folding up his newspaper.

"Nuthin' 'tall, Mars John, 'ceppin deze yer sunshine niggers. Dey begs my terbacker, en borrys my tools, en steals my vittles, en hit's done come ter dat pass dat I gotter pack up en go. I'm agwine down ter Putmon, dat's w'at."

Uncle Remus was accustomed to make this threat several times a day, but upon this occasion it seemed to remind Mr. Huntingdon of something.

"Very well," he said, "I'll come around and help you pack up, but before you go I want you to tell Sister here how you went to war and fought for the Union.— Remus was a famous warrior," he continued, turning to Miss Theodosia; "he volunteered for one day, and commanded an army of one. You know the story, but you have never heard Remus's version.''

Uncle Remus shuffled around in an awkward, embarrassed way, scratched his head, and looked uncomfortable.

"Miss Doshy ain't got no time fer ter set dar an year de ole nigger run on.''

"Oh, yes, I have, Uncle Remus!'' exclaimed the young lady; "plenty of time.''

The upshot of it was that, after many ridiculous protests, Uncle Remus sat down on the steps, and proceeded to tell his story of the war. Miss Theodosia listened with great interest, but throughout it all she observed—and she was painfully conscious of the fact, as she afterward admitted—that Uncle Remus spoke from the standpoint of a Southerner, and with the air of one who expected his hearers to thoroughly sympathize with him.

"Co'se,'' said Uncle Remus, addressing himself to Miss Theodosia, "you ain't bin to Putmon, en you dunner whar de Brad Slaughter place en Harmony Grove is, but Mars John en Miss Sally, dey bin dar a time er two, en dey knows how de lan' lays. Well, den, it 'uz right 'long in dere whar Mars Jeems lived, en whar he live now. When de war come 'long he wuz livin' dere longer Ole Miss en Miss Sally. Ole Miss 'uz his ma, en Miss Sally dar 'uz his sister. De war come des like I tell you, en marters sorter rock along same like dey allers did. Hit didn't strike me dat dey wuz enny war gwine on, en ef I hadn't sorter miss de nabers, en seed fokes gwine outer de way fer ter ax de news, I'd a 'lowed ter myse'f dat de war wuz 'way off 'mong some yuther country. But all dis time de fuss wuz gwine on, en Mars Jeems, he wuz des eatchin' fer ter put in. Ole Miss en Miss Sally, dey tuck on so he didn't git off de fus' year, but bimeby news come down dat times wuz gittin putty hot, en Mars Jeems he got up, he did, en say he gotter go, en go he

did. He got a overseer fer ter look atter de place, en he
went en jined de army. En he 'uz a fighter, too, mon,
Mars Jeems wuz. Many's en many's de time," continued
the old man, reflectively, "dat I hatter take'n bresh dat
boy on accounter his 'buzin' en beatin' dem yuther boys.
He went off dar fer ter fight, en he fit. Ole Miss useter
call me up Sunday en read w'at de papers say 'bout Mars
Jeems, en it hope 'er up might'ly. I kin see 'er des like it
'uz yistiddy.

"'Remus,' sez she, 'dish yer's w'at de papers say
'bout my baby,' en den she'd read out twel she couldn't
read fer cryin'. Hit went on dis way year in en year out,
en dem wuz lonesome times, sho's you bawn, Miss
Doshy—lonesome times, sho. Hit got hotter en hotter
in de war, en lonesomer en mo' lonesomer at home, en
bimeby 'long come de conscrip' man, en he des
everlas'nly scoop up Mars Jeems's overseer. W'en dis
come 'bout, ole Miss, she sont atter me en say, sez she:

"'Remus, I ain't got nobody fer ter look arter de
place but you,' sez she, en den I up'n say, sez I:

"'Mistiss, you kin des 'pen' on de ole nigger.'

"I wuz ole den, Miss Doshy—let 'lone w'at I is now;
en you better b'leeve I bossed dem han's. I had dem
niggers up en in de fiel' long 'fo' day, en de way dey did
wuk wuz a caution. Ef dey didn't earnt der vittles dat
season den I ain't name Remus. But dey wuz tuk keer
un. Dey had plenty er cloze en plenty er grub, en dey
wuz de fattes' niggers in de settlement.

"Bimeby one day, Ole Miss, she call me up en say de
Yankees done gone en tuck Atlanty—dish yer ve'y
town; den present'y I hear dey wuz a marchin' on down
todes Putmon, en, lo en beholes! one day, de fus news I
know'd, Mars Jeems he rid up wid a whole gang er men.
He des stop long nuff fer ter change hosses en snatch a
mouffle er sump'n' ter eat, but 'fo' he rid off, he call me
up en say, sez he:

"'Daddy'—all Ole Miss's chilluns call me daddy—

'Daddy,' he say, ' 'pears like dere's gwineter be mighty rough times 'roun' yer. De Yankees, dey er done got ter Madison en Mounticellar, en 'twon't be many days 'fo' dey er down yer. 'Tain't likely dey'll pester mother ner sister; but, daddy, ef de wus come ter de wus, I speck you ter take keer un um,' sezee.

"Den I say, sez I: 'How long you bin knowin' me, Mars Jeems?' sez I.

" 'Sence I wuz a baby,' sezee.

" 'Well, den, Mars Jeems,' sez I, 'you know'd 'twa'nt no use fer ter ax me ter take keer Ole Miss en Miss Sally.'

"Den he tuck'n squoze my han' en jump on de filly I bin savin' fer 'im, en rid off. One time he tu'n 'roun' en look like he wanter say sump'n', but he des waf' his han'—so—en gallop on. I know'd den dat trouble wuz brewin'. Nigger dat knows he's gwineter git thumped kin sorter fix hisse'f, en I tuck'n fix up like de war wuz gwineter come right in at de front gate. I tuck'n got all de cattle en hosses tergedder en driv' um to de fo'-mile place, en I tuck all de corn en fodder en w'eat, en put um in a crib out dar in de woods; en I bilt me a pen in de swamp, en dar I put de hogs. Den, w'en I fix all dis, I put on my Sunday cloze en groun' my axe. Two whole days I groun' dat axe. De grinestone wuz in sight er de gate en close ter de big 'ouse, en dar I tuck my stan'.

"Bimeby one day, yer come de Yankees. Two un um come fus, en den de whole face er de yeath swawm'd wid um. De fus glimpse I kotch un um, I tuck my axe en march inter Ole Miss settin'-room. She done had de sidebode move in dar, en I wish I may drap ef twuzn't fa'rly blazin' wid silver—silver cups en silver sassers, silver plates en silver dishes, silver mugs en silver pitchers. Look like ter me dey wuz fixin' fer a weddin'. Dar sot Ole Miss des ez prim en ez proud ez ef she own de whole county. Dis kinder hope me up, kaze I done seed Ole Miss look dat away once befo' w'en de overseer struck me in de face wid a w'ip. I sot down by de fier wid my axe 'tween my knees. Dar we sot w'iles de Yankees ransack de place. Miss Sally, dar, she got sorter restless, but Ole Miss didn't skasely bat 'er eyes. Bime-by, we hear steps on de peazzer, en yer come a couple er young fellers wid strops on der shoulders, en der sodes a draggin' on de flo', en der spurrers a rattlin'. I won't say I wuz skeer'd," said Uncle Remus, as though endeav-oring to recall something he failed to remember, "I wont say I wuz skeer'd, kaze I wuzent; but I wuz took'n wid a mighty funny feelin' in de naberhood er de giz-zard. Dey wuz mighty perlite, dem young chaps wuz; but Ole Miss, she never tu'n 'er head, en Miss Sally, she look straight at de fier. Bimeby one un um see me, en he say, sezee:

" 'Hello, ole man, w'at you doin' in yer?' sezee.

" 'Well, boss,' sez I, 'I bin cuttin' some wood fer Ole Miss, en I des stop fer ter wom my han's a little,' sez I.

" 'Hit is cole, dat's a fack,' sezee.

"Wid dat I got up en tuck my stan' behime Ole Miss en Miss Sally, en de man w'at speak, he went up en wom his han's. Fus thing you know, he raise up sudden, en say, sezee:

" 'W'at dat on yo' axe?'

" 'Dat's de fier shinin' on it,' sez I.

" 'Hit look like blood,' sezee, en den he laft.

"But, bless yo' soul, dat man wouldn't never laft dat day ef he'd know'd de wukkins er Remus's mine. But dey didn't bodder nobody ner tech nuthin', en bime-by dey put out. Well, de Yankees, dey kep' passin' all de mawnin' en it look like ter me dey wuz a string un um ten mile long. Den dey commence gittin' thinner en thinner, en den atter w'ile we hear skummishin' in de naberhood er Armer's fe'y, en Ole Miss 'low how dat wuz Wheeler's men makin' persoot. Mars Jeems wuz wid dem Wheeler fellers, en I know'd ef dey wuz dat close I wa'n't doin' no good settin' 'roun' de house toas'n my shins at de fier, so I des tuck Mars Jeems's rifle fum behime de do' en put out ter look atter my stock.

"Seem like I ain't never see no raw day like dat, needer befo' ner sence. Dey wa'n't no rain, but de wet des sifted down; mighty raw day. De leaves on de groun' 'uz so wet dey don't make no fuss, en I got in de woods, en w'enever I year de Yankees gwine by, I des stop in my tracks en let um pass. I wuz stan'in' dat away in de aidge er de woods lookin' out 'cross a clearin', w'en— *piff!*—out come a little bunch er blue smoke fum de top er wunner dem big lonesome-lookin' pines, en den— *pow!*

"Sez I ter myse'f, sez I: 'Honey, youer right on my route, en I'll des see w'at kinder bird you got roostin' in you,' en w'iles I wuz a lookin' out bus' de smoke—*piff!* en den—*bang!* Wid dat I des drapt back inter de woods, en sorted skeerted 'roun' so's ter git de tree 'twix' me en de road. I slid up putty close, en wadder you speck I see? Des ez sho's youer settin' dar lissenin' dey wuz a live Yankee up dar in dat tree, en he wuz a loadin' en a shootin' at de boys des ez cool as a cowcumber in de jew, en he had his hoss hitch out in de bushes, kaze I year de creetur tromplin' 'roun'. He had a spy-glass up dar, en w'iles I wuz a watchin' un 'im, he raise 'er up en look thoo 'er, en den he lay 'er down en fix his gun fer ter shoot. I had good eyes in dem days, ef I ain't got um now, en 'way up de big road I see Mars Jeems a comin'. Hit wuz too fur fer ter see his face, but I know'd 'im by de filly w'at I raise fer 'im, en she wuz a prancin' like a school-gal. I know'd dat man wuz gwineter shoot Mars Jeems ef he could, en dat wuz mo'n I could stan'. Manys en manys de time dat I nuss dat boy, en hilt 'im in dese arms, en toted 'im on dis back, en w'en I see dat Yankee lay dat gun 'cross a lim' en take aim at Mars Jeems I up wid my ole rifle, en shet my eyes en let de man have all she had."

"Do you mean to say," exclaimed Miss Theodosia,

indignantly, "that you shot the Union soldier, when you knew he was fighting for your freedom?"

"Co'se, I know all about dat," responded Uncle Remus, "en it sorter made cole chills run up my back; but w'en I see dat man take aim, en Mars Jeems gwine home ter Ole Miss en Miss Sally, I des disremembered all 'bout freedom en lammed aloose. En den atter dat, me en Miss Sally tuck en nuss de man right straight along. He los' one arm in dat tree bizness, but me en Miss Sally we nuss 'im en we nuss 'im twel he done got well. Des 'bout dat time I quit nuss'n 'im, but Miss Sally she kep' on. She kep' on," continued Uncle Remus, pointing to Mr. Huntingdon, "en now dar he is."

"But you cost him an arm," exclaimed Miss Theodosia.

"I gin 'im dem," said Uncle Remus, pointing to Mrs. Huntingdon, "en I gin 'im deze"—holding up his own brawny arms. "En ef dem ain't nuff fer enny man den I done los' de way."

HIS SAYINGS.

I.
JEEMS ROBER'SON'S
LAST ILLNESS.

A Jonesboro negro, while waiting for the train to go out, met up with Uncle Remus. After the usual "time of day" had been passed between the two, the former inquired about an acquaintance.

"How's Jeems Rober'son?" he asked.

"Ain't you year 'bout Jim?" asked Uncle Remus.

"Dat I ain't," responded the other; "I ain't hear talk er Jem sence he cut loose fum de chain-gang. Dat w'at make I ax. He ain't down wid de biliousness, is he?"

"Not dat I knows un," responded Uncle Remus, gravely. "He ain't sick, an' he ain't bin sick. He des tuck'n say he wuz gwineter ride dat ar roan mule er Mars John's de udder Sunday, an' de mule, she up'n do like she got nudder ingagement. I done bin fool wid dat mule befo', an' I tuck'n tole Jim dat he better not git tangle up wid 'er; but Jim, he up'n 'low dat he wuz a hoss-doctor, an' wid dat he ax me fer a chaw terbarker, en den he got de bridle, en tuck'n kotch de mule en got on her— Well," continued Uncle Remus, looking uneasily around, "I speck you better go git yo' ticket. Dey tells me dish yer train goes a callyhootin'."

"Hole on dar, Uncle Remus; you ain't tell me 'bout Jim," exclaimed the Jonesboro negro.

"I done tell you all I knows, chile. Jim, he tuck'n light on de mule, an' de mule she up'n hump 'erse'f, an den dey wuz a skuffle, an' w'en de dus' blow 'way, dar lay de nigger on de groun', an' de mule she stood eatin' at de troff wid wunner Jim's gallusses wrop 'roun' her behime-leg. Den atterwuds, de ker'ner, he come 'roun',

189

an' he tuck'n gin it out dat Jim died sorter accidental like. Hit's des like I tell you: de nigger wern't sick a minnit. So long! Bimeby you won't ketch yo' train. I got ter be knockin' long."

II.
UNCLE REMUS'S
CHURCH EXPERIENCE.

The deacon of a colored church met Uncle Remus recently, and, after some uninteresting remarks about the weather, asked:

"How dis you don't come down ter chu'ch no mo', Brer Remus? We er bin er havin' some mighty 'freshen' times lately."

"Hit's bin a long time sence I bin down dar, Brer Rastus, an' hit'll be longer. I done got my dose."

"You ain't done gone an' unjined, is you, Brer Remus?"

"Not zackly, Brer Rastus. I des tuck'n draw'd out. De members 'uz a blame sight too mutuel fer ter suit my doctrines."

"How wuz dat, Brer Remus?"

"Well, I tell you, Brer Rastus. W'en I went ter dat chu'ch, I went des ez umbill ez de nex' one. I went dar fer ter sing, an' fer ter pray, an' fer ter wushup, an' I mos' giner'lly allers had a stray shinplarster w'ich de ole 'oman say she want sont out dar ter dem cullud fokes 'cross de water. Hit went on dis way twel bimeby, one day, de fus news I know'd der was a row got up in de amen cornder. Brer Dick, he 'nounced dat dey wern't nuff money in de box; an' Brer Sim said if dey wern't he speck Brer Dick know'd whar it disappeared ter; an' den Brer Dick 'low'd dat he won't stan' no 'probusness, an' wid dat he haul off an' tuck Brer Sim under de jaw—*ker blap!*— an' den dey clinched an' drapped on de flo' an' fout under de benches an' 'mong de wimmen.

" 'Bout dat time Sis Tempy, she lipt up in de a'r, an' sing out dat she done gone an' tromple on de Ole Boy, an' she kep' on lippin' up an' slingin' out 'er han's twel bimeby—*blip!*—she tuck Sis Becky in de mouf, an' den Sis Becky riz an' fetch a grab at Sis Tempy, an' I 'clar' ter grashus ef didn't 'pear ter me like she got a poun' er wool. Atter dat de revivin' sorter het up like. Bofe un um had kin 'mong de mo'ners, an' ef you ever see skufflin' an' scramblin' hit wuz den an' dar. Brer Jeems Henry, he mounted Brer Plato an' rid 'im over de railin', an' den de preacher he start down fum de pulpit, an' des ez he wuz skippin' onter de flatform a hyme-book kotch 'im in de bur er de year, an' I be bless ef it didn't soun' like a bungshell'd busted. Des den, Brer Jesse, he riz up in his seat, sorter keerless like, an' went down inter his britches atter his razer, an' right den I know'd sho' nuff trubble wuz begun. Sis Dilsey, she seed it herse'f, an' she tuck'n let off wunner dem hallyluyah hollers, an' den I disremember w'at come ter pass.

"I'm gittin' sorter ole, Brer Rastus, an' it seem like de dus' sorter shet out de pannyrammer. Fuddermo', my lim's got ter akin, mo' speshully w'en I year Brer Sim an' Brer Dick a snortin' and a skufflin' under de benches like ez dey wuz sorter makin' der way ter my pew. So I kinder hump myse'f an' scramble out, and de fus man wa't I seed was a p'leeceman, an' he had a nigger 'rested, an' de fergiven name er dat nigger wuz Remus."

"He didn't 'res' you, did he, Brer Remus?"

"Hit's des like I tell you, Brer Rastus, an' I hatter git Mars John fer to go inter my bon's fer me. Hit ain't no use fer ter sing out chu'ch ter me, Brer Rastus. I done bin an' got my dose. W'en I goes ter war, I wanter know w'at I'm a doin'. I don't wanter git hemmed up 'mong no wimmen and preachers. I wants elbow-room, an' I'm bleedzd ter have it. Des gimme elbow-room."

"But Brer Remus, you ain't—"

"I mout drap in, Brer Rastus, an' den agin I moutn't, but w'en you duz see me santer in de do', wid my specs on, youk'n des say to de congergashun, sorter familious like, 'Yer come ole man Remus wid his hoss-pistol, an' ef dar's much uv a skuffle 'roun' yer dis evenin' youer gwineter year fum 'im.' Dat's me, an' dat's what you kin tell um. So long! 'Member me to Sis Abby."

III.
UNCLE REMUS AND
THE SAVANNAH DARKEY.

The notable difference existing between the negroes in the interior of the cotton States and those on the seaboard—a difference that extends to habits and opinions as well as to dialect—has given rise to certain ineradicable prejudices which are quick to display themselves whenever an opportunity offers. These prejudices were forcibly, as well as ludicrously, illustrated in Atlanta recently. A gentleman from Savannah had been spending the summer in the mountains of north Georgia, and found it convenient to take along a body-servant. This body-servant was a very fine specimen of the average coast negro—sleek, well-conditioned, and consequential—disposed to regard with undisguised contempt everything and everybody not indigenous to the rice-growing region—and he paraded around the streets with quite a curious and critical air. Espying Uncle Remus languidly sunning himself on a corner, the Savannah darkey approached.

"Mornin', sah."

"I'm sorter up an' about," responded Uncle Remus, carelessly and calmly. "How is you stannin' it?"

"Tanky you, my helt mos' so-so. He mo' hot dun in de mountain. Seem so lak man mus' git need* de shade. I enty fer see no rice-bud in dis pa'ts."

"In dis wi'ch?" inquired Uncle Remus, with a sudden affectation of interest.

"In dis pa'ts. In dis country. Da plenty in Sawanny."

"Plenty whar?"

"Da plenty in Sawanny. I enty fer see no crab an' no oscher; en swimp, he no stay 'roun'. I lak some rice-bud now."

"Youer talkin' 'bout deze yer sparrers, w'ich dey er all head, en 'lev'm un makes one mouffle,† I speck," suggested Uncle Remus. "Well, dey er yer," he continued, "but dis ain't no climate whar de rice-birds flies inter yo' pockets en gits out de money an' makes de change derse'f; an' de isters don't shuck off der shells en run over you on de street, an' no mo' duz de s'imp hull derse'f an' drap in yo' mouf. But dey er yer, dough. De scads 'll fetch um."

"Him po' country fer true," commented the Savannah negro; "he no like Sawanny. Down da, we set need de shade an' eaty de rice-bud, an' de crab, an' de swimp tree time de day; an' de buckra man drinky him wine, an' smoky him seegyar all troo de night. Plenty fer eat an' not much fer wuk."

"Hit's mighty nice, I speck," responded Uncle Remus, gravely. "De nigger dat ain't hope up 'longer high feedin' ain't got no grip. But up yer whar fokes is gotter scramble 'roun' an' make der own livin', de vittles wat's kumerlated widout enny sweatin' mos' allers gener'lly b'longs ter some yuther man by rights. One hoe-cake an' a rasher er middlin' meat las's me fum Sunday ter Sunday, an' I'm in a mighty big streak er luck w'en I gits dat."

The Savannah negro here gave utterance to a loud,

* Underneath.
† Mouthful.

contemptuous laugh, and began to fumble somewhat ostentatiously with a big brass watch-chain.

"But I speck I struck up wid a payır ' job las' Chuseday," continued Uncle Remus, in a hopeful tone.

"Wey you gwan do?"

"Oh, I'm a waitin' on a culled gemmun fum Savannah—wunner deze yer high livers you bin tellin' 'bout."

"How dat?"

"I loant 'im two dollars," responded Uncle Remus, grimly, "an' I'm a waitin' on 'im fer de money. Hit's wunner deze yer jobs w'at las's a long time."

The Savannah negro went off after his rice-birds, while Uncle Remus leaned up against the wall and laughed until he was in imminent danger of falling down from sheer exhaustion.

IV.
TURNIP SALAD AS A TEXT.

As Uncle Remus was going down the street recently he was accosted by several acquaintances.

"Heyo!" said one, "here comes Uncle Remus. He look like he gwine fer ter set up a bo'din-house."

Several others bantered the old man, but he appeared to be in a good humor. He was carrying a huge basket of vegetables.

"How many er you boys," said he, as he put his basket down, "is done a han's turn dis day? En yit de week's done commence. I year talk er niggers dat's got money in de bank, but I lay hit ain't none er you fellers. Whar you speck you gwineter git yo' dinner, en how you speck you gwineter git 'long?"

"Oh, we sorter knocks 'roun' an' picks up a livin'," responded one.

"Dat's w'at make I say w'at I duz," said Uncle

Remus. "Folks go 'bout in de day-time an' makes a livin', an' you come 'long w'en dey er res'in' der bones an' picks it up. I ain't no han' at figgers, but I lay I k'n count up right yer in de san' en number up how menny days hit'll be 'fo' you'er cuppled on ter de chain-gang."

"De ole man's holler'n now sho'," said one of the listeners, gazing with admiration on the venerable old darkey.

"I ain't takin' no chances 'bout vittles. Hit's proned inter me fum de fus dat I got ter eat, en I knows dat I got fer ter grub w'at I gits. Hit's agin de mor'l law fer niggers fer ter eat w'en dey don't wuk, an' w'en you see um 'pariently fattenin' on a'r, you k'n des bet dat ruinashun's gwine on some'rs. I got mustard, en poke salid, en lam's quarter in dat basket, en me en my ole 'oman gwineter sample it. Ef enny you boys git a invite you come, but ef you don't you better stay 'way. I gotter muskit out dar wa't's used ter persidin' 'roun' whar dey's a cripple nigger. Don't you fergit dat off'n yo' mine."

V.
A CONFESSION.

"W'at's dis yer I see, great big niggers gwine 'lopin' 'roun' town wid cakes 'n pies fer ter sell?" asked Uncle Remus recently, in his most scornful tone.

"That's what they are doing," responded a young man; "that's the way they make a living."

"Dat w'at make I say w'at I duz—dat w'at keep me grum'lin' w'en I goes in cullud fokes s'ciety. Some niggers ain't gwine ter wuk nohow, an' hit's flingin' 'way time fer ter set enny chain-gang traps fer ter ketch um."

"Well, now, here!" exclaimed the young man, in a dramatic tone, "what are you giving us now? Isn't it just as honest and just as regular to sell pies as it is to do any other kind of work?"

"Tain't dat, boss," said the old man, seeing that he was about to be cornered; " 'tain't dat. Hit's de nas'ness un it w'at gits me."

"Oh, get out!"

"Dat's me, boss, up an' down. Ef dere's ruinashun ennywhar in de known wurril, she goes in de comp'ny uv a hongry nigger w'at's a totin' pies 'roun'. Sometimes w'en I git kotch wid emptiness in de pit er de stummuck, an' git ter fairly honin' arter sump'n' w'at got substance in it, den hit look like unto me dat I kin stan' flat-footed an' make more cle'r money eatin' pies dan I could if I wuz ter sell de las' one twix't dis an' Chrismus. An' de nigger w'at k'n trapes 'round wid pies and not git in no alley-way an' sample um, den I'm bleedzd ter say dat nigger outniggers me an' my fambly. So dar now!"

VI.
UNCLE REMUS WITH THE TOOTHACHE.

When Uncle Remus put in an appearance one morning recently, his friends knew he had been in trouble. He had a red cotton handkerchief tied under his chin, and the genial humor that usually makes his aged face its dwelling-place had given way to an expression of grim melancholy. The young men about the office were inclined to chaff him, but his look of sullen resignation remained unchanged.

"What revival did you attend last night?" inquired one.

"What was the color of the mule that did the hammering?" asked another.

"I always told the old man that a suburban chicken-coop would fall on him," remarked some one.

"A strange pig has been squealing in his ear," suggested some one else.

But Uncle Remus remained impassive. He seemed to have lost all interest in what was going on around him, and he sighed heavily as he seated himself on the edge of the trash-box in front of the office. Finally some one asked, in a sympathetic tone:

"What is the matter, old man? You look like you'd been through the mill."

"Now you'er knockin' at de back do' sho'. Ef I ain't bin thoo de mill sence day 'fo' yistiddy, den dey ain't no mills in de lan'. Ef wunner deze yer scurshun trains had runned over me I couldn't er bin wuss off. I bin trompin' 'roun' in de low-groun's now gwine on seventy-fi' year, but I ain't see no sich times ez dat w'at I done spe'unst now. Boss, is enny er you all ever rastled wid de toof-ache?"

"Oh, hundreds of times! The toothache isn't anything."

"Den you des played 'roun' de aidges. You ain't had de kine w'at kotch me on de underjaw. You mout a had a gum-bile, but you ain't bin boddered wid de toofache. I wuz settin' up talkin' wid my ole 'oman, kinder puzzlin' 'roun' fer ter see whar de nex' meal's vittles wuz a gwineter cum fum, an' I feel a little ache sorter crawlin' long on my jaw-bone, kinder feelin' his way. But de ache don't stay long. He sorter hankered 'roun' like, en den crope back whar he come fum. Bimeby I feel 'im comin' agin, an' dis time hit look like he come up closer— kinder skummishin' 'roun' fer ter see how de lan' lay. Den he went off. Present'y I feel 'im comin', an' dis time hit look like he kyar'd de news unto Mary, fer hit feel like der wuz anudder wun wid 'im. Dey crep' up an' crep 'roun', an' den dey crope off. Bimeby dey come back, an' dis time dey come like dey wuzen't 'fear'd er de s'roundin's, fer dey trot right up unto de toof, sorter zamine it like, an' den trot all roun' it, like deze yer circuous hosses. I sot dar mighty ca'm, but I spected dat sump'n' wuz gwine ter happ'n."

"And it happened, did it?" asked some one in the group surrounding the old man.

"Boss, don't you fergit it," responded Uncle Remus, fervidly. "W'en dem aches gallop back dey galloped fer ter stay, an' dey wuz so mixed up dat I couldn't tell one fum de udder. All night long dey racked an' dey galloped, an' w'en dey got tired er rackin' an' gallopin', dey all cloze in on de ole toof an' thumped it an' gouged at it twel it 'peared unto me dat dey had got de jaw-bone loosened up, an' wuz tryin' fer ter fetch it up thoo de top er my head an' out at der back er my neck. An' dey got wuss nex' day. Mars John, he seed I wuz 'stracted, an' he tole me fer ter go roun' yere an' git sump'n' put on it, an' de drug man he 'lowed dat I better have 'er draw'd, an' his wuds wuzent more'n cole 'fo' wunner deze yer watchyoumaycollums—wunner deze dentis' mens—had retched fer it wid a pa'r er tongs w'at don't tu'n loose w'en dey ketches a holt. Leas'ways dey didn't wid me. You oughter seed dat toof, boss. Hit wuz wunner deze yer fo'-prong fellers. Ef she'd a grow'd wrong eend out'ard, I'd a bin a bad nigger long arter I jin'd de chu'ch. You year'd my ho'n!"

VII.
THE PHONOGRAPH.

"Unc Remus," asked a tall, awkward-looking negro, who was one of a crowd surrounding the old man, "wat's dish 'ere w'at dey calls de fonygraf— dish yer inst'ument w'at kin holler 'roun' like little chillun in de back yard?"

"I ain't seed um," said Uncle Remus, feeling in his pocket for a fresh chew of tobacco. "I ain't seed um, but I year talk un um. Miss Sally wuz a readin' in de papers las' Chuseday, an' she say dat's it's a mighty big watchyoumaycollum."

"A mighty big w'ich?" asked one of the crowd.

"A mighty big w'atzisname," answered Uncle Remus, cautiously. "I wuzent up dar close to whar Miss Sarah wuz a readin', but I kinder geddered in dat it wuz one er deze 'ere w'atzisnames w'at you hollers inter one year an' it comes out er de udder. Hit's mighty funny unter me how dese folks kin go an' prognosticate der eckoes inter one er deze yer i'on boxes, an' dar hit'll stay on twel de man comes 'long an' tu'ns de handle an' let's de fuss come pilin' out. Bimeby dey'll git ter makin' sho' nuff fokes, an' den dere'll be a racket 'roun' here. Dey tells me dat it goes off like one er deze yer torpedoes."

"You year dat, don't you?" said one or two of the younger negroes.

"Dat's w'at dey tells me," continued Uncle Remus. "Dat's w'at dey sez. Hit's one er deze yer kinder w'azisnames w'at sasses back w'en you hollers at it."

"W'at dey fix um up fer, den?" asked one of the practical negroes.

"Dat's w'at I wanter know," said Uncle Remus, contemplatively. "But dat's w'at Miss Sally wuz a readin' in de paper. All you gotter do is ter holler at de box, an' dar's yo' remarks. Dey goes in, an' dar dey er tooken and dar dey hangs on twel you shakes de box, an' den dey draps out des ez fresh ez deze yer fishes w'at you git fum Savannah, an' you ain't got time fer ter look at dere gills, nudder."

VIII.
RACE IMPROVEMENT.

"Dere's a kind er limberness 'bout niggers dese days dat's mighty cu'us," remarked Uncle Remus yesterday, as he deposited a pitcher of fresh water upon the exchange table. "I notisses it in de alley-ways an' on de street-cornders. Dey er rackin' up, mon, deze yer cullud fokes is."

"What are you trying to give us now?" inquired one of the young men, in a bilious tone.

"The old man's mind is wandering," said the society editor, smoothing the wrinkles out of his lavender kids.

Uncle Remus laughed. "I speck I is a gittin' mo frailer dan I wuz fo' de fahmin days wuz over, but I sees wid my eyes an' I years wid my year, same ez enny er dese yer young bucks w'at goes a gallopin' 'roun' hunt-in' up devilment, an' w'en I sees de limberness er dese yer cullud people, an' w'en I sees how dey er dancin' up, den I gits sorter hopeful. Dey er kinder ketchin' up wid me."

"How is that?"

"Oh, dey er movin'," responded Uncle Remus. "Dey er sorter comin' 'roun'. Dey er gittin' so dey b'leeve dat dey ain't no better dan de w'ite fokes. W'en freedom come out de niggers sorter got dere humps up, an' dey staid dat way, twel bimeby dey begun fer ter git hongry, an' den dey begun fer ter drap inter line right smart-ually; an' now," continued the old man, emphatically, "dey er des ez palaverous ez dey wuz befo' de war. Dey er gittin' on solid groun', mon."

"You think they are improving, then?"

"Youer chawin' guv'nment now, boss. You slap de law onter a nigger a time er two, an' larn 'im dat he's got fer to look atter his own rashuns an' keep out'n udder fokes's chick'n-coops, an' sorter coax 'im inter de idee dat he's got ter feed 'is own chilluns, an' I be blessed ef you ain't got 'im on risin' groun'. An', mo'n dat, w'en he gits holt er de fack dat a nigger k'n have yaller fever same ez w'ite folks, you done got 'im on de mo'ners' bench, an' den ef you come down strong on de p'int dat he oughter stan' fas' by de folks w'at hope him w'en he wuz in trouble de job's done. W'en you does dat, ef you ain't got yo' han's on a new-made nigger, den my name ain't Remus, an' ef dat name's bin changed I ain't seen her abbertized."

IX.
IN THE RÔLE
OF A TARTAR.

A Charleston negro who was in Atlanta on the Fourth of July made a mistake. He saw Uncle Remus edging his way through the crowd, and thought he knew him.

"Howdy, Daddy Ben?" the stranger exclaimed. "I tink I nubber see you no mo'. Wey you gwan? He hot fer true, ain't he?"

"Daddy who?" asked Uncle Remus, straightening himself up with dignity. "W'ich?"

"I know you in Charl'son, an' den in Sewanny. I spec I dun grow way frum 'membrance."

"You knowed me in Charlstun, and den in Savanny?"

"He been long time, ain't he, Daddy Ben?"

"Dat's w'at's a pesterin' un me. How much you reckon you know'd me?"

"He good whilé pas'; when I wer' pickaninny. He long time ago. Wey you gwan, Daddy Ben?"

"W'at does you season your recollection wid fer ter make it hole on so?" inquired the old man.

"I dunno: He stick hese'f. I see you comin' 'long 'n I say 'Dey Daddy Ben.' I tink I see you no mo', an' I shaky you by de han'. Wey you gwan? Dey no place yer wey we git wine?"

Uncle Remus stared at the strange darkey curiously for a moment, and then he seized him by the arm.

"Come yer, son, whar dey ain't no folks an' lemme drap some Jawjy 'intment in dem years er yone. Youer mighty fur ways fum home, an' you wanter be a lookin' out fer yo'se'f. Fus and fo'mus, youer thumpin' de wrong watermillion. Youer w'isslin' up de wrong chube. I ain't tromped roun' de country much. I ain't bin to Charlstun an' needer is I tuck in Savanny; but you couldn't rig up no game on me dat I wouldn't tumble on to it de minit I laid my eyeballs on you. W'en hit come ter dat I'm ole man Tumbler, fum Tumblersville—I is dat. Hit takes one er deze yer full-blooded w'ite men fer ter trap my jedgment. But w'en a nigger comes a jab-berin' 'roun' like he got a mouf full er rice straw, he ain't got no mo' chance 'long side er me dan a sick sparrer wid a squinch-owl. You gotter travel wid a circus 'fo' you gits away wid me. You better go 'long an' git yo' kyarpet-sack and skip de town. Youer de freshest nigger w'at I seen yit."

The Charleston negro passed on just as a policeman came up.

"Boss, you see dat smart Ellick?"

"Yes; what's the matter with him?"

"He's one er deze yer scurshun niggers from Charl-stun. I seed you a stannin' over agin de cornder yander, an' ef dat nigger'd a drawd his monty kyards on me, I wuz a gwineter holler fer you. Would youer come, boss?"

"Why, certainly, Uncle Remus."

"Dat's w'at I 'lowd. Little more'n he'd a bin aboard er de wrong waggin. Dat's wat he'd a bin."

X.
A CASE OF MEASLES.

"You've been looking like you were rather under the weather for the past week or two, Uncle Remus," said a gentleman to the old man.

"You'd be sorter puny, too, boss, if you'der bin whar I bin."

"Where have you been?"

" 'Pear ter me like ev'eybody done year 'bout dat. Dey ain't no ole nigger my age an' size dat's had no rattliner time dan I is."

"A kind of picnic?"

"Go 'long, boss! w'at you speck I be doin' sailin' 'roun' ter dese yer cullud picnics? Much mo' an' I wouldn't make bread by wukkin fer't, let 'lone follerin' up a passel er boys an' gals all over keration. Boss, ain't you year 'bout it, sho' 'nuff?"

"I haven't, really. What was the matter?"

"I got strucken wid a sickness, an' she hit de ole nigger a joe-darter 'fo' she tu'n 'im loose."

"What kind of sickness?"

"Hit look sorter cu'ous, boss, but ole an' steddy ez I is, I tuck'n kotch de meezles."

"Oh, get out! You are trying to get up a sensation."

"Hit's a natal fack, boss, I declar' ter grashus ef 'tain't. Dey sorter come on wid a cole, like—leas'ways dat's how I commence fer ter suffer, an' den er koff got straddle er de cole—one deze yer koffs wa't look like hit goes ter de foundash'n. I kep' on linger'n' 'roun' sorter keepin' one eye on de rheumatiz an' de udder on de distemper, twel, bimeby, I begin fer ter feel de trestle-wuk give way, an' den I des know'd dat I wuz gwineter gitter racket. I slipt inter bed one Chuseday night, an' I never slip out no mo' fer mighty nigh er mont'.

"Nex' mornin' de meezles 'd done kivered me, an' den ef I didn't git dosted by de ole 'oman I'm a Chinee. She gimme back rashuns er sassafac tea. I des natally hankered an' got hongry atter water, an' ev'y time I sing out fer water I got b'ilin' hot sassafac tea. Hit got so dat w'en I wake up in de mornin' de ole 'oman 'd des come 'long wid a kittle er tea an' fill me up. Dey tells me 'roun' town dat chilluns don't git hurted wid de meezles, w'ich ef dey don't I wanter be a baby de nex' time dey hits dis place. All dis yer meezles bizness is bran'-new ter me. In ole times, 'fo' de wah, I ain't heer tell er no seventy-fi'-year-ole nigger grapplin' wid no meezles. Dey ain't ketchin' no mo', is dey, boss?"

"Oh, no—I suppose not."

" 'Kaze ef dey is, youk'n des put my name down wid de migrashun niggers."

XI.
THE EMIGRANTS.

When Uncle Remus went down to the passenger depot one morning recently, the first sight that caught his eye was an old negro man, a woman, and two children sitting in the shade near the door of the baggage-room. One of the children was very young, and the quartet was altogether ragged and forlorn-looking. The sympathies of Uncle Remus were immediately aroused. He approached the group by forced marches, and finally unburdened his curiosity:

"Whar is you m'anderin' unter, pard?"

The old negro, who seemed to be rather suspicious, looked at Uncle Remus coolly, and appeared to be considering whether he should make any reply. Finally, however, he stretched himself and said:

"We er gwine down in de naberhoods er Tallypoosy, an' we ain't makin' no fuss 'bout it, nudder."

"I disremember," said Uncle Remus, thoughtfully, "whar Tallypoosy is."

"Oh, hit's out yan," replied the old man, motioning his head as if it was just beyond the iron gates of the depot. "Hit's down in Alabam. When we git dar, maybe we'll go on twel we gits ter Massasip."

"Is you got enny folks out dar?" inquired Uncle Remus.

"None dat I knows un."

"An' youer takin' dis 'oman an' deze chillun out dar whar dey dunno nobody? Whar's yo' perwisions?" eying a chest with a rope around it.

"Dem's our bed-cloze," the old negro explained, noticing the glance of Uncle Remus. "All de vittles what we got we e't 'fo' we started."

"An' you speck ter retch dar safe an' soun'? Whar's yo' ticket?"

"Ain't got none. De man say ez how dey'd pass us thoo. I gin a man a fi'-dollar bill 'fo' I lef' Jonesboro, an' he sed dat settled it."

"Lemme tell you dis," said Uncle Remus, straightening up indignantly: "you go an' rob somebody an' git on de chain-gang, an' let de 'oman scratch 'roun' yer an' make 'er livin'; but don't you git on dem kyars—don't you do it. Yo' bes' holt is de chain-gang. You kin make yo' livin' dar w'en you can't make it nowhars else. But don't you git on dem kyars. Ef you do, youer gone nigger. Ef you ain't got no money fer ter walk back wid, you better des b'il' yo' nes' right here. I'm a-talkin' wid de bark on. I done seed deze yer Arkinsaw emmygrants come lopin' back, an' some un 'em didn't have rags nuff on 'em fer ter hide dere nakidness. You leave dat box right whar she is, an' let de 'oman take wun young un an' you take de udder wun, an' den you git in de middle er de big road an' pull out fer de place whar you come fum. I'm preachin' now."

Those who watched say the quartet didn't take the cars.

XII.
AS A MURDERER.

Uncle Remus met a police officer recently.

"You ain't hear talk er no dead nigger nowhar dis mawnin', is you, boss?" asked the old man, earnestly.

"No," replied the policeman, reflectively. "No, I believe not. Have you heard of any?"

"Pears unter me dat I come mighty nigh gittin' some news 'bout dat size, and dats w'at I'm a huntin' fer. Bekaze ef dey er foun' a stray nigger layin' 'roun' loose, wid 'is bref gone, den I wanter go home an' git my brekfus, an' put on some clean cloze, an' 'liver myse'f up ter wunner deze yer jestesses er de peace, an' git a f'ar trial."

"Why, have you killed anybody?"

"Dat's wat's I'm a 'quirin' inter now, but I wouldn't be sustonished ef I ain't laid a nigger out some'rs on de subbubs. Hit's done got so it's agin de law fer ter bus' loose an' kill a nigger, ain't it, boss?"

"Well, I should say so. You don't mean to tell me that you have killed a colored man, do you?"

"I speck I is, boss. I speck I done gone an' done it dis time, sho'. Hit's bin sorter growin' on me, an' it come ter a head dis mawnin', less my name ain't Remus, an' dat's w'at dey bin er callin' me sence I wuz ole er 'nuff fer ter scratch myse'f wid my lef' han'."

"Well, if you've killed a man, you'll have some fun, sure enough. How was it?"

"Hit wuz dis way, boss: I wuz layin' in my bed dis mawnin' sorter ruminatin 'roun', when de fus news I

know'd I year a fus 'mong de chickens, an' den my bris-
sels riz. I done had lots er trubble wid dem chickens, an'
w'en I years wun un um squall my ve'y shoes comes on-
tied. So I des sorter riz up an' retch fer my ole muskit,
and den I crope out er de back do', an' w'atter you
reckin I seed?"

"I couldn't say."

"I seed de biggest, blackest nigger dat you ever laid
eyes on. He shined like de paint on 'im was fresh. He
hed done grabbed fo'er my forwardes' pullets. I crope
up nigh de do', an' hollered an' axed 'im how he wuz a
gittin' on, an' den he broke, an' ez he broke I jammed de
gun in de small er his back and banged aloose. He let a
yell like forty yaller cats a courtin', an' den he broke.
You ain't seed no nigger hump hisse'f like dat nigger.
He tore down de well shelter and fo' pannils er fence, an'
de groun' look like wunner deze yer harrycanes had lit
dar and fanned up de yeath."

"Why, I thought you killed him?"

"He bleedzed ter be dead, boss. Ain't I put de gun
right on im? Seem like I feel 'im give way w'en she went
off."

"Was the gun loaded?"

"Dat's w'at my ole 'oman say. She had de powder in
dar, sho', but I disremember wedder I put de buckshot
in, er wedder I lef' um out. Leas'ways, I'm gwineter call
on wunner deze yer jestesses. So long, boss."

XIII.
HIS PRACTICAL
VIEW OF THINGS.

"Brer Remus, is you heern tell er deze doin's out
yer in de udder eend er town?" asked a colored
deacon of the church the other day.

"W'at doin's is dat, Brer Ab?"

"Deze yer signs an' wunders whar dat cullud lady died day 'fo' yistiddy. Mighty quare goin's on out dar, Brer Remus, sho's you bawn."

"Sperrits?" inquired Uncle Remus, sententiously.

"Wuss'n dat, Brer Remus. Some say dat jedgment-day ain't fur off, an' de folks is flockin' 'roun' de house a hollerin' an' a shoutin' des like dey wuz in er revival. In de winder glass dar you kin see de flags a flyin', an' Jacob's lather is dar, an' dar's writin' on de pane w'at no man can't read—leas'wise dey ain't none read it yit."

"W'at kinder racket is dis youer givin' un me now, Brer Ab?"

"I done bin dar, Brer Remus; I done seed um wid bofe my eyes. Cullud lady what wuz intranced done woke up an' say dey ain't much time fer ter tarry. She say she meet er angel in de road, an' he p'inted straight fer de mornin' star, an' tell her fer ter prepar'. Hit look mighty cu'us, Brer Remus."

"Cum down ter dat, Brer Ab," said Uncle Remus, wiping his spectacles carefully, and readjusting them— "cum down ter dat, an' dey ain't nuthin' dat ain't cu'us. I ain't no spishus nigger myse'f, but I 'spizes fer ter year dogs a howlin' an' squinch-owls havin' de ager out in de woods, an' w'en a bull goes a bellerin' by de house den my bones git cole an' my flesh commences fer ter creep; but w'en it comes ter deze yer sines in de a'r an' deze yer sperrits in de woods, den I'm out—den I'm done. I is, fer a fack. I bin livin' yer more'n seventy year, an' I year talk er niggers seein' ghos'es all times er night an' all times er day, but I ain't never seed none yit; an' deze yer flags an' Jacob's lathers, I ain't seed dem, nudder."

"Dey er dar, Brer Remus."

"Hit's des like I tell you, Brer Ab. I ain't 'sputin 'bout it, but I ain't seed um, an' I don't take no chances deze days on dat w'at I don't see, an' dat w'at I sees I got ter 'zamine mighty close. Lemme tell you dis, Brer Ab:

don't you let deze sines onsettle you. W'en old man Gabrile toot his ho'n, he ain't gwineter hang no sine out in de winder-panes, an' when ole Fadder Jacob lets down dat lather er his'n you'll be mighty ap' fer ter hear de racket. An' don't you bodder wid jedgment-day. Jedgment-day is lierbul fer ter take keer un itse'f."

"Dat's so, Brer Remus."

"Hit's bleedzed ter be so, Brer Ab. Hit don't bodder me. Hit's done got so now dat w'en I gotter pone er bread, an' a rasher er bacon, an' nuff grease fer ter make gravy, I ain't keerin' much w'edder fokes sees ghos'es er no."

XIV.
THAT DECEITFUL JUG.

Uncle Remus was in good humor one evening recently when he dropped casually into the editorial room of "The Constitution," as has been his custom for the past year or two. He had a bag slung across his shoulder, and in the bag was a jug. The presence of this humble but useful vessel in Uncle Remus's bag was made the occasion for several suggestive jokes at his expense by the members of the staff, but the old man's good humor was proof against all insinuations.

"Dat ar jug's bin ter wah, mon. Hit's wunner deze yer ole timers. I got dat jug down dar in Putmon County w'en Mars 'Lisha Perryman wuz a young man, an' now he's done growed up, an' got ole an' died, an' his chilluns is growed up an' dey kin count dere gran'chilluns, an' yit dar's dat jug des ez lively an' ez lierbul fer ter kick up devilment ez w'at she wus w'en she come fum de foundry."

"That's the trouble," said one of the young men. "That's the reason we'd like to know what's in it now."

"Now youer gittin' on ma'shy groun'," replied Uncle

Remus. "Dat's de p'int. Dat's w'at make me say w'at I duz. I bin knowin' dat jug now gwine on sixty-fi' year, an' de jug w'at's more seetful dan dat jug ain't on de topside er de worrul. Dar she sets," continued the old man, gazing at it reflectively, "dar she sets des ez natchul ez er ambertype, an' yit whar's de man w'at kin tell w'at kinder confab she's a gwineter carry on w'en dat corn-cob is snatched outen 'er mouf? Dat jug is mighty seetful, mon."

"Well, it don't deceive any of us up here," remarked the agricultural editor, dryly. "We've seen jugs before."

"I boun' you is, boss; I boun' you is. But you ain't seed no seetful jug like dat. Dar she sets a bellyin out an' lookin' mighty fat an' full, an' yit she'd set dar a bellyin' out ef dere wuzent nuthin' but win' under dat stopper. You knows dat she ain't got no aigs in her, ner no bacon, ner no grits, ner no termartusses, ner no shellotes, an' dat's 'bout all you duz know. Dog my cats ef de seetfulness er dat jug don't git away wid me," continued Uncle Remus, with a chuckle. "I wuz comin' 'cross de bridge des now, an' Brer John Henry seed me wid de bag slung onter my back, an' de jug in it, an' he ups an' sez, sezee:

" 'Heyo, Brer Remus, ain't it gittin' late for watermillions?'

"Hit wuz de seetfulness er dat jug. If Brer John Henry know'd de color er dat watermillion, I speck he'd snatch me up 'fo' de confunce. I 'clar' ter grashus ef dat jug ain't a caution!"

"I suppose it's full of molasses now," remarked one of the young men, sarcastically.

"Hear dat!" exclaimed Uncle Remus, triumphantly—"hear dat! W'at I tell you? I sed dat jug wuz seetful, an' I sticks to it. I bin knowin' dat—"

"What has it got in it?" broke in some one; "molasses, kerosene, or train-oil?"

"Well, I lay she's loaded, boss. I ain't shuk her up sence I drapt in, but I lay she's loaded."

"Yes," said the agricultural editor, "and it's the meanest bug-juice in town—regular sorghum skimmings."

"Dat's needer yer ner dar," responded Uncle Remus. "Po' fokes better be fixin' up for Chrismus now w'ile rashuns is cheap. Dat's me. W'en I year Miss Sally gwine 'bout de house w'isslin' 'W'en I k'n Read my Titles Cler,'— an' w'en I see de martins swawmin' atter sundown—an' w'en I year de peckerwoods confabbin' tergedder dese moonshiny nights in my een' er town— den I knows de hot wedder's a breakin' up, an' I knows it's 'bout time fer po' fokes fer ter be rastlin' 'roun' and huntin' up dere rashuns. Dat's me, up an' down."

"Well, we are satisfied. Better go and hire a hall," remarked the sporting editor, with a yawn. "If you are engaged in a talking match you have won the money. Blanket him, somebody, and take him to the stable."

"An' w'at's mo'," continued the old man, scorning to notice the insinuation, "dough I year Miss Sally w'isslin', an' de peckerwoods a chatterin', I ain't seein' none er deze yer loafin' niggers fixin' up fer ter 'migrate. Dey kin holler Kansas all 'roun' de naberhood, but ceppin' a man come 'long an' spell it wid greenbacks, he don't ketch none er deze yer town niggers. You year me, dey ain't gwine."

"Stand him up on the table," said the sporting editor; "give him room."

"Better go down yer ter de calaboose, an' git some news fer ter print," said Uncle Remus, with a touch of irony in his tone. "Some new nigger mighter broke inter jail."

"You say the darkeys are not going to emigrate this year?" inquired the agricultural editor, who is interested in these things.

"Shoo! dat dey ain't! I done seed an' I knows."

"Well, how do you know?"

"How you tell w'en crow gwineter light? Niggers bin

prom'nadin' by my house all dis summer, holdin' dere
heads high up an' de w'ites er dere eyeballs shinin' in de
sun. Dey wuz too bigitty fer ter look over de gyardin'
palin's. 'Long 'bout den de wedder wuz fetchin' de nat'al
sperrits er turkentime outen de pine-trees an' de groun'
wuz fa'rly smokin' wid de hotness. Now dat it's gittin'
sorter airish in de mornin's, dey don't 'pear like de same
niggers. Dey done got so dey'll look over in de yard, an'
nex' news you know dey'll be tryin' fer ter scrape up
'quaintence wid de dog. W'en dey passes now dey looks
at de chicken-coop an' at de tater-patch. W'en you see
niggers gittin' dat familious, you kin 'pen' on dere
campin' wid you de ballunce er de season. Day 'fo' yistiddy I kotch one un um lookin' over de fence at my
shoats, an' I sez, sez I:

" 'Duz you wanter purchis dem hogs?'

" 'Oh, no,' sezee, 'I wuz des lookin' at dere p'ints.'

" 'Well, dey ain't pintin' yo' way,' sez I, 'an, fuddermo', ef you don't bodder 'longer dem hogs dey ain't
gwineter clime outer dat pen an' 'tack you, nudder,' sez I.

"An' I boun'," continued Uncle Remus, driving the
corn-cob stopper a little tighter in his deceitful jug and
gathering up his bag—"an' I boun' dat my ole muskit'll
go off 'tween me an' dat same nigger yit, an' he'll be at
de bad een', an' dis seetful jug'll 'fuse ter go ter de
funer'l."

XV.
THE FLORIDA WATERMELON.

"Look yer, boy," said Uncle Remus yesterday,
stopping near the railroad crossing on Whitehall
Street, and gazing ferociously at a small colored youth;
"look yer, boy, I'll lay you out flat ef you come flingin'
yo' watermillion rimes under my foot—you watch ef I

don't. You k'n play yo' pranks on deze yer w'ite fokes, but w'en you come a cuttin' up yo' capers roun' me you'll lan' right in de middle uv er spell er sickness— now you mine w'at I tell you. An' I ain't gwine fer ter put up wid none er yo' sassness nudder—let 'lone flingin' watermillion rimes whar I kin git mixt up wid um. I done had nuff watermillions yistiddy an' de day befo'."

"How was that, Uncle Remus?" asked a gentleman standing near.

"Hit wuz sorter like dis, boss. Las' Chuseday, Mars John he fotch home two er deze yer Flurridy watermillions, an him an' Miss Sally sot down fer ter eat um. Mars John an' Miss Sally ain't got nuthin' dat's too good fer me, an' de fus news I know'd Miss Sally wuz a hollerin fer Remus. I done smelt de watermillion on de a'r, an' I ain't got no better sense dan fer ter go w'en I years w'ite fokes a hollerin—I larnt dat w'en I wa'n't so high. Leas'ways I galloped up ter de back po'ch, an' dar sot de watermillions des ez natchul ez ef dey'd er bin raised on de ole Spivey place in Putmon County. Den Miss Sally, she cut me off er slishe —wunner deze yer ongodly slishes, big ez yo' hat, an' I sot down on de steps an' wrop myse'f roun' de whole blessid chunk, 'cepin' de rime." Uncle Remus paused and laid his hand upon his stomach as if feeling for something.

"Well, old man, what then?"

"Dat's w'at I'm a gittin' at, boss," said Uncle Remus, smiling a feeble smile. "I santered roun' 'bout er half n'our, an' den I begin fer ter feel sorter squeemish— sorter like I done bin an' swoller'd 'bout fo' poun's off'n de ruff een' uv er scantlin'. Look like ter me dat I wuz gwineter be sick, an' den hit look like I wuzent. Bimeby a little pain showed 'is head an' sorter m'andered roun' like he wuz a lookin' fer a good place fer ter ketch holt, an' den a great big pain jump up an' take atter de little one an' chase 'im 'roun' an' roun', an' he mus' er kotch 'im, kaze bimeby de big pain retch down an' grab dis yer lef' leg—so—an' haul 'im up, an' den he retch down an' grab de udder one an' pull him up, an' den de wah begun, sho nuff. Fer mighty nigh fo' hours dey kep' up dat racket, an' des ez soon ez a little pain 'ud jump up de big un 'ud light onter it an' gobble it up, an' den de big un 'ud go sailin' roun' huntin' fer mo'. Some fokes is mighty cu'us, dough. Nex' mornin' I hear Miss Sally a laughin', an' singin' an' a w'isslin' des like dey want no watermillions raise in Flurridy. But somebody better pen dis yer nigger boy up w'en I'm on de town—I kin tell you dat."

XVI.
UNCLE REMUS PREACHES TO A CONVERT.

"Dey tells me you done jine de chu'ch," said Uncle Remus to Pegleg Charley.

"Yes, sir," responded Charley, gravely, "dat's so."

"Well, I'm mighty glad er dat," remarked Uncle Remus, with unction. "It's 'bout time dat I wuz spectin' fer ter hear un you in de chain-gang, an', stidder dat, hit's de chu'ch. Well, dey ain't no tellin' deze days whar a nigger's gwineter lan'."

"Yes," responded Charley, straightening himself up and speaking in a dignified tone, "yes, I'm fixin' to do better. I'm preparin' fer to shake worldliness. I'm done quit so'shatin' wid deze w'ite town boys. Dey've been a goin' back on me too rapidly here lately, an' now I'm a goin' back on dem."

"Well, ef you done had de speunce un it, I'm mighty glad. Ef you got 'lijjun, you better hole on to it 'twell de las' day in de mornin'. Hit's mighty good fer ter kyar' 'roun' wid you in de day time an' likewise in de night time. Hit'll pay you mo' dan politics, an' ef you stan's up like you oughter, hit'll las' longer dan a bone-fellum. But you wanter have one er deze yer ole-time grips', an' you des gotter shet yo' eyes an' swing on like wunner deze yer bull-tarrier dogs."

"Oh, I'm goin' to stick, Uncle Remus. You kin put your money on dat. Deze town boys can't play no more uv dere games on me. I'm fixed. Can't you lend me a dime, Uncle Remus, to buy me a pie? I'm dat hongry dat my stomach is gittin' ready to go in mo'nin'.'"

Uncle Remus eyed Charley curiously a moment, while the latter looked quietly at his timber toe. Finally, the old man sighed and spoke:

"How long is you bin in de chu'ch, son?"

"Mighty near a week," replied Charley.

"Well, lemme tell you dis, now, 'fo' you go enny fud-der. You ain't bin in dar long nuff fer ter go 'roun' takin up conterbutions. Wait ontwell you gits sorter seasoned like, an' den I'll hunt 'roun' in my cloze an' see ef I can't run out a thrip er two fer you. But don't you levy taxes too early."

Charley laughed, and said he would let the old man off if he would treat to a watermelon.

XVII.
AS TO EDUCATION.

As Uncle Remus came up Whitehall Street recently, he met a little colored boy carrying a slate and a number of books. Some words passed between them, but their exact purport will probably never be known. They were unpleasant, for the attention of a wandering policeman was called to the matter by hearing the man bawl out:

"Don't you come foolin' longer me, nigger. Youer flippin' yo' sass at de wrong color. You k'n go roun' yer an' sass deze w'ite people, an' maybe dey'll stan' it, but w'en you come a slingin' yo' jaw at a man w'at wuz gray w'en de fahmin' days gin out, you better go an' git yo' hide greased."

"What's the matter, old man?" asked a sympathizing policeman.

"Nothin', boss, 'ceppin I ain't gwineter hav' no nigger chillun a hoopin' an' a hollerin' at me w'en I'm gwine 'long de streets."

"Oh, well, school-children—you know how they are."

"Dat's w'at make I say w'at I duz. Dey better be home pickin' up chips. W'at a nigger gwineter l'arn outen books? I kin take a bar'l stave an' fling mo' sense inter a nigger in one minnit dan all de school-houses betwixt dis en de State er Midgigin. Don't talk, honey! Wid one bar'l stave I kin fa'rly lif' de vail er ignunce."

"Then you don't believe in education?"

"Hits de ruination er dis country. Look at my gal. De ole 'oman sont 'er ter school las' year, an' now we dassent hardly ax 'er fer ter kyar de washin' home. She done got beyant 'er bizness. I 'aint larnt nuthin' in books, 'en yit I kin count all de money I gits. No use talkin', boss. Put a spellin'-book in a nigger's han's, en right den en dar' you loozes a plow-hand. I done had de spe'unce un it."

XVIII
A TEMPERANCE REFORMER.

"Yer come Uncle Remus," said a well-dressed negro, who was standing on the sidewalk near James's bank recently, talking to a crowd of barbers. "Yer come Uncle Remus. I boun' he'll sign it."

"You'll fling yo' money away ef you bet on it," responded Uncle Remus. "I ain't turnin' nothin' loose on chu'ch 'scriptions. I wants money right now fer ter git a pint er meal."

" 'Tain't dat."

"An' I ain't heppin fer ter berry nobody. Much's I kin do ter keep de bref in my own body."

" 'Tain't dat, nudder."

"An' I ain't puttin' my han' ter no reckommends. I'm fear'd fer ter say a perlite wud 'bout myse'f, an' I des know I ain't gwine 'roun flatter'n up deze udder niggers."

"An' 'tain't dat," responded the darkey, who held a paper in his hand. "We er gittin up a Good Tempeler's lodge, an' we like ter git yo' name."

"Eh-eh, honey! I done see too much er dis nigger tempunce. Dey stan' up mighty squar' ontwell dere dues commence ter cramp um, an' dey don't stan' de racket wuf a durn. No longer'n yistiddy I seed one er de head men er one er dese Tempeler's s'cieties totin' water fer a bar-room. He had de water in a bucket, but dey ain't no tellin' how much red licker he wuz a totin'. G'long, chile —jine yo' s'ciety an' be good ter yo'se'f. I'm a gittin' too ole. Gimme th'ee er fo' drams endurin er de day, an' I'm mighty nigh ez good a tempunce man ez de next un. I got ter scuffle fer sump'n t'eat."

XIX.
AS A WEATHER PROPHET.

Uncle Remus was enlightening a crowd of negroes at the car-shed yesterday.

"Dar ain't nuthin'," said the old man, shaking his head pensively, "dat ain't got no change wrote on it.

Dar ain't nothin' dat ain't spotted befo' hit begins fer ter commence. We all speunces dat p'overdence w'at lifts us up fum one place an' sets us down in de udder. Hit's continerly a movin' an a movin'."

"Dat's so!" "Youer talkin' now!" came from several of his hearers.

"I year Miss Sally readin' dis mawnin," continued the old man, "dat a man wuz comin' down yer fer ter take keer er de wedder—wunner deze yer Buro mens w'at goes 'roun' a puttin' up an' pullin' down."

"W'at he gwine do 'roun' yer?" asked one.

"He's a gwineter regelate de wedder," replied Uncle Remus, sententiously. "He's a gwineter fix hit up so dat dere won't be so much worriment 'mong de w'ite fokes 'bout de kinder wedder w'at falls to dere lot."

"He gwine dish em up," suggested one of the older ones, "like man dish out sugar."

"No," answered Uncle Remus, mopping his benign features with a very large and very red bandana. "He's a gwineter fix um better'n dat. He's a gwineter fix um up so you kin have any kinder wedder w'at you want widout totin' her home."

"How's dat?" asked some one.

"Hit's dis way," said the old man, thoughtfully. "In co'se you knows w'at kinder wedder you wants. Well, den, w'en de man comes 'long, w'ich Miss Sally say he will, you des gotter go up dar, pick out yo' wedder, an' dere'll be a clock sot fer ter suit yo' case, an' w'en you git home, dere'll be yo' wedder a settin' out in de yard waitin' fer you. I wish he wuz yer now," the old man continued. "I'd take a p'ar er frosts in mine, ef I kotched cold fer it. Dat's me!"

There were various exclamations of assent, and the old man went on his way singing, "Don't you Grieve Atter Me."

XX.
THE OLD MAN'S TROUBLES.

"What makes you look so lonesome, Brer Remus?" asked a well-dressed negro, as the old man came shuffling down the street by James's corner yesterday.

"Youer mighty right, I'm lonesome, Brer John Henry. W'en a ole nigger like me is gotter paddle de canoe an' do de fishin' at de same time, an' w'en you bleedzd ter ketch de fish and dassent turn de paddle loose fer ter bait de hook, den I tell you, Brer John, youer right whar de mink had de goslin'. Mars John and Miss Sally, dey done bin gone down unto Putmon County fer ter see dere kinfolks mighty nigh fo' days, an' you better b'leeve I done bin had ter scratch roun' mighty lively fer ter make de rashuns run out even."

"I wuz at yo' house las' night, Brer Remus," remarked Brer John Henry, "but I couldn't roust you outer bed."

"Hit was de unseasonableness er de hour, I speck," said Uncle Remus, dryly. " 'Pears unto me dat you all chu'ch deacons settin' up mighty late deze cole nights. You'll be slippin' round arter hours some time er nudder, an' you'll slip bodaciously inter de calaboose. You mine w'at I tell you."

"It's mighty cole wedder," said Brer John Henry, evidently wishing to change the subject.

"Cole!" exclaimed Uncle Remus; "hit got pas' cole on de quarter stretch. You oughter come to my house night 'fo' las'. Den you'd a foun' me 'live an' kickin'."

"How's dat?"

"Well, I tell you, Brer John Henry, de cole wuz so cole, an' de kiver wuz so light, dat I thunk I'd make a raid on Mars John's shingle pile, an' out I goes an' totes in a whole armful. Den I gits under de kiver an' tells my ole 'oman fer ter lay 'em onto me like she was roofin' a house. Bimeby she crawls in, an' de shingles w'at she put on her side fer ter kiver wid, dey all drap off on de flo'. Den up I gits an' piles 'em on agin, an' w'en I gits in bed my shingle draps off, an' dat's de way it wuz de whole blessid night. Fus' it wuz me up an' den de ole 'oman, an' it kep' us pow'ful warm, too, dat kinder exercise. Oh, you oughter drapt roun' 'bout dat time, Brer John Henry. You'd a year'd sho' nuff cussin'!"

"You don't tell me, Brer Remus!"

"My ole 'oman say de Ole Boy wouldn't a foun' a riper nigger, ef he wer' ter scour de country fum Ferginny ter de Alabam!"

XXI.
THE FOURTH OF JULY.

Uncle Remus made his appearance recently with his right arm in a sling and his hand bandaged to that extent that it looked like the stick made to accompany the Centennial bass-drum. The old man evidently expected an attack all around, for he was unusually quiet, and fumbled in his pockets in an embarrassed manner. He was not mistaken. The agricultural editor was the first to open fire:

"Well, you old villain! what have you been up to now?"

"It is really singular," remarked a commencement orator, "that not even an ordinary holiday— a holiday, it seems to me, that ought to arouse all the latent instincts of patriotism in the bosom of American citizens—can occur without embroiling some of our most valuable citizens. It is really singular to me that such a day should be devoted by a certain class of our population to broils and fisticuffs."

This fine moral sentiment, which was altogether an impromptu utterance, and which was delivered with the air of one who addresses a vast but invisible audience of young ladies in white dresses and blue sashes, seemed to add to the embarrassment of Uncle Remus, and at the same time to make an explanation necessary.

"Dey ain't none er you young w'ite men never had no 'casion fer ter strike up wid one er deze Mobile niggers?" asked Uncle Remus. " 'Kaze ef you iz, den you knows wharbouts de devilment come in. Show me a Mobile nigger," continued the old man, "an' I'll show you a nigger dat's marked for de chain-gang. Hit may be de fote er de fif' er July, er hit may be de twelf' er Jinawerry, but w'en a Mobile nigger gits in my naberhood right den an' dar trubble sails in an' 'gages bode fer de season. I speck I'm ez fon' er deze Nunited States as de nex' man w'at knows dat de Buro is busted up; but long ez Remus kin stan' on his hine legs no Mobile nigger can't flip inter dis town longer no Wes' P'int 'schushun an' boss 'roun' 'mong de cullud fokes. Dat's me, up an' down, an' I boun' dere's a nigger some'rs on de road dis blessid day dat's got dis put away in his 'membunce."

"How did he happen to get you down and maul you in this startling manner?" asked the commencement orator, with a tone of exaggerated sympathy in his voice.

"Maul who?" exclaimed Uncle Remus, indignantly. "Maul who? Boss, de nigger dat mauled me ain't bornded yit, an' dey er got ter have anudder war 'fo' one is bornded."

"Well, what was the trouble?"

"Hit wuz sorter dis way, boss. I wuz stannin' down dere by Mars John Jeems's bank, chattin' wid Sis Tempy, w'ich I ain't seed 'er befo' now gwine on seven year, an' watchin' de folks trompin' by, w'en one er deze yer slick-lookin' niggers, wid a bee-gum hat an' a brass watch ez big ez de head uv a beer-bar'l, come 'long an' bresh up agin me—so. Dere wuz two un um, an' dey went 'long gigglin' an' laffin' like a nes'ful er yaller-hammers. Bimeby dey come 'long agin an' de smart El-lick brush up by me once mo'. Den I say to myse'f, 'I lay I fetch you ef you gimme anudder invite.' An', sho' 'nuff, yer he come agin, an' dis time he rub a piece er watermillion rime under my lef' year.''

"What did you do?"

"Me? I'm a mighty long-sufferin' nigger, but he hadn't no mo'n totch me 'fo' I flung dese yer bones in his face." Here Uncle Remus held up his damaged hand triumphantly. "I sorter sprained my han', boss, but dog my cats if I don't b'leeve I spattered de nigger's eyeballs on de groun', and w'en he riz his count'nence look fresh like beef-haslett. I look mighty spindlin' an' puny now, don't I, boss?" inquired the old man, with great apparent earnestness.

"Rather."

"Well, you des oughter see me git my Affikin up. Dey useter call me er bad nigger long 'fo' de war, an' hit looks like ter me dat I gits wuss an' wuss. Brer John Henry say dat I oughter supdue my rashfulness, an' I don't 'spute it, but tu'n a Mobile nigger loose in dis town, fote er July or no fote er July, an', me er him, one is got ter lan' in jail. Hit's proned inter me.''

FOR THE BEST IN PAPERBACKS, LOOK FOR THE

In every corner of the world, on every subject under the sun, Penguin represents quality and variety—the very best in publishing today.

For complete information about books available from Penguin—including Puffins, Penguin Classics, and Arkana—and how to order them, write to us at the appropriate address below. Please note that for copyright reasons the selection of books varies from country to country.

In the United Kingdom: Please write to *Dept. JC, Penguin Books Ltd, FREEPOST, West Drayton, Middlesex UB7 0BR.*

If you have any difficulty in obtaining a title, please send your order with the correct money, plus ten percent for postage and packaging, to *P.O. Box No. 11, West Drayton, Middlesex UB7 0BR*

In the United States: Please write to *Consumer Sales, Penguin USA, P.O. Box 999, Dept. 17109, Bergenfield, New Jersey 07621-0120.* VISA and MasterCard holders call 1-800-253-6476 to order all Penguin titles

In Canada: Please write to *Penguin Books Canada Ltd, 10 Alcorn Avenue, Suite 300, Toronto, Ontario M4V 3B2*

In Australia: Please write to *Penguin Books Australia Ltd, P.O. Box 257, Ringwood, Victoria 3134*

In New Zealand: Please write to *Penguin Books (NZ) Ltd, Private Bag 102902, North Shore Mail Centre, Auckland 10*

In India: Please write to *Penguin Books India Pvt Ltd, 706 Eros Apartments, 56 Nehru Place, New Delhi 110 019*

In the Netherlands: Please write to *Penguin Books Netherlands bv, Postbus 3507, NL-1001 AH Amsterdam*

In Germany: Please write to *Penguin Books Deutschland GmbH, Metzlerstrasse 26, 60594 Frankfurt am Main*

In Spain: Please write to *Penguin Books S.A., Bravo Murillo 19, 1° B, 28015 Madrid*

In Italy: Please write to *Penguin Italia s.r.l., Via Felice Casati 20, I-20124 Milano*

In France: Please write to *Penguin France S.A., 17 rue Lejeune, F-31000 Toulouse*

In Japan: Please write to *Penguin Books Japan, Ishikiribashi Building, 2-5-4, Suido, Bunkyo-ku, Tokyo 112*

In Greece: Please write to *Penguin Hellas Ltd, Dimocritou 3, GR-106 71 Athens*

In South Africa: Please write to *Longman Penguin Southern Africa (Pty) Ltd, Private Bag X08, Bertsham 2013*